TRAILS MERGE

What Reviewers Say About Bold Strokes Books

"With its expected unexpected twists, vivid characters and healthy dose of humor, *Blind Curves* is a very fun read that will keep you guessing." – *Bay Windows*

"In a succinct film style narrative, with scenes that move, a character-driven plot, and crisp dialogue worthy of a screenplay ... the Richfield and Rivers novels are ... an engaging Hollywood mystery ... series." – *Midwest Book Review*

Force of Nature "...is filled with nonstop, fast paced action. Tornadoes, raging fire blazes, heroic and daring rescues... Baldwin does a fine job of describing the fast-paced scenes and inspiring the reader to keep on turning the pages." – *L-word.comLiterature*

In the Jude Devine mystery series the "...characters seem fully capable of walking away from the particulars of whodunit and engaging the reader in other aspects of their lives." – *Lambda Book Report*

Mine "...weaves a tale of yearning, love, lust, and conflict resolution ... a believable plot, with strong characters in a charming setting." – *JustAboutWrite*

"While these two women struggle with their issues, there is some very, very hot sex. If you enjoy complex characters and passionate sex scenes, you'll love *Wild Abandon*." – *MegaScene*

"*Course of Action* is a romance ... populated with a host of captivating and amiable characters. The glimpses into the lifestyles of the rich and beautiful people are rather like guilty pleasures ... a most satisfying and entertaining reading experience." – *Midwest Book Review*

The Clinic is "...a spellbinding novel." – *JustAboutWrite*

"*Unexpected Sparks* lived up to its promise and was thoroughly enjoyable ... Dartt did a lovely job at building the relationship between Kate and Nikki." – *Lambda Book Report*

"*Sequestered Hearts* ... is everything a romance should be. It is teeming with longing, heartbreak, and of course, love. As pure romances go, it is one of the best in print today." – *L-word.comLiterature*

"*The Exile and the Sorcerer* is a mesmerizing read, a tour-de-force packed with adventure, ordeals, complex twists and turns, and the internal introspection of appealing characters." – *Midwest Book Review*

The Spanish Pearl is "...both science fiction and romance in this adventurous tale ... A most entertaining read, with a sequel already in the works. Hot, hot, hot!" – *Minnesota Literature*

"A deliciously sexy thriller ... *Dark Valentine* is funny, scary, and very realistic. The story is tightly written and keeps the reader gripped to the exciting end." – *JustAbout Write*

"*Punk Like Me* ... is different. It is engaging. It is life-affirming. Frankly, it is genius. This is a rare book in that it has a soul; one that is laid bare for all to see." – *JustAboutWrite*

"*Chance* is not a novel about the music industry; it is about a woman discovering herself as she muddles through all the trappings of fame." – *Midwest Book Review*

Sweet Creek "... is sublimely in tune with the times." – *Q-Syndicate*

"*Forever Found* ... neatly combines hot sex scenes, humor, engaging characters, and an exciting story." – *MegaScene*

Shield of Justice is a "...well-plotted...lovely romance...I couldn't turn the pages fast enough!" – Ann Bannon, author of *The Beebo Brinker Chronicles*

The 100th Generation is "...filled with ancient myths, Egyptian gods and goddesses, legends, and, most wonderfully, it contains the lesbian equivalent of Indiana Jones living and working in modern Egypt." – *Just About Write*

Sword of the Guardian is "...a terrific adventure, coming of age story, a romance, and tale of courtly intrigue, attempted assassination, and gender confusion ... a rollicking fun book and a must-read for those who enjoy courtly light fantasy in a medieval-seeming time." – *Midwest Book Review*

"*Of Drag Kings and the Wheel of Fate*'s lush rush of a romance incorporates reincarnation, a grounded transman and his peppy daughter, and the dark moods of a troubled witch—wonderful homage to Leslie Feinberg's classic gender-bending novel, *Stone Butch Blues*." – *Q-Syndicate*

In *Running with the Wind* "...the discussions of the nature of sex, love, power, and sexuality are insightful and represent a welcome voice from the view of late-20-something characters today." – *Midwest Book Review*

"Rich in character portrayal, *The Devil Inside* is an unusual, unpredictable, and thought-provoking love story that will have the reader questioning the definition of right and wrong long after she finishes the book." – *JustAboutWrite*

Wall of Silence "...is perfectly plotted and has a very real voice and consistently accurate tone, which is not always the case with lesbian mysteries." – *Midwest Book Review*

By the Author

Learning Curve

Trails Merge

Visit us at www.boldstrokesbooks.com

TRAILS MERGE

by

Rachel Spangler

2008

ISBN 10: 1-60282-039-2
ISBN 13: 978-1-60282-039-5

This Trade Paperback Original Is Published By
Bold Strokes Books, Inc.
P.O. Box 249
Valley Falls, NY 12185

First Edition: December 2008

CREDITS
EDITORS: SHELLEY THRASHER AND STACIA SEAMAN
PRODUCTION DESIGN: STACIA SEAMAN
COVER DESIGN BY SHERI (GRAPHICARTIST2020@HOTMAIL.COM)

Acknowledgments

Trails Merge has had several drafts and the story has evolved somewhat from my original concept, but at its heart it remains a story about families. There are families we're born into, the families we join, and the families we create. Like my characters, I am a part of many families, and I am greatly indebted to each of them.

The first is a family I've been lucky enough to join at Bold Strokes Books. Thank you to Rad for creating this family of writers and letting me be a part of it. Thanks also go out to my amazing editor Shelley Thrasher for her endless patience with me and to Jennifer Knight for her continued oversight. As always, Sheri's covers are impressive, and she gets extra thanks this time for incorporating my own picture of a trails merge sign that was impeccably shot by Will Banks, another person I consider myself lucky to have as part of several of my families. I also owe a debt of gratitude to Stacia Seaman for her fine eye and penchant for detail. Another member of that family of choice, Toni Whittaker, is not only an endless source of friendship and support, but she did me the great honor of serving as a beta reader. Finally, I am so proud to be a part of the family of amazing writers and fans on the Bold Strokes Authors Connect mailing list. They keep me inspired with conversations about craft and entertained with discussions of everything else; I am grateful for both.

Moving on to my family of birth, I am proud to say all of the sweet and supportive family members you see in this book are inspired by my own family members. While many people have friends they consider family, I also have family that are among my best friends. My parents, my brother, my large extended network of grandparents, aunts, uncles, and cousins have all played a part in making me who I am today. I know I could call any one of them, at any time, for any reason, and they would be there for me. I am truly blessed to have each and every one of them in my life.

Last and most important is the family I've created. Susie, the love of my life, you give me the strength and the inspiration to chase my dreams. Without your influence I'd be only a shadow of my true self. And Jackson, the light of my life, you've shown me the meaning of unconditional love. I became whole the minute I became your mom. You two have reaffirmed that nothing in this life is more consuming or fulfilling than the connections that tie us together as one. Come what may.

Dedication

To Susie and Jackson
You are my greatest adventure.

And Susie, it's still your fault!

PROLOGUE

Where was Lynn? She should have been home hours ago. Campbell Carson paced the living room like a caged bear. She had run out of things to do in her small apartment in Madison, Wisconsin. She had packed their suitcases, watered the plants, and gassed up the car. All she was waiting on was Lynn Meyers, her partner of five years.

She had waited on Lynn a lot over the past few years, so she should have been used to it. But Campbell always played Charlie Brown and trusted Lucy to hold the football upright. And she never did. Like a fool, Campbell had still hoped when Lynn said she would be home by noon she actually would be. Now it was late afternoon and Lynn had only just called to say she was leaving the office.

Lynn put in long hours as a gay-and-lesbian-rights advocate for Wisconsin Equality, a special-interest group with political and philanthropic agendas. Campbell understood that. But did Lynn really have to work these particular hours on this particular Saturday afternoon? She was obviously trying to put off their upcoming visit to Campbell's family at Bear Run.

Campbell had been named godmother to her newest cousin, and the christening was tomorrow morning, followed by a celebration at the small family-run ski resort. Lynn didn't enjoy the trips to see Campbell's family but had promised to make the most of this occasion. Surely she knew how important it was to Campbell.

Campbell hadn't seen her family in five months, and even then Lynn had been too busy to go with her. She resented the time away from the city, and she resented Campbell's connection with her large, extended family. She always found something to complain about—the lack of cell-phone reception, the way Campbell's mother hovered over her children, or the lack of nightlife on the mountain. Lynn didn't have a good relationship with her own relatives, and she couldn't understand Campbell's desire to stay close to hers.

Still, Campbell thought a weekend on the mountain would be good for them. Lynn was overworked and they hadn't spent any quality time together in weeks. They needed to reconnect. Campbell was lonely and ready for some time away from the fund-raisers, business dinners, and late-night phone calls that had taken over their life in the past year as Lynn climbed the career ladder.

Campbell's days weren't bad, since she worked with an underprivileged youth program at the local YMCA and enjoyed the time she spent with the kids. But her nights were long, and the weekends dragged on forever, with Lynn working so much. They got out often, but usually for a political event Lynn needed to attend, and their peer group consisted entirely of her business associates and colleagues who were as busy and driven as Lynn.

"Hey, honey." Lynn bustled through the door and immediately began to change clothes.

Campbell smiled at the flash of porcelain skin she glimpsed as Lynn traded one dress shirt for another. Lynn was every bit as stunning as the day they met in college.

She was still every bit as passionate and outspoken, too, and hot tempered as her flame-red hair indicated, which was why Campbell instantly fell in love with her, and that love hadn't wavered.

"I know you don't want to hear this, but I just got an interview with a staffer of one of the senators who's been stalling the hate-crimes bill."

"That's great," Campbell said. "You've been working on this bill all spring. Why wouldn't I want to hear that?"

"Because the meeting is tonight at eight thirty," Lynn said, heading toward their bedroom.

Campbell's heart sank, but she wasn't eager to start a fight. They'd been having a lot of them lately. "Okay, I guess we'll just go up late tonight."

Lynn's brow gathered in disbelief. "You don't get it, do you?"

"What?" Campbell thought she might be getting it, but she didn't want to admit that possibility yet.

"I'm not going to Bear Run this weekend." Lynn pulled a suit jacket off a hanger in the closet before she added, "If I never go there again, I wouldn't mind."

"I know you don't like Bear Run, but I'm the godmother. I have to be at the baptism."

"Well, that's your fault for going along with that antiquated idea. But you won't catch me sitting in some small-town church pretending to be interested in a ceremony I don't even agree with." Lynn began to raise her voice, a sign she was about to go on a tear.

"Okay, you don't have to, and when we have kids, we don't have to have them baptized," Campbell said, trying to pacify her, but she knew immediately that she'd said something wrong.

"Are you serious?" Lynn stopped dead and her light green eyes flashed with anger. "Are you freaking serious? When we have kids? You see? That's why I don't want you going up there. You spend two days on Walton Mountain and you start acting like a goddamn straight girl."

"Hey, that's not fair." Campbell was tired of having this argument. "You can be a lesbian and still have a relationship with your family."

"And live in a small town, take over the ski business, raise another generation of Carson kids? Give me a break. If you want to act straight, you need to find someone else to do it with," Lynn snapped.

Campbell recoiled. "You don't mean that," she finally whispered.

"I do, Campbell. I mean it. No self-respecting lesbian would ever settle for the life you're dreaming of. If you take that road, you'll spend the rest of your life alone." Lynn grabbed her briefcase. "I'm off to my meeting now. While I'm gone, decide whether you want to be a dyke or play heterosexual homemaker at Bear Run."

Campbell barely heard the door slam as Lynn left. The pain would come eventually, but she felt nothing as she processed the ultimatum. She could either be with the woman she loved in a life she hated, or she could live the life she loved with the people she loved, but she would do it alone. She wasn't eager to choose, but Lynn had left her few options.

Sadly she picked up her suitcase, leaving Lynn's on the floor, then slipped the key to the apartment from her pocket, placed it on the coffee table, and closed the door behind her.

CHAPTER ONE

Six Months Later

Parker Riley shouldered open the door to her new office, a box of her personal belongings in one arm and a stack of file folders in the other. She dropped the box and folders on top of an old wooden desk and looked around. The walls had probably been white at one point, but they were now dingy and yellowish. The thick brown carpet shaded from light to dark in various parts of the room, depending on the amount of direct sunlight it had been subjected to over the years. The ceilings, in keeping with the alpine theme of the old building, peaked high and then sloped drastically downward, with a window set back in the dormers on each of the outside walls.

She walked over to a window and had to admit the view wasn't unattractive. The fall colors were almost at their brightest, painting brilliant reds, yellows, and oranges across the rows of trees that climbed the steep incline of the terrain.

"Not bad," she mumbled to herself, then shook her head, "but it's not Chicago."

She trudged back to her desk and flopped into a rickety swivel chair. It gave more than she expected, and she grabbed the sides of the desk to keep from tumbling backward. After steadying herself, she rubbed her forehead and wondered if this near fall was a metaphor for her life. Fallen politicians, leading to a fall in her career, topped off by the falling apart of a two-year relationship. Now she was reduced to falling out of old desk chairs at Bear Run Ski Hill in Wisconsin.

The possibility was almost too depressing to contemplate, but before she had time to dwell on it, a knock interrupted her pity party. Emery Carson, her new boss, stepped through the doorway.

"Well, I guess you found the place all right," he said as he glanced around the office.

"Yeah, thanks," Parker replied, not sure what else to say to the man who stood there. He wore Carhart overalls and muddy work boots, not exactly business attire where Parker came from, but she would probably see a lot more of it. Emery wasn't as old as she had assumed during her initial interview, maybe in his mid to late forties. He was clean shaven and smelled pleasantly of Cool Water cologne, but he was far from the slick and polished Ivy Leaguers she usually worked for. And while she immediately liked him, she was at a loss about what to say to him. Finally, she fell back on the one thing she knew—her job.

"I should start researching the clientele demographics to see what I have to deal with. Where can I get the spec sheets of season-pass holders for the past five years? Also, the conference bookings for as far back as you have them would be helpful."

"The conference ledgers are in the main office, but our bookkeeper doesn't come in on weekends," Emery said, running his fingers through his perfectly coiffed golden hair. "And we've never compiled any spec sheets on season-pass holders. We have a list of names and phone numbers on the computer, though."

"Okay, that's a start." Parker tried not to let her frustration with the lack of record-keeping show. "Can I have those?"

"They're in the front office, too. I can get you a key, but if you wait until Monday, the secretary will print everything out for you. Why don't you take some time to settle in?"

Parker thought of all the boxes the movers had unceremoniously dropped in the living room of her apartment less than a mile from the resort. "Okay, I guess I can wait until tomorrow."

"Not tomorrow. Tomorrow's Sunday."

Parker paused, trying to follow Emery's logic.

"Nobody works Sundays here during the off season. It's a day of rest."

Parker stood up. Sitting down when someone else was standing put her in a one-down position. "I'm not really a religious person."

"Neither am I." Emery chuckled. "But once the snow flies, we won't get a break around here for a solid six months, so take the time now."

Parker nodded, not wanting to disagree so early on her first day. "If you say so."

"Sleep in or unpack in the morning. Then you can meet the rest of the year-round staff at the softball game in the afternoon."

"Softball game?"

"Yeah, there's a makeshift field over by the summer picnic area. Everyone who's available meets there around one o'clock on Sundays for a pickup game."

"Oh, I'm not good at sports." Parker tried to back out gracefully.

"None of us are." Emery laughed. "It's mostly a bunch of middle-aged men trying to recapture our youth. You can just watch. Some of the wives join in, and some of them sit around and make fun of us. Either way, you can meet some folks before you start work on Monday."

"Sounds fun." Parker tried to force a smile, even though she would rather poke herself with a sharp stick than spend an afternoon playing jock with a bunch of farm boys.

"Great." Emery smiled. "See you tomorrow."

"See you then." Parker kept her fake smile until Emery shut the door behind him. Then she dropped back into the desk chair, remembering to catch herself before it tipped her backward. What had she gotten herself into this time?

❖

Parker cringed at the sight of her apartment. The movers had been oblivious to the official labels she had painstakingly created and attached to each box to detail its contents and which room it belonged in. Instead, they had dropped everything in a series of haphazard piles just inside the door. Parker slipped through the available space left by the half-open door and wove between stacks of boxes, picking a path through the mess toward the kitchen.

When she finally made it to the refrigerator, she found a lone carton of beef chow mein she'd picked up on her drive from Chicago to Bear Run. She grabbed it and sniffed before she succumbed to the inevitable and tossed it into the microwave. The only other item not still in a box was an unopened bottle of red wine she had bought at one of the wine-and-cheese huts that seemed to be the only type of shops that survived in this part of Wisconsin.

"Well," Parker mumbled to herself as she grabbed the bottle of wine, "red meat does call for red wine." She closed the door to the now completely barren fridge and searched through the maze of boxes for a corkscrew and a wineglass. When she didn't find the glasses right away, she realized most of her fragile items had probably ended up beneath several heavier boxes, perhaps her books or her free weights.

She wandered back into the kitchen and retrieved the steaming beef and noodles and uncorked the wine. Sitting at the kitchen table, she used a plastic fork that came with the carryout and shrugged at how desperate she would look to anyone who might see her. But that thought didn't stop her from swigging directly from the bottle.

When she was about halfway through her meal, her cell phone rang shrilly.

She finished swallowing a mouthful of noodles as she fished the phone from her pocket. "Parker Riley."

"Green Acres is the place to be," sang someone on the other end of the line.

Parker chuckled at her best friend. She could picture Alexis Reynolds clearly, her platinum blond hair falling over her shoulders and down her lithe frame while her sharp blue eyes danced with laughter. "Hi, Alexis."

"Hello, darling. Have you fed the chickens and milked the cows yet?"

"I don't have any chickens or cows, Alexis. In fact I haven't seen a single chicken since I got here."

"But be honest. You have seen cows, haven't you?" Alexis said playfully.

Parker looked down at the piece of beef on her fork. "I guess you could say that."

"I knew it. So what does the new dyke about town have planned for her first Saturday night in Wisconsin?"

"Um"—Parker glanced around the room—"I'll probably unpack."

"Oh, come on, not even a dinner date?" Alexis sounded a little worried.

"No. I'm having Chinese food at home."

"Oh, dear." Alexis sighed heavily. "I just had the most horrible vision of you sitting alone surrounded by boxes, eating old moo shoo and drinking whiskey out of a Dixie cup."

"It's not whiskey. I'm drinking a very nice cabernet," Parker replied in an attempt to reassert her dignity. Then she added more softly, "And I can't find my cups."

"Honey, you're positively depressing. When do you plan to stop punishing yourself?"

"Alexis, we've been through this already. I'm not punishing myself," Parker said seriously. "I'm starting over, clean slate, back to the basics—"

"Off to find yourself in the great wild yonder," Alexis added with fake enthusiasm.

"Yes."

"And isolating yourself to wallow in self-pity is part of this rejuvenation process?"

"I'm not wallowing."

"Sitting at home and drinking alone on a Saturday night doesn't constitute wallowing?"

"I'm simply enjoying some peace and quiet for once."

"I have a feeling you plan to do that a lot in the upcoming months."

"Don't make me sound like a hermit, Alexis. I've only been here two days. I'm still getting settled."

"I know. I'm just worried about you." Alexis's voice softened. "I can't stand the thought of you up there alone. You're a social creature, honey. You'll go crazy if you sentence yourself to solitary confinement."

"I know. But I really am okay. In fact, I'm already filling my social calendar."

"Really?" Alexis sounded skeptical.

"Really. I'm going to a softball game tomorrow afternoon," Parker said, without adding that her boss had told her to.

"A softball game?" Alexis sounded perplexed.

"Yes, apparently it's in season. The whole staff gets together to play every Sunday." Parker tried to make the event sound appealing.

"Yes, yes." Alexis affected a snooty air. "I've heard of such things among country lesbians. Sporting events accompanied by the traditional potluck. I think the requisite attire is flannel and work boots."

Parker laughed. "Then I'd better head to Wal-Mart. I haven't unpacked my flannel yet."

"Don't you dare. I'd rather you drink alone than spend your Saturday night at Wal-Mart."

"You're right. I'll just have to forgo the flannel."

"But how will you signal to the other women that you're one of them? Mating call? Secret handshake?"

"No." Parker sighed, despite her friend's humor. "I'm through with mating calls for a while."

"Uh-oh, we're back to wallowing."

"No, not wallowing at all. This is exactly what I want from my life right now."

"Loneliness."

"Independence."

"Thank you, Mia," Alexis mumbled under her breath.

"It's not about Mia. Really. I'm just focused on rebuilding my career and reputation. You know I want to make a difference in the world. Another relationship right now would only keep me from getting myself back together."

"Especially if she shows more interest in frat parties than partisan politics."

"Alexis, I mean it. Leave Mia out of it. This isn't her fault," Parker said, even though the ache in her chest suggested that statement wasn't completely true.

"Who said anything about Mia? I was speaking hypothetically," Alexis responded dryly. "But if the shoe fits—"

"Can we change the subject? Why don't you tell me what you plan to do tonight?"

"Well, some of the girls from the office have tickets to that *Wizard of Oz* musical, but I'd rather hit the clubs."

Parker tried not to let her voice reflect her twinge of sadness. Getting away from Chicago had been the right choice, even if it hadn't been easy to make. "I hear that's supposed to be amazing."

"Why don't you come down next weekend and we'll see it together?"

"Alexis, you know I can't. I have a job here."

"You won't see any hit musicals at Bear Run," Alexis answered sullenly.

"No, probably not, but you should go and then tell me all about it."

"If you say so." Alexis sighed again. "I'd better run. Hugs and kisses."

"You, too." Parker hung up and took another swig of wine directly from the bottle before she stood up. Dwelling on her doubts wouldn't improve the situation, so she resigned herself to an evening of unpacking.

CHAPTER TWO

C ampbell," the pitcher shouted when the ball hit the palm of his glove. "Cool it. We're just warming up."

Campbell laughed at her brother as he shook his gloved hand to relieve the sting. "Sorry, Sammy. I forget how fragile you are," she teased.

"You know I can take any heat you've got. Just let me warm up first." Sammy defended his ego.

"Whatever you say." Campbell crouched behind home plate. She then pounded her fist into the pit of her mitt, signaling for him to quit talking and start throwing.

Sammy wound up and, using a swift underhand motion, hurled a softball directly over the plate and into Campbell's mitt with a crisp pop. After slipping her mask over her head, she shouted to a group of men standing near a sideline. "We're ready."

"Uh-oh," someone sitting on the makeshift bleachers behind a chain-link fence said. "Campbell's got Sammy worked up again."

Campbell chuckled and put her mask back down. "Batter up."

The first hitter approached the plate, a man in his mid thirties with a beer belly bulging under his long-sleeved T-shirt. Campbell flashed her index finger from her fist, just below her catcher's mitt, signaling for Sammy's signature pitch. He wound up and delivered the ball swiftly across the inside of the plate. The batter swung several seconds too late.

"Strike one," Campbell called as she tossed the ball back to Sammy.

Knowing that she had bolstered her brother's confidence, she once again lowered her index finger, this time flashing it slightly to the left. Sammy let loose another fireball. The batter swung with a loud grunt but didn't even come close.

Campbell smiled as she flashed the next sign. An index finger, held steady, pointing directly downward. Her brother wasn't the only one with a competitive streak, though Campbell didn't show hers as readily. Sammy gave her an almost unperceivable grin before he brought the heat right down the middle of the plate. The batter's knees almost buckled as the ball flew by him. He'd barely gotten the bat off his shoulder when Campbell called out, "One down, two to go."

The second hitter, another man in his thirties, went out swinging on strikes, but Campbell realized Sammy was getting too comfortable. She needed to rattle him before he got too cocky.

The third batter, a young woman, stepped up to the plate and dug in with her back heel. This time Campbell flashed two fingers downward just below her mitt. They both knew Sammy couldn't throw a curveball. He rolled his eyes and threw another one right down the pipe at breakneck speed. The woman caught a piece of the ball and sent it straight up in the air. Campbell hopped to her feet and threw off her mask in the same motion. Aligning her body directly under the ball, she trapped it neatly with one hand.

Campbell winked at her brother on her way to the sidelines. "If you'd learn to throw a curve, I wouldn't have to bail you out like that." *That should keep him hyped up for the next inning.*

"Bail me out?" Sammy asked as he joined her in the dugout.

Campbell shrugged as she slipped off her mitt and grabbed a bat.

"One person got a bat on the ball all inning, but you bailed me out?"

"Am I going to have to separate you two?" their uncle, Emery Carson, asked, clasping Campbell's shoulder.

"Yeah," Sammy grumbled, and stalked off. Campbell and Emery both smiled as they watched him go. "You know, this is just a friendly game. There's no need to get him all riled up like that," Emery said when Sammy was out of earshot.

"Yeah, but that's what big sisters are for."

Emery laughed and threw his arm around her shoulder. While

Campbell was close with all her family members, she and Emery shared an unspoken camaraderie that reached back to her early childhood. "Hey, I just saw someone I want you to meet after the game."

"Who?" Campbell had known everyone around the resort for years.

"The new marketing woman just got here." He nodded toward a slender woman who stood off to the side of the bleachers with a pair of low-rise blue jeans slung loosely over her hips and a fitted gray shirt tight enough to show her curves without clinging to them. Her long dark hair was in a loose ponytail, and the corners of her mouth were turned slightly upward in a look of amusement that didn't quite qualify as a smile. Her eyes were hidden behind sunglasses, but Campbell thought she was looking in their direction. She immediately felt a strange twinge in the pit of her stomach, but she couldn't determine why her attraction to the stunning woman unsettled her.

"Hey, you still here?" Emery asked, waving a hand in front of her eyes.

Campbell blushed when she realized she'd been caught staring. "Yeah, sorry. What did you say?"

Emery raised a questioning eyebrow. "You're up."

"Oh." She clutched her bat and headed toward the field before she turned back to Emery. "How many outs?" she asked sheepishly.

"One. Sammy's on first."

Campbell nodded and tried to refocus on the game. She set her feet in the batter's box and took a warm-up swing, then turned her attention to the pitcher. After the windup she saw the ball leave the pitcher's hand, but it was over the plate before she even got the bat off her shoulder.

"Strike one," the catcher called out, a little too enthusiastically.

Campbell glanced back at him. "Thanks for clearing that up."

She returned her attention to the pitcher and tried to determine the ball's speed as soon as it left his hand. Once again, in the split second she had to make a judgment on the trajectory of the ball it was over the plate, her bat too far behind it to make any contact.

"That's two," the catcher yelled.

Campbell tightened her jaw and set her sights on the pitcher. The attractive new stranger had shaken her up, but she was determined not to let another ball past. This time when the pitcher released the ball she was already moving the bat, but in mid-swing she realized the ball was outside the strike zone. Too far gone to pull back, she fully extended her arms over the plate and felt the end of the bat collide with the ball. She knew it wouldn't go far, so she quickly dropped the bat and sprinted toward first base.

As she ran, the shortstop scooped up the ball and tossed it to the second baseman, who tagged the bag before Sammy was even halfway there, then hurled it toward first for the double play. Campbell powered up her stride, but even as her foot touched the bag she knew the baseman had the out locked up. After she burned out her speed, she didn't even look back. Instead, she jogged toward the bench to grab her mitt and mask.

As she turned to leave the dugout, Sammy stood in front of her with his arms folded. "You sure bailed me out that time."

After the game, Campbell threw her gear into an old gym bag and strode over to speak with a few spectators lingering behind the backstop. She smiled at the older couple standing side by side talking to Sammy.

"Twenty-eight years old and still swinging at pitches in the dirt." Her dad's easy laugh rolled over her as he hugged her.

"Thanks." Campbell returned the hug.

"You notice he wasn't out there swinging," her mother added. Campbell towered over her, but that didn't stop her mom from hugging her as well.

"That's because your mother won't let me anymore."

"His knees won't let him, but he likes to blame me." As she winked at Campbell and Sammy, her brilliant blue eyes shone with mischief.

Emery joined them, bringing with him the woman he'd pointed out earlier. "Everybody, this is Parker Riley. She's our new marketing gal, up from Chicago. Parker, this is my brother Greg, sister-in-law Irene, and their kids, Sammy and Campbell."

Parker slipped her sunglasses up to rest on her head and flashed a full smile directly at Campbell. "It's nice to meet you." The gaze of the woman's soft brown eyes was unnerving, though Campbell still couldn't pinpoint why.

"I heard you got a place at the slope-side condos," Greg said.

Parker gave him an inquisitive look. "I did."

"News travels fast around here, honey." Irene's piecing blue eyes, the same ones Campbell saw in the mirror each morning, sparkled when she laughed.

"I guess it does. I only got here Friday night."

"Do you need help unpacking?" Sammy asked, edging closer to her.

"I've got it under control."

"Well, if you need anything, just give me and Campbell a call. We live a short walk through the timber from where you are."

"And we're only a bit farther up the mountain," Greg added, "though I don't do much walking anymore."

"Thanks, that's nice of you," Parker responded, politely but dismissively. There was a defiance in her stance that made Campbell suspect this woman didn't often depend on other people for help.

"We'd better get on home," Irene said. "Do you need a ride somewhere, Parker?"

"No, I'm on foot."

"We are, too, Mom." Sammy said. "We'll head back with her."

Campbell rolled her eyes at her brother's transparent attempt at chivalry.

"All right, it was nice to meet you, Parker, and we'll see you two later," Irene said.

The family said good-bye to one another with hugs all around before Parker, Campbell, and Sammy took the road that circled the resort and surrounding residences. The breeze was beginning to turn chilly in the shadows, but the late-afternoon sun was enough to warm them where it reached between the trees and the buildings they passed.

Campbell was unsure what to make of Parker. She was beautiful, but also reserved. If not for her practiced smile, she would have come across as aloof. Despite her cordial interactions with them, she seemed distracted, as if she'd rather be somewhere else. Her clothes were a designer attempt at casual, and her perfectly manicured nails indicated that she wasn't used to spending much time outdoors.

Campbell tried to figure out why this woman disconcerted her, but finally concluded that Parker seemed slightly uncomfortable with her company and not very eager to make small talk.

Sammy, on the other hand, appeared determined to keep up a conversation with the newcomer, asking, "So, what do you think of the mountain?"

"It's very pretty with all the leaves changing colors," she responded with seeming sincerity.

"I bet you didn't get much foliage in Chicago, did you?"

"No, I lived right downtown, a few blocks off the lakeshore, and didn't make it far from there very often."

"Were you in marketing?"

"I was in politics," Parker said, a hint of tension in her voice.

Campbell wondered what it was about politics that the woman didn't want to discuss. People in politics usually didn't want to discuss anything else.

Thankfully, Sammy appeared to be oblivious to her discomfort as he rambled on. "Then what brought you up here to our little mountain in the woods?"

"It was time for a change, and this was a big one," Parker stated flatly, then added that contrived smile.

Campbell heard the noncommittal comment for what it was, an attempt to dodge the heart of the question. The woman wasn't introverted, but guarded, and that fact piqued Campbell's suspicions. Sammy was right to wonder why a woman like this would come to a place like Bear Run. Something didn't add up, but she obviously didn't want to talk about her personal situation, and Campbell didn't intend to push the subject any further.

"Yeah? Well, I imagine this place will be very different from what you're used to," Sammy continued. "What about your family? They must be sad to see you move."

"Sam," Campbell finally cut in, "leave the poor woman alone. She's not even unpacked."

"Sorry, I was just trying to make conversation."

"You can pick it up some other time." Campbell motioned to the small, one-lane road that headed up into some timber and a group of one- and two-story houses. "This is our turn."

"Thanks for walking me this far," Parker said with a polite smile that seemed slightly more genuine than the others she'd produced. Maybe she was warming up, or maybe she was just happy to be rid of them.

"Anytime," Sammy said genially. "If you ever need anything, we're the fifth cabin up on the left."

"Thanks, I'll keep that in mind."

"It was nice to meet you," Campbell added as Parker turned to leave.

"You, too."

After Parker left, Campbell and Sammy slowly started up the hill, settling into an easy silence that came from spending so much of their lives together. When they reached their cabin, they both kicked off their softball cleats and dropped their gear just inside the doorway. Sammy grabbed a can of soda from the fridge, cracking it open as he flopped on the couch.

Campbell ran her hand through her shoulder-length golden brown hair, matted down from the ball cap she'd worn, and glanced down at her shirt and pants, covered in the red clay of the softball diamond. "I'm going to take a shower."

"Hey, Cam," Sammy called as she started to climb the stairs to her loft.

"What?"

"You think Parker plays for your team or mine?"

Campbell shrugged, slightly uncomfortable with the implications of his question. The possibility that Parker would be dating material uncovered that old hurt she had worked so hard to bury. "What difference does it make? I'm sure a woman like that wouldn't be interested in ski bums like us."

"Speak for yourself. I'm quite a catch."

Campbell wondered if Sammy had heard her slight bitterness. She was a little disconcerted to detect it herself. Something about Parker had sparked it. What was more, the guarded new marketing director was responsible for an even more unsettling response. For the first time in six months, Campbell's pulse was racing.

Chapter Three

Parker was the first one to arrive for her meeting with the entire resort management staff. She had been at Bear Run for just over two weeks and completely immersed herself in her work. She pored over the disorganized records of season-pass holders and spent days sifting through the names of anyone who had skied here for the past few seasons. After inputting the names into a simple spreadsheet, then adding the ages, or approximate ages, of the pass holders, she ran some correlations and created a few graphs. Once she compiled the data, she spotted a trend immediately. She wanted to talk about it during today's meeting.

"Good morning, Parker," Emery Carson said with his warm smile as he shrugged off his light denim jacket and tossed it over the back of his chair.

"Hi, Emery." Parker returned his smile. They had virtually nothing in common, but she was finding it hard not to like him. He was easygoing but steady, in or out of the office, and his gentle presence made her feel at ease. He had checked on her daily and provided helpful information on incorrect registration forms of several of the season-pass holders. Apparently few people came and went around the resort without Emery knowing them or their mother or their brother.

"How's the season-pass work coming along?"

"Finished it last night. I'm moving on the conference ledgers today."

"Great. Our bookkeeper should be a big help. She's got a memory like you wouldn't believe. She can tell you not only what happened

when and where, but how polite or messy people were while doing it."
He chuckled.

"She's been wonderful so far. I'm sure I'll depend on her expertise
a lot during this first season," Parker admitted, thinking of the resort
secretary. She wasn't the most meticulous bookkeeper in the world, but
she would do anything for you. Almost everyone at Bear Run was like
that, though part of Parker was still waiting for the other shoe to drop.

"Hey, you two." Irene and Greg walked in together and both
hugged Emery before taking their seats, though Parker sensed a slight
reserve in Greg's greeting.

"Are you settled in, Parker?" Irene asked.

"I'm almost completely unpacked."

Irene had dropped by the apartment one evening with a loaf of
fresh-baked bread and a chicken casserole. It was the first home-cooked
food Parker had eaten since she'd arrived, and she lived off it for days.
Judging by their few interactions, Irene was the mother of the entire
mountain, always cooking for, or cleaning up after, or checking in on
someone.

Parker could hear Sammy and Campbell bickering all the way
down the hall, as they usually were. Not an angry argument, more
like good-natured sibling rivalry. They seemed inseparable, though
Campbell seemed more elusive, even mysterious, than her forthright
brother. Parker wondered if she ever tired of spending all her time with
this perpetual adolescent.

"Hi, Parker. How's it going?" Sammy said, plopping down next
to her.

"Good. How are you?"

"Great," he replied, with his usual grin.

"What about you, Campbell?" she asked. The woman had barely
spoken to her since she arrived, and Parker had yet to decide if she was
shy, uninterested, or distrustful.

Campbell had slipped out of her jacket and was taking off her
baseball cap. When she turned to face Parker, she smiled politely. "I'm
fine, thanks for asking."

Parker noticed again how naturally attractive Campbell was, in
an unrefined way. Her wavy, sand-colored hair curled back behind her
ears and hung just above her shoulders. Her deeply tanned face and
arms set off her bright blue eyes, and her smile was contagious when

she let it show in full force. But those occasions were usually reserved for family members.

Would she ever receive such a smile? The thought surprised her. Why would she care whether Campbell smiled at her? The woman had barely spoken since she arrived.

"I'm back. Did you all miss me?" An energetic woman who appeared to be just a few years older than Parker's own twenty-nine years bustled through the door. Everyone jumped up to greet her with more hugs all around.

What a huggy group this was. They seemed to embrace each other for no apparent reason, even if they'd seen one another the day before. No one had tried to hug her yet, but she was beginning to wonder if it was simply a matter of time before they did. She didn't know how comfortable she was with that possibility.

"You must be Parker," the latest arrival said. "I'm Janelle, Greg and Emery's baby sister."

Parker shook the outstretched hand firmly. Janelle was obviously a Carson. She had sandy hair like the rest, with a natural muscle tone, slightly thrown off by a bit of extra girth around her waist, though she was in better shape than Greg, who appeared to be fifteen years her senior.

"I've been on maternity leave, hence the leftover baby weight. But I can't miss another ski season, so I took one final vacation with the hubby and the kids last week before starting back to work."

"Did you enjoy the beach?" Irene asked.

"It was heaven, warm and sunny the whole time. The kids loved the waves and the sand. I could hardly drag them away."

"What about your husband?" Greg asked with a smile. "Was it hard to drag him away from all the bikinis?"

"You know it." Janelle laughed loudly. "He was drooling as much as the baby half the time we were there. I told him to keep dreaming. Can you imagine? Him and his pasty white beer belly in his ten-year-old swim trunks."

The whole family laughed along with her. Parker shifted in her seat, slightly uncomfortable. She'd heard people talk like this, but usually those conversations took place in a bar, not a business meeting.

Janelle settled into her seat. "Greg, I saw one of the lifts running this morning. That's a good sign."

"Oh yeah, I know it runs, which is a step up on last year. We'll start inspecting them this week before it gets too cold."

"What about you, Irene?" Emery asked. "How's the licensing renewal coming for the daycare?"

"So far so good. We're up to code and three sitters are returning, so we know they'll clear background checks. I've got some good applicants from the community college to fill the other slots. We'll start bringing them in for interviews shortly."

Parker listened absently to the casual exchange between the older siblings of the Carson family for several minutes before she realized they weren't just chatting. They had begun the actual meeting. She immediately put her pen to work, taking notes and trying to recall what had already been said. The tone of the conversation didn't change whether they were talking about their brother-in-law on the beach or the renewal of their childcare license. Parker was more than a little disconcerted. She was good at her job, but she wasn't the most adept at all this family-oriented banter, and the two seemed completely interwoven here.

Janelle added, "My two shift managers are back in the kitchen, and I need to start reviewing applications for servers and cleanup staff. I plan to drop by the college and the high school later this week and put ads in the newspaper."

"What about the county food inspectors?"

"Oh, I'll call Don in a week or two and have him come out after I've given the kitchen a good scrub."

"Have Dahlia and Juan help. I don't want you doing it all by yourself," Emery said, sounding more like a brother than a boss.

Parker had no idea who Don, Dahlia, or Juan was, but everyone else seemed to, so she didn't want to interrupt. She was successful in any job because she learned as much as she could about every aspect of the business, not just the parts she was directly responsible for. She would have to approach this resort as a student would a textbook.

"What about you, Uncle Emery, how's the lodge looking?" Campbell asked. Her uncle oversaw all of the lodging, including the conference facilities, the housekeeping staff, and the general upkeep of the main lodge and cabins. It was the first time she had spoken since the meeting started, and the sound of her voice almost startled Parker.

"Well, I guess since everyone else is hiring, I'd better get a jump on the cleaning staff. We'll start getting reservations for Christmas anytime now, so I'll start working on the rentals, checking fireplaces and plumbing and whatnot."

"Cam and I are in the same boat," Sammy added. "We have to get in touch with lift staff and ski instructors, but we won't be able to start training for a while."

"Sounds good," Emery said. "Anything else?"

Everyone stared at Parker expectantly, and she froze. It wasn't that she didn't have anything to say. She had too much to say, and her brain jammed with the weight of the presentation she had worked on for days. She had prepared charts and graphs and projections and a formal speech. She wore a business suit and low heels. Now she had to quickly reassess the formality of the situation while they all stared at her.

"You need more women," she blurted.

Everyone chuckled.

"I've been telling them that for years," Sammy said. "Whatever you have planned, count me and Campbell in."

Campbell scowled at her brother, and Parker's heart beat faster. Campbell and Sammy were interested in getting more women to the mountain? Did that mean Campbell was gay? Why hadn't she picked up on that possibility sooner? Campbell had been playing softball the first time she saw her, and she was so sexy in those tight white baseball pants. Surely that was a sign. She grinned in spite of herself at the stereotype she had just used.

Quickly she realized she had lost her train of thought and shifted her attention to the situation at hand. As she passed around the packet of graphs and charts she had printed for everyone, she tried not to pay attention to their bemused expressions.

"I could go through each of these, but basically your local demographics show that only children, college students, and men in the twenty to forty-five age and thirty-five to fifty-five thousand dollar income range buy season passes. You're missing a major portion of the population—adult women."

Parker paused. "You could boost your pass holders by as much as twenty percent if you find a way to tap into that market."

Emery pulled his reading glasses from the front pocket of his flannel shirt and slipped them on. He flipped through the packet of information. "Well, don't stop now. You're on a roll."

"Women stop coming to the resort when they start having children. Obviously women stop skiing because they don't have the time or resources."

Irene and Janelle both nodded, seeming to immediately understand where she was going.

"We ought to offer a women's special one day a week." Parker paused again and studied the expressions of the people around her.

"We'd offer free childcare for any woman who has a lift ticket," Irene said.

"And maybe a discount for lessons," Campbell added.

Parker smiled. They might be casual business people, but they were still business people.

Greg cleared his throat. "This is a pretty major decision to make so soon."

Parker regarded him carefully. "It's all in the numbers here. You're maxed out on men and children. If you want to increase your business, you need to target women."

"I hear what you're saying, but it'll take a lot of work and money to try a program like this. We'll have to advertise heavily and hire extra employees on your ladies' days in hopes that housewives really have some hidden desire to be downhill skiers." Greg sat back in his chair and folded his arms across his chest. "That's a lot of time, money, and manpower for something I doubt local gals would even be interested in."

"I assume you took all this into account in your cost-benefit analysis?" Emery asked.

"Absolutely. The bulk of your net income comes from lift tickets. Childcare, lodging, and food sales just have to break even."

"And having mothers and children on the mountain for an extra day will keep the concessions busy," Janelle said.

Greg shook his head. "I have a hard time believing all these women want to ski and we haven't heard anything about it until now."

"Maybe that's because no one ever thought to ask them," Parker said, trying to force a smile. "That's what you're paying me for."

Emery offered a compromise. "I think it's worth looking into. Let's give it a shot on a trial basis, and if it doesn't work, we'll cut it."

Greg threw up his hands. "Fine, just so long as it doesn't come out of my budget."

"Point taken," Emery said, then turned to Parker. "This is your baby. Get the word out and make it fit into the budget, and you can do whatever you want."

With that, everyone began to get up and leave. Parker was packing her briefcase, and when she finished, she and Emery were the only ones left.

"Good job today," he said.

"Thanks. I'm glad you approve, but I don't think everyone shares your opinion."

Emery chuckled. "Don't mind Greg. He's the oldest and the most stuck in his ways. He wasn't quite sold on hiring a marketing person, so he'll probably be slow to agree to new marketing ideas. But he'll come around when we show him your idea is good for the mountain. We're a big family. Have you ever met a family that agrees on everything all the time?"

"I'll just have to let the results prove me right on this one," Parker replied resolutely. She might not know much about skiing, but she trusted the numbers.

"Good. Now, is everything else okay?" Emery asked, switching gears. "Are you getting to know folks around here?"

"Everyone has been wonderful. The lack of bookkeeping has been frustrating, but the staff has been helping me fill in the blanks."

"Glad to hear it." Emery nodded in approval. "But there's more to life than work. Are you enjoying yourself at all?"

They started walking down the hallway toward Parker's office, continuing their conversation.

"I've been so busy with work and unpacking that I haven't had time for much else, but I am enjoying the job. You don't have to worry about me." Parker didn't feel ready to discuss her social life, or lack thereof, with her boss, even if she did feel connected to him in ways she couldn't quite put into words.

"Well, all the same, maybe you should call Sammy or Campbell and go out this weekend. You deserve a break."

Parker paused at the mention of Campbell, reflecting on the meeting and Sammy's comments. Campbell hadn't seemed pleased at being outed, but she had remained silent, as she always did.

Parker decided to take a chance and probe deeper. "Sammy's been great about checking up on me. Campbell is a lot quieter, though. She doesn't talk much, does she?"

Emery stopped, his quizzical gaze a little unsettling as he seemed to hear more to the question than she had spoken. "She certainly was quiet today, now that you mention it, but usually, no. She's only been back on the mountain six months, but she's always been outgoing. Hell, when she was little, you couldn't get her to shut up."

Parker forced a smile as she reached her office door. "Okay, I was just wondering."

"Well, like I said, have some fun this weekend." And with that he was gone.

Parker walked over to the window. She should be thrilled. Her first proposal had just been approved, even if only on a trial basis. This new project would be a challenge, which she usually thrived on. She had so much to do, so many details to bring into focus. So why was she thinking about Campbell, who was apparently an outgoing lesbian? How had she missed that?

CHAPTER FOUR

Campbell's skis cut through the fresh powder so deep in places that she could make out only the tips of her old Rossignols as they parted the surface. Occasionally she saw her breath, a translucent cloud blowing back into her face as she sliced down the side of the mountain. She didn't feel the cold, just an overwhelming sense of invigoration. Slowly the image faded, along with the feeling of movement, and finally when all sense of the experience was gone, she opened her eyes.

She had been back at Bear Run for half a year now, though it hardly seemed that long. The first few months had passed in a haze, days spent rehashing her decision to leave and replaying every fight she and Lynn had ever had. Almost from the very beginning of their relationship a pattern had emerged. Their core values had always been different. Lynn was driven, self-possessed, and thrived in go-it-alone battles. Campbell, on the other hand, needed to feel connected, wanted to be tied to something outside herself, and loved being part of a family. She hoped Lynn would come to appreciate those connections as well. She knew Lynn didn't see herself as a mother, but deep down Campbell hoped she would embrace the idea as she settled down and aged. Now she realized she had always wanted Lynn to grow into someone she wasn't. It had been as unfair to try and change Lynn as it had been for Lynn to try to keep her away from the people and places she loved.

Now back among her family, she was beginning to feel secure in herself once more. The pain of losing her first love was fading, and while lessons she associated with the loss were still fresh, she was finally finding the strength to consider her future. She loved her work at Bear

Run and could imagine taking over the resort someday and moving it from a winter playground to a year-round outdoors destination. She looked forward to watching her family grow and change, to helping her cousins grow into adults and being there for Sammy and his kids when that time came. Only occasionally, on the most restless of nights, did she let herself long for more.

She still dreamed of having it all, the lesbian *Leave it to Beaver* scenario, as she secretly referred to it. In that dream her wife was her partner in both love and life, someone with whom she could share everything. Someone who sent her heart racing with just one look and heated her up even on the coldest winter nights. Someone who accepted and loved her for who she was while still challenging her to be better. Someone to create a family and grow old with.

She never indulged in those fantasies for long. They weren't productive. She had the love and support of her family, and she had a job she was passionate about. Wasn't that enough? Nobody ever really had it all.

The sun was only beginning to creep through the half-open window of her bedroom. She lay still, breathing deeply, each breath filling her lungs with the crisp, cool air. The temperature had dropped at least twenty degrees and the scent of frost washed over her. Snow was still a few weeks off, but today, for the first time all fall, she could feel it coming. It was only the first weekend in November, but the sensation was unmistakable. It ran through to her bones. Snow was on the way.

Campbell pulled on a pair of jeans and a sweatshirt she had left on the floor. She couldn't go back to sleep. This morning held too much energy, too much promise for the season ahead. And everyone else on the mountain would know it, too, because they had spent their life on the slopes. Her family, their livelihood, everything was tied to the weather on this mountain and the change of every season. Early snow meant good times ahead. It always had, and after several years away Campbell was ready to face that promise.

She went outside, pulling on an orange windbreaker as she climbed onto an old four-wheeler. Slowly she rolled the ATV onto the slope that ran along the back of her house. A solid layer of frost coated the grass that was already turning brown. Life ebbed and flowed on the mountain in ways it didn't seem to in other places. Just now as the leaves were falling and the grass had stopped growing, the world seemed to be brown and dying, but actually in a few months everyone who lived here would be filled with life. They cared for the land, and in turn the land cared for them. This symbiotic relationship had served her family well for three generations, starting with her grandfather, who had built the lodge and installed the first rickety lift.

She urged the four-wheeler across the slope and turned along the line of trees that ran up the side of the mountain. Moving slowly, she breathed deeply as she climbed higher. As the sun peeked over the ridge, its light reflected off the frost and shimmered across the ground.

Campbell was completely lost in the peaceful beauty of her surroundings when she noticed movement in the woods up ahead. She slowly edged closer, not wanting to disturb whatever was working its way through the timber. It was probably a deer, which were thick in the woods this time of year. Her family worked hard to take only as many as they needed and to leave what the land could sustain. The hunters had just a few weeks to bag their prize, so they made the most of that time, and even though she hadn't seen any yet this morning, there were likely several out there.

Something was moving among the trees again as she slowed to a stop and squinted into the woods along one of the many narrow cross-country trails they had cut between the trees. As her vision adjusted, she realized she wasn't looking at an animal, but a person. And as the person moved closer, she could discern a woman jogging along the trail, dressed in a designer, chocolate-colored track suit. Campbell immediately hopped off the four-wheeler, her heart beating faster as she realized that if she had mistaken the jogger for a deer, a hunter could very easily do the same.

"Get out of there," she shouted, just before she recognized the woman. Parker glanced up, seeming startled to see her standing so close, then pulled some small headphones from her ears.

"Hi, Campbell." She smiled and slowed to a walk as she approached.

Campbell grabbed Parker's arm and pulled her onto the cleared slope. "What the hell are you doing? Are you trying to get yourself killed?"

Parker stared at her like she had gone crazy. "I was just jogging. I run here every day."

"In the woods? Dressed in brown? In the middle of hunting

season?" Campbell fought to control the tone of her voice, but she couldn't hide her fear and disbelief.

The color drained from Parker's face. "Hunting season?"

"Yes, it's deer season. Don't you watch the news?" Campbell knew she was yelling, but she couldn't get her nerves under control just yet.

"Of course I watch the news. I have CNN on constantly." Parker sounded incredulous.

"Well, I'm sure you think our local news is below you, but if you turned it on occasionally, you would know there are hunters all over these woods right now, and they'll shoot anything not wearing an orange jacket." Campbell was unsure where her anger came from. She hadn't intended to lash out at Parker.

"I can't imagine anyone allowing hunting when they could stop it. It's a barbarous activity that I won't even dignify with the term 'sport.' Killing helpless, innocent animals just for the fun of it, and to somehow prove your superiority. It certainly says a lot about your family to let it happen so close to home. That's practically teaching the children to do it when they get big enough to hold a gun. Why, someone could have shot me?"

"Sorry to upset your fragile bourgeois sensibilities, but hunting is necessary in this barbaric part of the world. The deer no longer have any natural predators, so if we don't control the population, they begin to starve to death." Campbell didn't understand why people from the city had such a hard time understanding the cycle of interaction between people and nature. "Hunting is a more humane manner of death, and we use them as food and clothing rather than leaving them to rot. That would be inhumane. Still, my family regulates hunting on our land. We grant only fifty permits a year, just enough to keep the deer from overpopulating the place but not enough to eliminate them. We sold all of the permits for this fall months ago, and the hunters have to abide by strict rules."

As Campbell talked, she noticed how stunning Parker was. Her dark hair was pulled back in a long ponytail, and her fair skin was slightly flushed from her workout and her anger. Her dark eyes were deep enough for Campbell to drown in.

"Everyone has their reason for doing things. That doesn't mean

I have to like it," Parker muttered. "I'll be more careful. And I might even watch the local news once in a while. That is, if you'll promise to watch CNN."

"Deal." Campbell nodded and took a deep breath to help regain her composure. This woman wouldn't last at Bear Run until Christmas. She'd probably run back to her sophisticated Chicago lifestyle any day now. "Where were you headed?"

"To the office."

"At seven on a Saturday morning?" This woman was unreal. A wave of frustration rose in Campbell, but she wasn't sure why she cared what Parker did on her weekends.

"I've got work to do," Parker said. "I don't have time to play."

Campbell shook her head. "How can you spend a day like this in an office?"

"I spend almost all of my days in an office. It's what I do. It's who I am."

"Really? It's pretty sad that you don't have anything more meaningful in your life than conference ledgers and marketing campaigns," Campbell snapped, then realized how nasty the comment sounded.

"Did you forget that those marketing campaigns benefit your precious mountain?"

Campbell nodded toward the four-wheeler. "Climb on."

Parker hesitated, eyeing the ATV suspiciously. Campbell swung a leg over, straddling the seat, then motioned for Parker to follow her.

The woman took a deep breath as if preparing herself for the worst, then climbed on. Campbell was about to show her how to hold on to the carrier rack on the back of the four-wheeler when Parker's hands came to rest lightly on her waist and caused an unexpected chill. She knew Parker's action was completely innocent, but she couldn't stop the goose bumps that rose on her skin as she started up the mountain. She hadn't felt a woman's touch in a long time, and her body reacted on its own accord.

She drove faster toward the top of the mountain, then along the top of the ridge. The sun was shining higher above them when Campbell stopped. She dismounted the ATV and nodded for Parker to follow her, right up to the edge of a steep drop-off.

As they gazed out over the edge, they could view the entire resort and beyond that more woods for as far as they could see. The view was breathtaking, even to Campbell, who had enjoyed it her entire life. They could make out a few towns dotting the landscape that rose and fell with each hill and valley, but mostly the vista painted with the last hues of autumn's pallet was undisturbed. She wondered if Parker could appreciate what she was seeing. She certainly couldn't find a view like this in Chicago.

"This is pretty. I've seen scenes like it on TV and wondered if they were real. Of course, it probably doesn't hold a candle to Aspen or the other resorts in the Rockies. I bet those offer some real scenery."

Campbell flinched. This woman was impossible. She would never realize that being on the mountain wasn't work, but a way of life. Well, let her stick to her office and work herself to death. "You'd know better than I would. I'm not much on overpriced places and overindulgent people. I guess you'd be right at home."

Campbell stalked over to the ATV.

Following her, Parker said, "Actually, I've never managed to get up there on my Colorado trips. I'd rather see a place firsthand than buy into stereotypes."

As they started down the mountain, Parker once again slipped her arms around Campbell's waist, but this time Campbell felt none of the thrill she had on the way up. Instead, she wondered how she could have ever been drawn to a woman who was so self-absorbed she couldn't see what was right in front of her.

When they reached the lodge, Parker let go. "Well, that was different, Campbell. Thanks for the break."

"No problem." Campbell was ready to get away from this irritating woman who didn't appreciate anything the mountain had to offer.

Parker began to walk away, but then, as if remembering something, she stopped and turned around.

"Campbell, it may be none of my business," she said quickly, "but in the meeting this week, your brother implied—"

"That I'm a lesbian?"

"Yes."

Campbell blushed. "I am."

Parker's smile formed slowly, as though she were fighting it but couldn't stop herself. "Me, too."

Campbell's pulse quickened and her irritation melted. She wasn't surprised by the statement, but by her own reaction to it. "Okay."

"Now that's out of the way," Parker transitioned awkwardly, "have a nice day."

"You, too," Campbell replied, then as an afterthought added, "Be careful on the way home."

Parker chuckled. "Thanks. I'll stick to the main roads until you tell me it's safe in the woods."

As Campbell pulled away, she wondered at her luck. Finally, a smart, attractive, passionate lesbian at Bear Run. This should have been everything she'd been dreaming of, yet after a few minutes of conversation, Campbell had been dying to get away from her. The whole situation felt like a great cosmic joke.

❖

"Where did you go this morning?" Sammy asked Campbell over breakfast at her parents' house.

Everyone stopped eating and waited for her answer.

Campbell's face warmed as she remembered the brief, confusing moments she had shared with Parker. "I went up to the drop-off to enjoy the view."

Her parents glanced at each other quickly. They had clearly been worried about her since she'd returned to the mountain unexpectedly six months earlier. While they would never say it, they hadn't agreed with her decision to leave when she first moved away to the city. Her dad had even tried to talk her out of it, saying the university was a waste of time, that they couldn't teach her anything he couldn't about running a ski resort. And he wouldn't even charge her, he'd said, trying to kid her into seeing his point of view. Her mother, however, had merely remarked that it wouldn't hurt her to see something besides Bear Run.

When Campbell moved back, her dad didn't say "I told you so," but he didn't have to. Whatever her parents thought, they let her know she was welcome there anytime.

"I saw the four-wheeler parked at the base lodge when I went by this morning," Emery said absentmindedly.

"I dropped Parker off there before I came over," Campbell

answered, realizing that even a casual statement was bound to spark more questions.

"You took Parker up the mountain with you?" Sammy asked, sounding more than a little surprised.

"Well, I didn't intend to. I saw her jogging on one of the cross-country trails." She took a bite of pancake, hoping to avoid the subject, since her interaction with Parker had stirred emotions she was still trying to sort out.

"That's a pretty damn dumb thing to do this time of the year," Greg mumbled with his mouth full.

"Our next-door neighbor is out there hunting right now," Irene said, sounding worried. "That's a great way for Parker to get herself shot."

"I told her that. She didn't even know it was hunting season."

"It's been all over the news," her mother said, shaking her head.

"I told her that, too. You know, we should do some workshops on nature conservancy, maybe hold educational programs. People from the city would love that, and if they're anything like Parker, they could use some instructions on how to get along out here," Campbell suggested.

"We're a ski resort, not a nursery school." Greg waved off the idea. "We should stick to doing what we know. It's not our fault Parker's too dumb to keep from getting shot at."

"Well, I hope she'll be more careful from now on," Emery said.

"I think she will." Campbell dropped the education idea. Her father was stuck in his ways, and now wasn't the time to try to push him out of them.

"So you took her to the office?" Greg asked. "She ought to get out more. No good can come of her being at work all the time. She's probably got a full day ahead of her thinking up ways to fix things that were working fine to begin with."

"I told her she shouldn't be working on a day like this," Campbell answered shortly, taking a bite of bacon even though that tactic hadn't helped so far.

"You talked an awful lot," Sammy said, a hint of suspicion in his voice. "I thought you didn't like her much."

Campbell stared at him blankly. "I never said that."

"Well, now that you mention it, I talked to Parker last week and I think she might have gotten the same impression," Emery said. "She mentioned something about you being awfully quiet around her. I thought that was odd."

Irene came to her daughter's defense. "Why would Campbell have any reason to dislike Parker?"

"Because Parker reminds her of Lynn," Sammy suggested bluntly.

The room fell quiet. Campbell didn't miss the look of deep concern that passed between her parents. She knew they worried about the pain her breakup with Lynn had caused her, and she tried not to let the sting of the comment show.

Likewise the expression on Sammy's face said he would do anything to take his words back. "I'm sorry, Cam. I don't know why I said that."

"It's fine." Campbell shrugged, her throat tight. "Don't worry about it."

She tried to shake the comment from her head. Though the mention of Lynn stung, she was afraid Sammy might be right. Had she been rude to Parker because she was afraid of being around another woman like her ex? Another power suit–clad lesbian with a ladder to climb and an ax to grind? Parker came from a similar background, highly educated and politically minded, and she never seemed to leave work. She had yet to mention her own family.

Campbell shuddered as she realized she was comparing Parker to the woman who had torn her heart apart only half a year ago. Then as if on cue she recalled the way she had snapped at her earlier, her comment about the local news being below Parker, and her anger about Parker working on a Saturday morning. Was that where her outburst had come from? Had she been venting old frustration about Lynn to the next similar target? That would explain that mysterious sense of unease she felt every time Parker was around.

Now that she thought about it, she realized she hadn't done a single thing to reach out to Parker since she arrived. Campbell was the only one in her family who hadn't offered to help her move in. Even Sammy had stopped by to check on her, and Campbell hadn't gone along. At the time she hadn't given it any thought. As the pieces began to fall into place, she was disappointed in herself. She knew what it was like to move to a new town, to start a new job, to be far away from everything familiar. She'd obviously let her own biases cloud her perception of Parker, and while she wasn't yet ready to consider what that meant about her own residual feelings for Lynn, she did realize that she needed to make more of an effort to see Parker for who she was and not the image she had projected onto her.

Campbell stayed at the table until breakfast was over, then made an excuse about wanting to get some stuff done around the house. She hugged everyone good-bye and didn't fail to notice that each of her parents gave her an extra squeeze before she left. It was nice to know they cared, but now that the wound had been reopened, she had to deal with it one way or another. Even if Parker irritated her, she would try to reach out to her. They had to make peace with one another. Who knew, maybe they could become friends. Parker certainly didn't qualify for anything more permanent than that.

CHAPTER FIVE

Parker paced around the living room of her small apartment with CNN playing on her TV, the sound turned low so she could hear NPR on her radio. Today the rest of the nation was choosing the politicians who would control Washington D.C. and by extension influence much of the world. Today was midterm election day. And here she was, stuck in the boonies, poring over ledgers and finishing tedious work that seemed inconsequential. With Greg opposing her, she might never to make any meaningful changes that would help Bear Run grow into the type of enterprise it could become.

Occasionally she would sit down on the couch long enough to mouse over a new article on her laptop. She was being silly since the East Coast results wouldn't even start coming in for another hour, but she couldn't help herself. She was going stir-crazy with nothing productive to do. She felt helpless. This was the first election since she was old enough to vote that she wasn't in the streets passing out information or in the war room of some campaign coordinating the final thrust of an operation to elect whatever official she'd thrown her weight behind.

That old version of herself, the true believer, had been hidden since she'd arrived in Wisconsin. That part of her had been badly beaten, left for dead. But today, election day, it would not be suppressed. Her political-wonk side was determined to resurface, if only for a few hours. Early projections were positive for progressive candidates across the country, and the old Parker had the new Parker holding her breath in anticipation.

She wanted to call Alexis, or any other old friend who she knew would be feeling the same sickening excitement she did. She had even picked up the phone and started dialing the 312 area code of Chicago, but she stopped, knowing that anyone who felt like she did in Chicago today wouldn't have time to chat about it. Everyone was busy, not busy watching results but busy shaping them.

Parker was surrounded by people who had no understanding of the outside world. Even Campbell, the only lesbian she had met in her first month at Bear Run, might as well have been a straight girl for all her Midwestern sensibilities. The world was changing so rapidly, but at Bear Run time seemed to crawl like a snail. While Parker was busy trying to pull herself back together, she might be missing out on the chance to make a difference in some way that actually mattered.

Everyone had warned her that those feelings would overcome her eventually. She was surprised she hadn't experienced them before. The overwhelming regret, the longing to be back in the hunt, to be canvassing the campaign trail, the high that came from throwing herself into something so much greater than herself—it was a trip, an addiction, the reason she had to get as far away from that world as possible.

Had she stayed in Chicago, she would have no doubt caved by now. She knew her own weakness. She would have jumped on the first campaign wagon hauling a promising candidate who said the right thing at the right time, and she would have been welcomed aboard. She was aware of her own powers, especially her ability to help put people in positions of power. She had worked on over half a dozen major campaigns and claimed a share of the victory in each one, a fact she had been proud of until six months ago. Like every time before, she had picked a winner, one who, like all the others, said the right things at the right time, one who could go far beyond the state senate and was prepared to take Parker with him all the way to the top. He would be a winner, all right. He would win at any cost. Parker shuddered.

She realized she had been reliving her fall from grace longer than she thought. It was seven o'clock and the polls along the East Coast were closing. Results were beginning to come in. She turned up the sound on her TV in time to hear that the projections appeared to be holding true as governors' races went to Democrats in New York and Maryland. The bright blue congressional seating chart graphic flashed across the screen, showing that Democrats had also picked up senate seats in New Hampshire and Rhode Island and congressional seats in at least four states. Parker smiled broadly. The political system might be badly broken, but it was the only one available at the moment, and it seemed to be swinging in favor of her views.

The phone rang, and she jumped to pick it up. "Hello?"

"Darling, if you get in the car now, you can be here around midnight. The party will just be getting good by then."

"Alexis. What are you doing?"

"I'm on my way home to change and soak my feet."

"But the polls are open for another half hour," Parker reprimanded lightly. There was still a chance to sway a few more votes.

Alexis laughed. "You're such a good soldier, always fighting to the death. You're much more suited for this job than I. Why don't you come take over for me?"

"You're great at your job, Alexis."

"Oh, what do you care?" She faked a pout. "I thought you were done with the glamorous world of politics."

"Just because I can't work with you anymore doesn't mean I don't care." Parker meant that. She did care. She cared too much, believed too much, so much that she couldn't trust her own judgment anymore.

"*He's* going to win, you know?" Alexis said softly.

Parker sighed, knowing exactly who she was talking about. "Yeah, I know. I'm the one who told him how."

"I just didn't want you to be surprised when you saw the results come in."

"Thanks. I'll be fine. So where are you going tonight?" Parker changed the subject because she couldn't let her mind go back there again, not tonight.

She didn't hear her friend's response due to a loud knock at her door. "Hey, Alexis, hold on a sec. Someone's here."

"Get back to me when you have a chance. They're calling some of the Pennsylvania and Ohio races on the radio, and I want to hear what they have to say."

"Okay." Parker hung up and opened her door. She wasn't expecting anyone in particular but was caught off guard to see Campbell standing there. She sported a well-worn pair of blue jeans and a white button-down shirt under a brown leather jacket, and her wavy golden brown hair was combed back and tucked behind her ears. Parker, struck by how handsome she was, was surprised when her pulse quickened.

"Hi, Parker." Campbell shifted her weight from one foot to the other, seeming unsure.

"Hey, Campbell. Come in," Parker said. "To what do I owe this honor?"

"I tried to catch you at work today, but I missed you."

They both stepped back into the apartment, closing the door. "I left right at five today to watch the election-day coverage." Parker's attention was mostly on Campbell, but she was still watching the TV out of the corner of her eye.

"I didn't mean to interrupt anything," Campbell said, obviously aware that Parker's attention was divided. "I'll let you get back to it."

Parker faced her fully. The coverage was important, but what Campbell had come over for probably was, too. "No, what did you need?"

"Nothing, really." Campbell shrugged nervously. "I was just going to a football game. My cousins play, and I thought you might like to come along."

"Normally, I would, but…" Parker absorbed a bulletin that flashed across the screen. Two more congressional races were being called in favor of Democratic candidates.

"No, it's okay," Campbell said, turning to leave. "It was silly of me to stop by tonight. You have much bigger things on your mind than a middle-school football game."

"It was really nice of you to think of me. Maybe this weekend we could—" Parker's phone was ringing. She glanced at the caller ID. Alexis was calling again. She hesitated for a moment, not sure what to do.

"I'll let you get that," Campbell said.

"No, Campbell, the machine can get it." She wasn't sure why she handled Campbell gently, but she wanted to please the woman standing across the room from her. Maybe it was her soft blue eyes, or that she seemed fragile, despite her chiseled features. Politics were a big part of Parker's past, but Campbell would be a big part of her future if she stayed at Bear Run. Though today, even more than most days, she wasn't sure she wanted that. Small-town football games and stifling families weren't her thing.

"Really, I should get going. The game starts soon." Campbell was already heading for the door.

"Okay, thanks for coming by. I wish I could go with you," Parker said, and realized she almost meant it. There was something special about Campbell that she couldn't put her finger on. The game might be bearable, sitting next to her.

Campbell smiled. "Maybe some other time."

"Parker, darling, pick up the phone," Alexis called from the answering machine.

Parker flushed as she realized Campbell would be able to hear everything Alexis was about to say. Silently she cursed herself, knowing her friend's propensity for running her mouth. She should have just answered the phone.

"Have you drowned in the black hole of civilization up there?" Alexis continued. "I'm not sure if they have these newfangled things called televisions where you are, but here in the real world we're taking back control of Congress. Answer the phone and I'll tell you all about it."

Campbell raised an eyebrow, blushing slightly, but Parker didn't know if she was angry, embarrassed, or something else. "Sounds important."

"Campbell, she's just..." Parker fumbled.

"It's fine. They don't play small-town football games on 'newfangled' televisions, so I have to leave if I want to see the boys in action." With that she was gone, closing the door softly.

Parker flopped limply onto the couch and picked up the phone. "Alexis—"

"Oh, good, you're still alive." Alexis laughed.

"Yes," she sighed, "I'm alive."

"Did you see the news? We're a third of the way to controlling Congress, and only fifteen percent of the races have been called. We're on pace to take it all."

"I did see that on my television, Alexis. Not only do I have one in my living room, but in the bedroom, too," she snapped, irritated that Campbell had been finally reaching out to her, only to close right back up.

"What's with the sour mood all of a sudden? Is watching TV all you've been doing in your bedroom lately?"

"Alexis, I had company," Parker answered flatly.

"A woman?" Alexis's tone grew serious.

"As a matter of fact, yes, but it's not what you're thinking. It was Campbell."

"And tell me again, which one is Campbell?"

Parker had spoken with Alexis on a regular basis since moving, but her friend had little interest in learning about the day-to-day operations of a small-time ski resort. "She's the niece of the resort manager. Her dad supervises the lifts, and her mom runs the child care. She's been working on the slopes and is a ski instructor in the winter."

There was silence on Alexis's end of the line.

Parker continued. "She's the one who took me up the mountain on the four-wheeler."

"She's the lesbian," Alexis shouted, sounding giddy.

"Yes, she's the lesbian." Parker should have known that was the only detail Alexis would remember.

"Are you sleeping with her?"

"No," Parker practically yelled. "Alexis, does your mind have a permanent mailing address in the gutter?"

"I was just asking. She sounds hot, like a lesbian Marlboro Man."

Parker chuckled in spite of her effort to be perturbed. The description was disturbingly accurate.

"Hey, speaking of lesbians you love who never leave home," Alexis segued into a topic Parker was equally uncomfortable with, "Mia will be at the party tonight. Do you want me to spill punch on her shoes or something?"

Parker's smile faded. "She has every right to be there, Alexis. This is a big night for her."

"It's a big night for her daddy," Alexis corrected, an unmistakable bitterness creeping into her voice.

"Mia is her father's daughter. You can't separate the two." Parker felt none of the animosity of her friend and only a hint of sadness.

"Right. Daddy and his followers do all the work, then Mia buys a new dress and hops up onstage to take all the credit. It's a pretty tight bond." Alexis's tone was biting. She and Mia had rarely gotten along, and since Mia and Parker's breakup, Alexis no longer felt obligated to be polite to her.

"That's not really fair. Don't forget that you and I both owe a lot to that family. There isn't a single person in the Chicago Democratic

Party that doesn't," Parker said, partly out of loyalty to the party and partly because completely discrediting Mia would remind her of her own lapse in judgment.

Alexis sighed. "I know. Technically the man is my boss's boss, but I still can't stand the way Mia played the part of his little lapdog when the senator got caught with his hand in the cookie jar this summer. She was your lover, for God's sake. That should have meant something."

"It's over, Alexis." Parker fought to keep her voice level despite the familiar thickness beginning to engulf her throat. "I've moved on. You should, too."

"Still," Alexis's tone lightened, "I could just spill a little punch—"

"Alexis," Parker laughed again, "go enjoy the party. You've earned it. This is a big night. Live it up for both of us."

"Okay. I'll call you tomorrow with all the gossip."

Parker hung up and turned up CNN just in time to hear the first results from the central time zone. More Democratic victories. She snuggled in on the couch. It would be a long night, and she planned to do everything possible to enjoy it. She thought back briefly to Campbell's visit and hoped that Alexis hadn't offended her too much. She and Campbell had little in common, but it wouldn't hurt to have a friend here at Bear Run. The thought of a middle-school football game on a day like today was almost comical, but Campbell had at least tried to reach out to her, which had to count for something.

CHAPTER SIX

"A ll right, Noel, drive us up to Uncle Greg." Campbell pulled the fair-haired little girl onto her lap. The five-year-old gripped the steering wheel and turned it gently to the left. Campbell gave the rusty old pickup truck a little gas, and they started slowly up the mountain.

Campbell had been away from the mountain for most of Noel's life, but since she'd returned she'd tried to build a relationship with her young cousin. Noel represented the future of the family, the next generation of Carsons. She already seemed interested in the family business and, even at five, showed a respect for the land that had been in their family for three generations. Campbell sought to nurture that connection early, the way her older family members had done for her, hoping that someday Noel would bring her own dreams to the family business, just as Campbell had returned home to do.

The PoleCat snowmaker they were towing—a black, cannonlike structure—was rolling steadily along. They weren't going far, but it was important to keep every snowmaker in tip-top condition. They would be dependent on the PoleCats to help create the base of snow that would blanket the resort for the next five or six months.

Noel seemed to take her job as driver seriously as she turned the steering wheel no more than an inch or two at a time. Campbell smiled as they reached their destination and Sammy and her father waved for them to stop. She shifted into park and secured the hill brake before giving Noel a little squeeze. "Good driving, kiddo."

"Hey, Noel," Sammy called as they climbed out of the truck, "want to help me hook up the hoses?"

"Yeah." The child bounced over to him, excited to be involved in another important task.

Campbell and her father unhitched the snow cannon and rolled it the few feet to where Sammy and Noel were uncoiling a series of black and green hoses. Greg silently patted her back, then headed off to oversee Sammy.

Campbell stood in the middle of what would be known as the bunny slope in a few weeks. This would be her domain until the end of March. She took in the wide clearing, considering every bump and curve. To her right was a raised conveyor belt that would serve as a carpet lift for the youngest skiers. A more traditional chairlift would carry the beginners halfway up the mountain when they were ready. Last year, she had missed all this, and now she wanted to take in every aspect of the experience.

When she surveyed the land, she noticed how the terrain dipped lightly from one of the beginner trails into a stand of fir trees before it leveled out onto the bottom of an intermediate run. The summer rain had eroded part of the hillside over the past few years as the trees grew large enough to divert the water, but Campbell hadn't been around to see the change until now. The new layout could help skiers work on their speed control and transitions. With a few minor adjustments, it could be a wonderful learning tool.

"Hey, Dad." Campbell pointed to the spot she'd been inspecting. "If we took out those four trees, we'd have a perfect cut-through between these two trails."

Greg glanced up for only a few seconds before he went back to work on the snow gun. "We don't need a cut-through. Both those runs end up in the same space."

"It would be a fun little drop for folks who're just getting up their speed but can't handle a full slope yet," Campbell reasoned. "It wouldn't be hard to do. Sammy and I could have those trees out in an afternoon."

"Cam, I know you're excited, but things are working fine as they are. Don't be in such a hurry to change the place," Greg said, then added in a softer tone, "It's a beautiful day. Why would you want to disrupt any of this?"

Campbell dropped the subject. There was no sense starting an argument. It was a perfect day. During the past week the temperature had hung steadily in the upper thirties during the day and the mid twenties at night. They would station all the PoleCats on the beginner trails today, and hopefully they would place some of the heavier single-barrel snow guns on the intermediate slopes. The entire family would help for the day, and with some of the winter employees they would finish securing the rest of the snowmakers later in the week.

"Hey, Parker's car is in the lodge parking lot," Emery called to Greg and Sammy. "Somebody get her out here. She should be a part of this, too."

Campbell knew her family was worried about her after last Saturday's breakfast conversation, so she tried to remain casual about the request. "You two keep working. I'll go see if she'd like to join us."

She started down the hill in the truck. Try as she might, she couldn't make sense of their last encounter, four days ago. Parker had seemed genuinely happy to see her, even if she was a little distracted by the television. Campbell could hardly hold that against her. The woman had spent her entire adult life working in politics and was entitled to be a little distant on election day. Even inviting Campbell in was a big gesture of good will, but the phone call… "Black hole of civilization." Was that really what Parker thought of Bear Run?

If Campbell's home and family business were so beneath her, why didn't she just hit the road? The Carsons had done fine without her, and they could do without her bad attitude right now. Besides, if the resort was so unworthy of her, why was she working sixty-five-hour weeks for a place she considered not even part of the "real world"? Like so many things about Parker, it just didn't add up, and Campbell was getting frustrated with all her inconsistencies.

The office door was open, and Parker smiled broadly at her.

"Good morning, Campbell." She sat behind her desk, wearing a purple and white sweatshirt that simply read "Northwestern" in large block letters. Despite Campbell's aggravation, she couldn't ignore the fact that Parker was truly beautiful. In fact, she was even more attractive in the sweatshirt than in her power suits, which seemed contrived, as though they were merely a calculated part of the message she tried to send. The casual attire made her appear more real and certainly more comfortable in her own skin.

"Hey, you went to Northwestern?" Campbell asked when she found her voice.

"Yeah, who wants to know?"

"One of your biggest rivals, that's who." Campbell took up a playfully defiant stance.

"Which one? University of Wisconsin?"

"Yep. With honors, no less."

"Cum laude?" Parker asked, as though that fact had piqued her interest.

"Magna." Campbell felt herself blush slightly. She wasn't used to bragging about herself like this.

"That's impressive."

"Don't sound so shocked," Campbell teased. "Did you think you were the only one on the mountain with a Big Ten background?"

"Well, no," she replied, flustered, but Campbell was positive from Parker's reaction that she probably had made assumptions about her level of education. She didn't buy it when Parker tried to cover by saying, "I just didn't know we were rivals."

"You can hardly consider Northwestern a real rival," Campbell said.

"Are you insulting my Wildcats?" Parker said with a hint of laughter.

"Never. I saw them play in Madison one year. They didn't need us to put them down. They managed to do that fine all by themselves."

"I'll get you for that one." Parker smiled. "Maybe we'll have to go down to Madison for the game next year."

Campbell's heart ached at the thought of returning to Madison. She knew her expression changed immediately, and she tried to cover it quickly but managed only to mumble a noncommittal, "Maybe."

Parker must have realized she'd said something that caused Campbell to withdraw, because she stopped chuckling immediately. They both fell into an awkward silence before Parker reassumed her professional persona. "What can I do for you?"

"You can stop coming to the office on Saturdays, for starters," Campbell replied matter-of-factly. The vivid reminder of Lynn had spoiled her kidding mood.

Parker regarded her seriously. "I do my job the best way I know how. If you have a problem with that—"

"I do."

"You do what?" Parker asked, seeming confused.

"I have a problem with how you're doing your job." Campbell was tired of this conversation.

Parker flushed, either with anger or frustration. "I don't see where working *too much* has ever deterred someone from researching effective marketing strategies. So unless your degree is in marketing, I suggest you stick to your own work and let me focus on mine."

Campbell chuckled at Parker's defensiveness. The hint of color rising in her cheeks was more flattering than the glow of the florescent lights. Were there any more pleasant ways to make her blush? "You're missing the point."

"I beg your pardon?"

"You're doing the wrong kind of research. The keys to marketing this place aren't in those books," she said, pointing to the conference ledgers Parker had strewn across her desk. "People come here, and come back, for the mountain, and the mountain is out there."

Parker glanced out the window as though she had barely noticed the onset of activity on the slopes. "What are they doing?"

"We're placing the snowguns today. It's the unofficial start of winter," Campbell explained patiently.

"You're going to start making snow?"

"No, *we're* going to start making snow."

At Parker's questioning expression, Campbell picked up her coat from where it had been draped over the back of her chair and handed it to her. "If you really want to learn about this mountain, put away the books and start experiencing it."

"You think this will give me some extra insight that will help my job?"

"I wouldn't be here if I didn't." Campbell was learning that she got a lot further with Parker when she appealed to her sense of professionalism. While Parker might pass on an opportunity to get out on the slopes, she wasn't likely to miss the chance to see another side of the business.

Parker shrugged. "I guess it never hurts to learn something new, especially if it might affect my livelihood." She took the coat Campbell held out to her, their fingers brushing lightly in the exchange and leaving Campbell to wonder if the contact was accidental or perhaps more intimate.

Once outside, Campbell motioned for Parker to help her with

a snow cannon. Together they shoved the carriage into position and hitched it to the back of the truck. "This is a PoleCat snowgun. We're going to take it up to where Sammy and my dad are."

"Okay." Parker shrugged and climbed into the truck.

"The PoleCats will be stationed all over the base area, the flats on the mountaintop, and the beginner slopes." As Campbell relayed the information, she watched Parker carefully for any sign of boredom, afraid she would find this type of work beneath her. Parker, however, seemed interested in taking it all in, which was promising.

"What about the intermediate trails?" Parker asked, glancing toward a trail with a sharper incline that was coming into view.

"These machines are too top-heavy to be placed on steep terrain. We'll station some of our single- and double-barrel guns on our longer, heavy-traffic blues and blacks."

"Blues and blacks?"

Was Parker serious? "Blue trails are intermediate ones, and black trails are for experts."

"Oh, right. That's how they show up on the trail map, right?"

"Right." Campbell nodded, caught off guard that someone who worked at a ski resort would be so clueless about the basic trail-rating system, but she didn't have time to probe further.

"Hi, Sammy. I hear you're getting ready to make some snow," Parker called as soon as the truck stopped.

"We should start tonight," Sammy said, with his characteristic broad, boyish smile. "Pretty exciting, huh?"

"Sure is."

Parker's smile fell somewhere short of exuberant.

"So this is a family affair," Parker noted as they started off down the mountain again.

"Most things around here are." Campbell wondered if Parker was ready to work alongside the family. She depended on the mountain now, just like the rest of them, and that bond could be as thick as any blood relation, but she doubted Parker understood that yet.

They stopped next to a large storage shed around the corner from the main lodge, where several of the snowguns were already uncovered and assembled on their metal sled frames, and quickly loaded several guns into the truck bed. Campbell watched appreciatively as Parker helped lift the heavy machinery. Despite her slender frame, she was anything but frail. When she pushed up the sleeves of her sweatshirt, revealing the subtle flex of her biceps, Campbell's temperature rose for reasons that had nothing to do with their shared physical exertion. "Those guns we just loaded were Snow Giant single-barrel snowguns," Campbell said. "They're a lot more powerful than the PoleCats, so we'll move them all over the mountain for most of the season."

"You won't need them all winter, will you?" Parker was quickly accepting the role of student.

"Man-made snow is much denser and therefore more resilient, so even when we have a good snowfall, we'll make snow at night too and mix it with the natural stuff," Campbell answered. "We don't like to have too many blowers running during the day while the skiers are here."

"Why?"

"Why what?" Campbell moved the steering wheel to send them up the mountain at a better angle.

"Why not run them when the skiers are here?"

Campbell chuckled. "You've obviously never skied in front of one of these before."

Parker stiffened, her deep brown eyes clouding over. "No, but I know about skiing. I spent two spring breaks in Colorado listening to my brother obsess over back bowls and moguls."

Campbell wasn't sure what had set Parker off, but she had clearly been offended. What nerve had she inadvertently hit? "I didn't mean to imply anything." She measured her words carefully. "These guns shoot a high-pressure mix of air and water that freezes almost immediately, pelting anyone nearby with considerable force. They're loud and strong and pumping out lake-water snow that doesn't taste very good if you breathe it in."

"That doesn't sound pleasant," Parker said, her tone much more level.

"That's why we run them at night as much as we can, but of course in the fall and spring we sometimes need to go around the clock to keep the base layer thick enough to ski on."

The conversation halted as they reached the first station and stopped the truck. Emery was waiting there with his twin sons and Noel, and after quick introductions they all set to work unloading the snowguns.

"Here's a station," Campbell said as she pointed to two pipes protruding a few feet out of the ground just on the edge of a line of trees. "One pipe is for the water pumped from the lake, and the other is for the compressed air. They both feed into the barrel of the gun here and are expelled into the air at very high speeds."

"And that freezes into snow and makes huge piles," one of the twins added.

The other boy jumped in. "Then you ski over them and get big air."

Campbell was pleased to see Parker reward the boys' enthusiasm with what appeared to be the beginnings of a genuine smile. She was even happier to see Parker turn that little grin toward her, causing her breath to emerge in shorter bursts. This less-guarded version of Parker was much more likeable than the one she had previously come to know.

The excitement in everyone's voice was evident. Even Noel joined the fun by saying, "I'm going down a blue this year."

Campbell laughed. "Only if you take me or Sammy with you."

"Or Parker?" the child asked, staring expectantly up at them.

Parker had an unmistakable expression of concern and, inexplicably, Campbell had a sudden urge to protect her. "Only if Parker wants to."

Parker smiled nervously at the child. "Campbell is probably a better teacher than I am."

Campbell realized Parker hadn't made the statement out of modesty. She appeared genuinely concerned, and her furrowed brow and tightly pressed lips were much less alluring than the earlier look of happy amusement. Something was wrong, but before Campbell could question her further, the kids were clambering to unload the snowguns. She returned her attention to the current task, but she definitely needed to figure out what was going on.

Campbell spent much of the rest of the day trying to piece together Parker's odd reactions. They had placed well over half of the snowguns, and Parker even became an asset to the team by the end of the day. She was a quick learner and eventually warmed to the more technical aspects of the task, learning the intricacies of snowmaking. Campbell doubted that Parker appreciated the finer points of working alongside the Carson family or felt any meaningful connection to the land, but at least she wasn't afraid to get her hands dirty. She hadn't seemed concerned about the physical labor either, never once shying away from lifting or towing anything. Had Campbell misjudged her? Parker obviously would never be a happy member of the Bear Run team, but perhaps she had more depth than the "fragile bourgeois sensibilities" Campbell had accused her of.

In fact, the only times Parker had seemed concerned was when they talked about skiing. Campbell couldn't figure out what would cause such reactions in a woman who was normally so self-assured. Then it all started to come together. Parker didn't know the color code of the slopes, the purpose of the snow guns, or if she could keep up with a five-year-old. Parker didn't know how to ski.

Campbell's temper flashed hot. She had been about to let Parker off the hook, only to find out Parker had misled her and her family about something so central to their lives. The woman was maddening. Early on, she could have simply stated that she didn't ski, and no one would have held it against her, but no, she was too stubborn to admit she was less than perfect in any way. Now she had dug herself into a hole she wasn't likely to find her way out of, and it served her right.

Campbell wanted so badly to give in to her sense of self-righteousness, wanted to feel vindicated in knowing she had simply misread Parker, and she wanted to take pleasure in exposing her. Instead, she felt frustrated that she was already thinking of ways to bail Parker out.

CHAPTER SEVEN

Parker stood up and stretched out her back. She had been hunched over her desk for hours and was starting to doze off. Yawning, she looked out the window at the mountain and its looming gray clouds. The snowguns had been blowing for almost a week, and huge piles of snow were appearing at random intervals all over the slopes. The entire scene was rather surreal. Not much natural snow had fallen yet, so the parking lot was covered by the occasional puddle, but on the other side of the building, a winter wonderland was springing up. The piles of snow hadn't developed out of thin air, and she was unusually proud of having helped create them.

Working alongside the Carson family made her feel part of something larger than herself. Her involvement wasn't as thrilling as her work in politics and certainly didn't matter as much in the grand scheme of things, but it was something. As she recalled the afternoon she helped place the snowguns, she realized again how much she had enjoyed working by Campbell's side. She had isolated herself since arriving at Bear Run, but now it was good to have someone to talk to, even if they did occasionally trade barbs.

Sammy and Campbell were driving the massive snow groomer on the beginners' hill. The large, yellow, tanklike machine that had been parked out back when she'd arrived that morning seemed rather ominous despite its cheerful color. Set on conveyor treads half as tall as she was, it featured a huge corrugated metal plow that Campbell and Sammy had been using to push the piles in the beginners' area for several hours so that they all blended into one even layer of man-made snow. The area now resembled a small frosted square of cake, with the rest of the icing heaped in haphazard globs.

Parker returned to her desk. She had finished analyzing the conference ledgers, having reorganized all the records and plugged the data into a spreadsheet that allowed her to study the information in a number of ways. No trend jumped out at her like she had discovered with the season passes. The conferences were exactly what she would expect. A lot of church groups, some Boy Scout and Girl Scout troops, and some academic departments from nearby colleges held events and annual retreats there. The small resort also pulled in some local businesses from time to time. As far as she could see, the conference center wasn't lacking anything, but it wasn't outstanding either.

She flipped through the information for the tenth time in the past two hours. She had obviously missed something, failed to consider some angle. A soft knock on the door roused her, and then Campbell stood in the doorway, her hair peeking out from underneath a stocking cap and her blue eyes hinting of mischief. In her hands was a pair of thick black plastic boots.

"New pair of shoes?" Parker asked, and smiled. Something about this woman made her feel warm inside. They hadn't exactly hit it off, so their connection was inexplicable, but unmistakable. Of course it didn't hurt that Campbell was built like a wilderness goddess. Her tan skin and rippling muscles were certainly hot enough to raise Parker's body temperature a few degrees.

"Yeah, they're Kenneth Cole and *so* this season." Campbell affected a superior tone.

"Oh, my God, they're divine. I've always wanted a pair just like that."

"Size eight?"

"Seven and a half."

Campbell grinned. "Close enough. I hope you're wearing thick socks."

"You were being serious?"

"Not about the Kenneth Cole part, but yeah, these are your ski boots. Come on, I've got more stuff for you downstairs." Then she disappeared.

Parker froze. *I'm so busted.* This had been coming from the moment she lied to Emery Carson in her first interview. But she'd thought she had another week or two to figure out a winning strategy.

So what if she had implied she could ski, maybe even suggested she enjoyed skiing on a regular basis? She had rationalized her deceit in several ways. She wasn't totally lying—she didn't hate to ski, or ski poorly. For all she knew she was a great skier. She simply hadn't tried to find out, and she wasn't that excited about doing so now.

Slowly she stood and put on her coat. Pausing at the top of the stairs, she watched Campbell pull on a pair of Gore-Tex ski pants over her jeans and felt a flash of panic. *This is really happening.* She had worked hard over the past two months to establish her credibility as a knowledgeable marketing strategist and would lose it when it became obvious that she didn't have a clue how to ski.

If she were to trip and break her leg while going down the stairs, she would have an excuse not to have to 'fess up to her big secret. *Oh, for God's sake, Parker, are you seriously considering bodily harm to avoid being found out?* She hurried down the stairs before she seriously considered the option.

Campbell smiled. "Suit up. We're about to make the first tracks of the season."

"Wow, that sounds like quite an honor." Parker hoped the nervousness in her voice wasn't too obvious. She pulled on the extra pair of pants Campbell had laid out for her, then tried to mimic Campbell's moves as she stepped into a pair of the heavy black boots like those she had brought for Parker. But when she slipped her feet inside she realized that, unlike Campbell's, which had a row of clips down the front, hers clasped in the back.

Before she had a chance to make sense of the straps, Campbell bent down next to her and said, "Lean forward." She did as told, and in one motion Campbell buckled her in. Then Campbell's hands tightened around the top of the boot, where it met her calf muscle. "How does that feel?"

"Uh, that's good," Parker replied softly, her mouth dry from the unexpected heat of their contact. She tried not to dwell on the fact that a woman knelt in front of her, but her body reacted on its own and her temperature rose rapidly. *Focus, Parker, you're about to be revealed as a fraud, and here you are thinking about Campbell's face between your legs.*

"Good. Here are some gloves," Campbell said, oblivious to the fact that her innocent touch had burned through both the ski pants and jeans and was still heating Parker's skin. She pulled on the gloves without letting her eyes wander to any part of Campbell's body. Perhaps Alexis was right and she *had* been sleeping alone for too long. She was about to be caught in a pretty big lie, and all she could think about was Campbell's hand on her leg.

"Hat and goggles," Campbell instructed, and Parker silently put on the last few items of ski gear while she tried to regain her composure.

They started toward the door but Parker stumbled slightly in her boots, which were heavy and caused her to pitch forward just enough to affect her balance. Campbell turned to her without judgment or mockery in her expression, merely a gentle grin. "They're always a little awkward at first."

Campbell led her onto the deck and down the stairs before she turned to offer her a hand. Parker thought about resisting. Though she couldn't ski, she wasn't helpless, but the gesture was so natural, so unassuming, that she accepted it and let herself be steadied as she took each stair with one foot, then the other. She actually felt slightly disappointed when she reached the bottom and broke the contact between them. It had been a long time since she had felt the casual touch of a woman, and even a helping hand was better than the emptiness when the contact was withdrawn.

Quietly she followed Campbell about forty yards to the base of the new snow that had been spread out just a few hours earlier. It was twilight on a Tuesday evening, and the mountain was quiet except for the distant rumble of the snowguns farther up the slopes. Only the rapid beating of her own heart—fear at being caught mixing with the excitement of sharing an intimate moment with Campbell—broke the serenity of the moment.

She noticed two pairs of skis on the ground, one pair drastically shorter than the other, and wondered why Campbell was the one she would have to confess to. She should have told Emery the truth. It would have been hard to admit she'd lied to her boss, but embarrassing herself in front of Campbell seemed worse. Gorgeous, strong, opinionated Campbell, and just when they were starting to make some progress.

This lie could cost them the guarded respect they had established and undercut any potential friendship.

Campbell stepped into a small wooden hut a few feet ahead of her, and some lights above them flickered to life. A second later the conveyor belt in front of the hut creaked and whirred as it began to turn slowly. She had to say something soon, but she couldn't find the right words, so when Campbell exited the hut she just blurted, "I can't ski."

Campbell smiled broadly. "I know."

"I don't see how that will impair my judgment as a marketing strategist, and it certainly doesn't make me less dedicated to doing my job and—what?"

Campbell laughed. "I know you can't ski. That's why I plan to teach you."

"How did you know?"

"I could tell last weekend when we were talking about the types of slopes and snow."

"Was I that obvious?" Parker asked. Maybe everyone had seen right through her.

"Not at all." Campbell smiled again. "You put up a very good front, and I don't see why anyone else needs to know," she answered matter-of-factly. "By the time the resort opens, you'll ski well enough that no one will suspect you haven't been doing it for years."

Parker stared into her eyes. Campbell was throwing her a lifeline without a hint of self-satisfaction. She was apparently completely oblivious to the power dynamic of the situation, which made Parker feel inexplicably safe in her presence. That was extremely exciting. She hadn't felt safe enough to be herself around anyone for months, and now that Campbell had given her the space to open up, she was inundated with emotions, most of them stemming from the knee-weakening smile Campbell was flashing her.

❖

Campbell picked up her ski poles, adjusting them so that her gloved hands fit directly into the grooves of the rubber grips. She then handed a slightly shorter pair to Parker and said, "Just do what I do, okay?"

Parker nodded and gripped the poles with her usual determined expression, but underneath it Campbell detected something more, something fragile. Learning to ski didn't have as much to do with ego as it did with self-respect, which was much more appealing than the self-centeredness Campbell had assumed as the motivation for Parker's lies. She would have to handle this lesson very carefully so Parker could gain ability without losing any dignity.

"Use one of the poles to help you balance as you lift your foot." Campbell demonstrated. "Go ahead and use the other pole to tap the side of your boot. This snow is pretty thick, and if it sticks to the bottom of your boot, you'll have trouble locking into your skis."

Parker did as she was told, appearing to use every ounce of her energy to concentrate.

Campbell watched her closely, not only studying her movements but also her facial expressions and body language. It was a beautiful body, lean and lithe, but she tried to stay focused on the technical aspects of Parker's actions. "Good. Now place your boot on the ski binding so your toe and heel fall between those metal pieces. Listen carefully as you push your foot down." For emphasis she stepped firmly onto her ski, causing it to snap into the binding with an audible click. "Just like that."

Parker mimicked her move perfectly, and her mouth twitched slightly upward in the hint of a smile when the boot clicked into position. Campbell was once again struck by her beauty. Parker's deep brown eyes were intense with focus, and Campbell wondered once more what it would be like to have that type of attention directed at her. "This may sound silly now, but soon you'll think that's the sweetest sound in the world."

Doubt was written plainly across Parker's face, but she didn't say anything, so Campbell continued. She quickly snapped into her other ski and moved over to help steady Parker while she did the same. "This one is just the same, but you'll be less balanced with your other boot already in the ski."

"I got it," Parker said when the other boot clicked into place, the relief evident in her voice. Then a flicker of fear returned to her beautiful eyes. "So what now?"

"First of all, just relax." Campbell smiled gently. "This isn't a job. Skiing is fun."

Parker rolled her eyes. "Thanks for the pep talk, but what do I need to do?"

Campbell bit her tongue. She was learning that Parker's abruptness was only a buffer to hide her apprehension. "Just wiggle around a little. Slide your skis back and forth to get used to the way they feel." Parker, bracing herself with her poles, made a few tentative moves with her feet and seemed slightly comforted when the skis didn't immediately fly out from under her. "See, they don't have minds of their own, even though it may seem like it at times."

"I'd like to reserve judgment on that." Parker smiled weakly. "When do I start hurtling down the mountain?"

Campbell gave a light laugh. "Let's learn the basics before we even think about the mountain."

"And what are the basics?"

"Well, they're very complicated," Campbell stated gravely, "very serious positions that will determine the amount of speed and control you have at any given point."

"Wonderful," Parker mumbled sarcastically, "what are they?"

Still refusing to crack a smile, Campbell said, "They're called 'pizza' and 'French fries.'"

Parker cocked her head to one side. "'Pizza' and 'French fries?'"

"Hey." Campbell finally allowed herself to grin. "I told you this isn't rocket science. Try to have fun."

"Fine," Parker sighed, "how do I do a French fry?"

"What about that?" Campbell pretended to be amazed. "You're already doing French fry."

Parker regarded her skis, which were exactly parallel and slightly less than shoulder width apart. "This is it?"

"That's it. You just point your skis ahead of you, down the hill, close enough to keep control of them, but with enough room that they don't get crossed up. See, they're like two French fries, side by side."

"And what does French fry do?"

"It makes you go really fast down the mountain." Campbell chuckled, knowing that wasn't the position Parker wanted to start off with.

"What?" Parker gasped. "That's not what I want to do."

"Then you'd better learn to pizza," Campbell teased.

Parker glared at her, but Campbell could tell she was fighting a smile. "You're really enjoying this, aren't you?"

"Of course I am. Why? Aren't you?"

Parker's cheeks were rosy from the cold, and she was still gripping her ski poles in a hypervigilant attempt to stay balanced, but her eyes danced with amusement and a slow smile played at the corners of her delicate mouth. "Surprisingly, I am."

"Good," Campbell said, hoping the extent of her relief wasn't too evident in her tone. "Then you'll love pizza, which we sometimes call snowplowing. All you have to do is point your skis so they angle in toward each other in the front." She demonstrated the move as Parker watched. "This position makes your skis form a triangle like a slice of pizza."

"Like this?" Parker turned her skis slightly inward but made small adjustments with her body.

"Just spread your legs wider." The words were out of Campbell's mouth before she thought about the suggestiveness of the command. Immediately her face flamed as she wondered if Parker could tell her mind had slipped into the gutter.

Thankfully she was too busy trying to mimic Campbell's stance. "Like this?"

"You got it. Be careful that the tips of your skis don't get crossed, or, as we tell the kids, don't let your skis kiss. No kissing on the slopes." That joke always went over well with the children in her ski group, but once again it took on a completely different meaning with Parker, or at least it did to Campbell as she envisioned what that would entail, and it had nothing to do with skis.

Campbell kept talking, hoping she didn't appear as frazzled as she felt. "You can keep an inch or two between them to avoid getting tangled up. If you dig in with your instep and put a little pressure into the stance, you should slow down to a nice gentle stop."

"Nice gentle stop," Parker repeated softly, as if for her own benefit.

"Now let's go for a magic carpet ride," Campbell said, nodding toward the conveyor belt to her left.

"Pizza, French fries, and magic carpets. Why does all this sound like a children's fantasy world?"

"Because it is." Campbell laughed. "And the sooner you learn to see it for what it is, the more you'll enjoy it."

"I'm not very in touch with my inner child," Parker confessed.

"Well, just scoot your skis up here." Campbell pushed forward with her poles until the conveyor belt caught her skis and started rolling her up the hill. "Maybe a few trips down the bunny slope will remind you what it feels like to be a kid."

Parker appeared skeptical, but she did as instructed and a wave of relief showed on her face when she successfully made it onto the carpet lift.

"Childlike lesson number one. Go with the flow," Campbell called. "At the top, the lift will slide you onto the snow. You'll pick up a little speed for a second, but if you ride it out, you'll be fine. If you fight it, you'll fall. It's that simple." Then she slid onto the snow and glided to a stop a couple of feet from where Parker approached the end of the lift.

"Okay, just relax. I'll be right here to help you get off." Campbell almost choked on the phrase as it left her mouth. *Oh, my God, I just offered to get her off*, she screamed internally. What was suddenly making everything sound so sexual? She had to get a grip. The last thing Parker needed right now was a teacher more focused on checking her out than helping her out.

Campbell struggled to turn her attention back to the lesson as Parker hit the edge of the tightly packed snow. The instant her skis began to move faster, Parker attempted to dig in with her poles and grind her feet into her skis, and she immediately toppled over. Campbell shook her head. Parker's need for constant control would make these lessons a lot harder than they had to be.

"I guess now would be a good time to show you how to take one of your skis off. It's a lot easier to get back up that way."

"Yeah, that would be helpful," Parker said through gritted teeth, and Campbell's customary frustration around her threatened to return.

"Take one of the poles and use it to reach back behind your bottom ski boot and push down on the release. When your boot's free, use that foot to help you stand back up."

Parker quickly did as she was told and hopped back onto her feet. Without waiting for further instructions, she lifted the foot she had just freed, tapped it with her pole, and pushed it into its ski again. She then defiantly faced Campbell. "Let's go."

Campbell shrugged and faced downhill. She wouldn't do Parker any favors by trying to restrain her obvious determination. That level of resolve came from years of self-reliance and self-preservation. To deny it or attempt to temper it would come across as condescending.

"All right, now, we're going to pizza all the way to the bottom, just so you can get a feel for it."

Parker nodded, her eyes focused somewhere toward the bottom of the hill. With a deep breath she pushed off, Campbell following a few yards behind. She watched Parker wobble and weave down the first part of the small slope. She performed the technical aspects exactly as she'd been instructed, but her balance was visibly shaky. When she approached the halfway point, her skis were edging too close together and she was picking up speed, so Campbell called out, "Pizza, Parker, pizza!"

Parker's skis turned slightly inward so that the tips were almost touching and her speed started to decrease, just as it should. Campbell kept going at her initial pace so she could pull in front of Parker and see her expression, but just as she paused beside her, Parker's skis crossed. *Oh no, she's going down.* Campbell's heart began to pound.

Parker started to slide sideways as she struggled to lift the top ski off the bottom one. Campbell helplessly watched her slip farther down the hill, her earlier expression of determination penetrated by fear, her face contorted with frustration. Finally, Parker lost her fight for balance as she dropped into the snow. Campbell winced and dug her skis to an almost instantaneous stop, but to her amazement Parker popped right back up, as if she had bounced off the snow. Her eyes wide with surprise, she had the presence of mind to turn her skis back into the pizza position, and with her momentum already slowed by her earlier struggles, she was able to glide to a stop only a foot or two from the bottom of the carpet lift.

Campbell pointed her skis in that direction and stopped right next to Parker, throwing an arm around her shoulder and pausing only to register the intoxicating feel of her lithe frame and sinewy limbs against her body while she tried to figure out how Parker had managed to stay upright. The tension of the previous moments dissipated and they burst out laughing. "How did you do that?"

"I didn't want to fall again," Parker said through a mix of deep breaths and heavy laughter.

Campbell pulled her closer into the crook of her arm. "I've skied my whole life, and I've never seen anyone stay upright through sheer force of will. I thought you were a goner."

"Then you underestimated me, Campbell Carson," Parker replied, her eyes still shining with the pure joy of her accomplishment.

Parker's words, combined with the contact between their bodies, caused a heat to spread through Campbell that she hadn't experienced in a long time and hadn't been sure she would ever feel again. Holding Parker had ignited something unexpected and slightly scary. It was more than the incidental contact they had toyed with until that point. This connection was purposeful and powerful. It was too good, too familiar, and too dangerous. The last time she felt like this she had opened herself to pain and devastation. She quickly broke the contact between them and said seriously, "You're right. I did underestimate you, but it won't happen again."

❖

"That's perfect," Campbell shouted as Parker followed her down the beginners' slope. "Make a full *C* with your turn, then finish it out all the way across the hill."

Parker easily made the turn, following exactly in the tracks Campbell had just made. Her skis were almost completely parallel, and she appeared perfectly balanced. It had been only a week since their first lesson, and already Parker had begun to show the form of an intermediate skier. They had moved from the bunny trail to the full-length beginner slope, and both of them were making the most of the opportunity to spend longer periods of time skiing and less time on the slow-moving carpet lift.

Campbell worked every day covering and grooming the slopes in preparation for the resort's season opening, and Parker seemed equally occupied, but they both made time to meet for nearly two hours every evening, and they stopped only when Campbell forced Parker to take a break. She was borderline obsessive when she set her mind to something, and she needed frequent reminders that she was just out there to have fun. Otherwise she could slip into an intensity that rivaled that of

Olympic athletes. Campbell had never seen anyone like Parker, whose determination impressed her and whose single-mindedness bothered her somewhat. Parker's intense focus was, however, appealing, and at times when she let her guard down and simply enjoyed herself, she embodied beauty and grace. During those times she was so striking that Campbell's breath caught.

"That was great. See? You don't have to fight your skis. Just flatten them out and be patient. They'll find the right line."

"I thought you said these things don't have a mind of their own," Parker called back.

"Touché." Campbell laughed. "Think you can handle a little more speed?"

"Bring it on."

Without another word they turned downhill, this time cutting their turns closer together and hitting the last little steep with some speed. They glided smoothly over the freshly groomed snow, cutting back and forth across the slopes in an elegant *S*-shaped pattern. Campbell felt like a teenager again. She was happy, relaxed, and even thrilled to share the slopes with Parker coming up quickly behind her. In that moment she was exactly where she wanted to be. She cut through the first natural snow of the year, about half an inch that had fallen the night before. She was showboating, but she couldn't restrain herself from swooshing to an abrupt stop, kicking up a wave of snow with the tails of her skis.

Parker stopped gracefully at her side, a full-fledged smile on her face. "I'm starting to see what you enjoy about this." She held her arms out. "It all fits in perfect harmony. The mountain, the snow, the trees swaying in the wind, and when you're on the powder, it's like you're riding right along with it."

Campbell caught her breath. She had almost seen something click inside Parker, as if Parker was seeing her surroundings for the first time. "Do you have plans for Thanksgiving?"

Parker seemed caught off guard by the abrupt change of subject. "I really haven't thought about it. I don't think I'll go back to Chicago, since that'll be two days before we open. I was planning to take the day off, though."

"Would you like to spend the day with me and my family?" Campbell asked without even thinking. "We do a whole big meal with all the trimmings, and then we spend the afternoon on the slopes. It's a time for us to have the resort to ourselves, just the family, before we all get too busy."

"Actually, I'd rather sleep in. I'm just not into the whole family thing. It's a little stifling for my tastes. Maybe I'll come by for some skiing later, if I get bored."

Parker's words sounded so much like Lynn's that Campbell felt as if she'd been punched in the stomach. She had to work hard to hide the flash of pain that surged through her.

Parker eyed the controls of the lift carefully. She knew how to turn it on. She'd seen Campbell do it many times over the past week. She also knew she probably shouldn't touch it. It was the evening before Thanksgiving, and Campbell was late for their lesson. Time was closing in on Parker. The resort would open the day after tomorrow, and she had been invited to ski with the Carsons before that. Her reputation was on the line. Losing her credibility in Chicago had shaken her to the core. She was at Bear Run to pull herself back together, and the last thing she needed was to make a fool of herself. Campbell had taught her so much since their lessons began, but Parker wasn't satisfied with just being passable. She wanted to come across as competent. Anything less would be a failure.

She glanced at her watch one more time. Campbell was fifteen minutes late. "Oh, screw it," she muttered, and began to flip switches on the lift's power terminal. She held her breath as the machine creaked to life. Parker was almost positive she had it running correctly before she allowed one of the chairs to whisk her up the mountain. She spent the ride reviewing everything Campbell had told her lately—"Relax, go with the flow, just enjoy yourself." Campbell wasn't giving her much technical instruction anymore. Most of her directions focused on attitude and demeanor, and it was a little disconcerting how well she was able to read Parker's moods.

She exited the chair at the top of the mountain and examined the trail below her, which seemed more daunting without Campbell by her side. She really didn't need Campbell there anymore, but she enjoyed her company. She was witty and always managed to crack a joke at the right time. She didn't shrink at Parker's nasty temper, and she could hold her own in an argument if she needed to, though thankfully they had been arguing less. Campbell was gorgeous all the time, but especially when she smiled, and she had been smiling at Parker a lot more lately. No matter how many times it happened, Parker was never quite prepared for the way her stomach tightened. She wished she could have the reassurance of that heart-stopping smile right now instead of just the vast expanse of trail before her.

Shaking her head, she pushed off lightly. Right now she needed to focus on skiing, not Campbell. Her skis glided over the top of the snow, which was running faster than usual. She turned in a wide arc to control her speed, just like she'd been taught, but her edges didn't dig in nearly as deep as she had hoped. Immediately she looked up for Campbell's reassurances or direction. The move had become so second nature that she'd momentarily forgotten Campbell wasn't there. Slowly she pulled herself together and completed the turn before she started into another one in the opposite direction. She followed this shaky pattern all the way to the bottom of the slope and was silently congratulating herself on not falling when Campbell rushed out of the little wooden terminal that housed the lift controls.

"What the hell do you think you're doing?" Campbell shouted, her crystal blue eyes filled with fury.

"I—I was, Jesus, I was just skiing," Parker stammered, completely taken off guard by the outburst.

"Alone?" Campbell closed the distance separating them so they were only a breath apart. "Did you start that lift?"

"Yes." Parker was thrown off by both Campbell's anger and her close proximity, and her body temperature began to rise.

"What's wrong with you? That's a half a million dollars' worth of machinery, and you just flip switches and press buttons like it's some kind of toy? What made you think you had the right to touch the lift controls without so much as asking for a lesson in how to use them?"

"You were late, and I needed some more practice, so I—"

"So you what? You felt entitled to it? You thought the rules didn't apply to you?"

"Oh, come on, Campbell." Parker had had enough and gave in to her own emotions. "It's not rocket science. Grease monkeys and college dropouts run these things all season."

"What the hell is that supposed to mean? That because you have a degree you're somehow better or more qualified than the rest of our staff?"

"No." Now Campbell was putting words into her mouth. "I just meant that it wasn't as complicated as you're making it out to be. I didn't break anything, did I? Nothing exploded. It's not that big a deal."

"You don't get it, do you?" Campbell took Parker's face in her hands and pulled her in so that their noses were almost touching, and her entire body tightened with anticipation. "You were the only one out here. You could have been hurt. You could have been killed messing around with something you don't understand because you're too self-centered to wait a few minutes."

Campbell's eyes were no longer filled with aggravation. They were pleading with her, seeming to search for any sign of understanding, and Parker melted into them. Her emotions were so raw there was no room for rational thought. The intensity in Campbell's embrace overwhelmed her senses. A lustful haze blurred her vision, and the dull roar of her own blood rushed through her ears.

Campbell didn't appear to be faring any better. Her breath was coming in quick, shallow bursts that brushed warm against Parker's skin, and her fingers trembled where they now grazed the edges of Parker's jaw and cheeks. Campbell closed her eyes and neared almost imperceptibly, her lips laying the barest of touches against Parker's so rapidly that if not for the heat that had passed between them, Parker would have wondered if they had actually kissed.

"I'm sorry," Campbell said, stepping back, her stunning blue eyes beginning to clear and focus. "I don't know what I was doing."

"Please don't apologize," Parker whispered, unable to speak louder. Campbell seemed about to cry, or faint, or run away. In the end she chose the latter.

"We're done for the day. If you want to ski any more, I'll see you tomorrow," Campbell stated flatly, and then she was gone.

As the shock and excitement of the encounter wore off, Parker watched her leave, feeling cold, empty, and confused.

CHAPTER EIGHT

Campbell sat on the back steps of her parents' house, fastening the buckles on her ski boots. It was a Carson tradition to ski the mountain as a family before the resort opened to the public. She'd missed the experience last year, like so many other things. She'd planned to be here, but Lynn had wanted to stay in Madison and spend the holiday with her colleagues. She shook her head at the memory, just like all the other times she'd passed on the things she cared about because she'd cared about Lynn more.

It wasn't entirely Lynn's fault. Campbell had worked hard to try and make her own dreams Lynn's too, but her ex had never misled her about what she did or didn't want in life. She didn't want to be part of a family, she resented sharing any of Campbell's attention, and nothing Campbell could have done would ever change that. It was her own fault for continuing to try. She wasn't angry, but she was sad when she recalled the years they had shared.

The back door opened and her father approached. His slight limp reminded her that he probably wouldn't be skiing with them today, and she knew that bothered him. He was still good-looking, in spite of his gray-streaked hair and the creases around his eyes, but he seemed so much older now that Campbell had spent some time away from him. He was nearing retirement age, but Campbell doubted he'd ever quit working. He loved his family and the mountain too much and was resisting Parker's new ideas because he didn't want to let go of any part of the business he had spent his entire life building. He fiercely protected everything he loved and was leery of anything or anyone who tried to change it. Campbell loved him dearly, but she also longed for the time when he would entrust some of that responsibility to her. She loved this mountain too and wanted people to see it as much more than a simple winter playground.

"Sammy and I are going down to start the lift. Why don't you take the boys out in a few minutes? Your mother and Janelle will be there as soon as the kids wake up from their nap."

Campbell stood up and stomped her boots to make sure they were fastened snugly. "Sounds good."

Instead of heading back inside, Greg regarded her thoughtfully, then hugged her. "Have I told you lately how happy I am that you're home?"

Campbell smiled. "Thanks Dad. I'm happy to be here."

Greg seemed as if he wanted to say something more, but then thought better of it. "Good, that's all that matters." Campbell knew he wasn't a man of many words, but he cared about her deeply. This was what she'd returned home for, the type of connection she'd missed with Lynn. Greg placed a kiss on her forehead before he released her. "I'll let the boys know you're ready."

The door had barely shut behind her father when Emery's boys came out in full ski gear. Parker was behind them, pulling on her gloves. Campbell was surprised to see her. After the way things had gone the day before she hadn't expected Parker to show up. The memories of their last heated encounter flooded over her and she flushed. She'd almost kissed Parker, but she didn't know why. One minute she'd been so angry she'd wanted to grab her and shake some sense into her. But when she touched the smooth skin of Parker's face and fell into those deep brown eyes, all those emotions that had burned inside her had fused into something primal, something raw, and the expression of it twisted until her lips were brushing Parker's. It wasn't a kiss, not really, but it came so close to one that she couldn't mistake where it had been headed. Since then, Campbell had alternately been embarrassed over what Parker must think of her (though she had made no move to pull away), angry at herself for letting her emotions boil over, and aroused at the pull between Parker's body and her own.

When Campbell finally willed herself to make eye contact with Parker, she returned her gaze with a weak smile. Parker was obviously nervous, and Campbell wasn't sure if Parker was reacting to her or to the fact that she was about to hit the slopes with the entire family. She had become a solid skier in under two weeks, due to her determination and the hours she'd spent practicing every night, but today was the first day she'd skied in front of anyone other than Campbell. That had to be weighing on her mind.

The four of them walked to the slope just a few yards from the back porch and clicked into their skis. The boys were off a second later. The joy of the first run of the year was entirely too much for them to wait for Parker and Campbell.

"How are you feeling about this?" Campbell asked. She wanted to put her arm around Parker's shoulder to offer some sense of comfort, but she simply didn't trust her body.

Parker took a deep breath and exhaled slowly. "I guess I'm ready."

"It's just like we practiced."

"Except your whole family and my boss will be watching. I don't want to embarrass us both." Parker tried to chuckle, but Campbell saw through her attempt.

"You won't embarrass either of us, and my family members aren't judgmental. You don't have to prove anything to anybody," she said softly. During their time together she had learned to recognize Parker's bravado as a defense mechanism. "They already like you, or you wouldn't be here today."

"They didn't invite me. You did," Parker answered jokingly, then a little more softly added, "Does that mean you like me?"

Campbell felt an unexpected blush rise in her cheeks as she tried not to overthink the question. "Yes, I do," she said. The memory of their near kiss reminded her just how much she liked Parker, but that wasn't what Parker needed from her right now. She cleared her throat self-consciously. "And I think you ski beautifully, or I wouldn't have you out here right now."

Parker shook her head, but she smiled, too. "I guess it's too late to turn back now." Then she pushed off and headed downhill toward the bottom of the lift with Campbell close behind.

The twins were already on the lift when they arrived, so Campbell and Parker slid into place as the next chair swung around. The nearness sent Campbell's body temperature through the roof again. She was sure Parker would see right through her attempts to focus on anything and everything neutral. "You coming up?" she called to Sammy.

"I'll be right behind you."

"He won't expect to go tearing down any black diamond runs, will he?" Parker asked.

"Yeah, probably." Campbell chuckled, thinking of Sammy's daredevil streak. "But not right away. He'll work his way up there as the afternoon wears on. I'd be more worried about the boys trying to go over the drop-off the first time out."

"Can they do that?" Parker sounded horrified at the idea.

"Not yet. It's not open, but they will before Christmas."

"How many of the trails will be open for the public tomorrow?"

"We're at almost sixty percent, so about fifteen or sixteen, which is good for this early in the year."

"Does that mean we'll have a good season?"

Campbell shrugged as they prepared to unload. "You can never know for sure, but the temperatures have been steady and we're getting a little natural snow already. Those are both good signs."

They stood as their skis slid across the gentle grade of the snow-covered lift exit. Leaning slightly forward, they let their momentum carry them over to where the twins stood adjusting their boots and pole straps. Campbell didn't even have to ask them where they wanted to go because she knew the answer. They were obviously planning a path that cut from a green slope to a more challenging blue one. Any avid skier would want to take this path back to the bottom of the lift, but she could sense Parker's uncertainty, and just as Sammy slid to a stop next to them, she decided to offer a more moderate route.

"Let's take it easy the first time down." The boys started to object, but she cut them off. "You haven't had those skis on for over six months. Take it slow the first time to make sure everything's okay with your gear." It was a lame excuse, since none of the Carsons would have strapped into anything other than perfectly tuned equipment, but the boys didn't argue. They started out together, but the guys quickly pulled ahead, tucking low into their stance and picking up speed. Parker followed them closely, her form solid but not aggressive.

Campbell was last, watching Parker carefully. They had practiced on this slope the last two evenings. She knew this was where the family would spend the day and wanted Parker to feel comfortable with her surroundings, and it seemed like she did. She moved gracefully into a wide arc to the periphery of Campbell's vision, and while Campbell tried to evaluate Parker's technical skills, she couldn't help but notice how nicely her ski pants fit over her hips. Campbell watched those hips curve lightly as Parker shifted her weight to follow the bend of the trail. It was a wide slope with a consistently gentle grade the entire length. It was also one of the longest runs on the mountain, measuring a little over one mile. On one side stood a row of cabins, some occupied by the Carsons, others used as rental properties for families and larger groups who wanted ski-in/ski-out access to their accommodations. The bottom of the slope flattened out nicely before a hedgerow provided a final barrier between skiers and the road that wrapped entirely around the resort.

Skiing along, Campbell gazed across the snowy terrain at the mild grade lined by large frosted pines, and her heart swelled. This was the view she remembered most vividly from her childhood, and when she was away, this image filled her hours of longing for home. The beauty of the scene and the pleasure it evoked made her want to be part of the family business and help move it into a strong future. They could branch out to a broader clientele and serve as educators as well as entertainers. Parker could be a big part of that broader approach, if she wanted to. Campbell returned her focus to the present as the entire group made it back to the start of the lift without any problems, and Parker even managed to slide to a stop gracefully, winning an appreciative nod from Sammy.

"You don't have to hold back for my sake," Parker said when they were on the lift again.

"I won't. You can hold your own, even on the blue trail right under the lift. We ran it yesterday and you did great."

"Then why were you going so slow?"

"Honestly?" Campbell asked. "I was reminiscing. I have a lot of good memories of days just like this."

"I envy you," Parker said. "We never had holiday traditions. We just went with whoever offered the best invitation."

Campbell frowned. She couldn't imagine that. "Well, I guess that could be exciting, to be with different friends all the time."

"I doubt that you would call them friends. I mean, I guess they were my parents' friends, as much as they had time for such. Mostly colleagues they spent long periods of time with on one project or another."

"You've never talked about your family before," Campbell said, glad that Parker was finally opening up about something other than work. They seemed to be getting closer, and not just in a physical sense, though that aspect of their friendship still weighed heavily on Campbell's mind.

"There's nothing to talk about, really," Parker said casually. "My mother's a lawyer, my father's a business consultant, and my brother's a stockbroker."

Parker had listed her family members' respective occupations and said nothing about their relationships, but they had reached the top of the lift and the boys were once again planning their descent. This time Campbell let them go. They had too much energy for her to rein them in any longer, and as soon as Sammy arrived they flew down the mountain again.

"We'll go with them, but follow my tracks, not Sammy's," Campbell instructed. Parker nodded and pushed off behind her.

They headed left, directly below the lift, with Campbell carving a large S-shaped path, using the turns to help control their speed. The terrain was more challenging than Parker was used to, but not enough that she should be worried. Campbell smiled to herself. Even if they were on the steepest part of the resort, Parker would find a way to keep up. She wouldn't fall if the entire mountain came crashing down behind her, not with the rest of the family watching. Campbell liked that about her. In fact, the more she learned about Parker, the more she liked. She was focused, driven, and determined, but now that Campbell was learning to see past her iron façade, she also detected a vulnerability that made Parker much more attractive. She seemed to genuinely care about her work at Bear Run, which endeared her to Campbell despite her early impressions of her. The flutter in Campbell's stomach whenever Parker got near enough to brush against her was harder to explain and much more difficult to ignore.

Parker mimicked her every move the entire way down, cutting and curving over the steeps and keeping her speed through the flats. In a few weeks Parker wouldn't need her as a guide, which made Campbell both proud and disappointed.

They barely stopped at the bottom of the lift as Greg waved them onto the next available chair. "You planning to ski, Dad?" Campbell asked as they flew away.

"I'm too old," he called, but she knew he would try at least once before the season was over.

"Do you see your family much?" Campbell asked, picking up their conversation from the previous lift ride in the way skiers often did.

"Not really." Parker seemed neither joyous nor sad as she simply stated the fact. "I used to run into my parents at fund-raisers or dinners occasionally back in Chicago, and I went out to visit my brother and his wife in Colorado twice when I was in college. But I haven't seen them since they moved back to Chicago this fall."

Campbell didn't know how to reply. She knew not everyone had family ties like she did, but she couldn't imagine living so near her parents and seeing them only by accident at official functions.

"It's not like we don't get along," Parker continued, seeming slightly uncomfortable with the topic. "We've just never been that close. We're all so busy, and they're very successful people."

Campbell wanted to challenge the idea that anyone could be considered successful without having a relationship with his or her children. Instead she said, "They must be proud of everything you've accomplished."

Parker tensed. Even through all Parker's layers of clothing, Campbell could feel her muscles tighten. "I'm sure they were at some point."

The conversation was closed, and judging by the hard-set line of Parker's mouth, it wouldn't be revisited anytime soon. The hardness of Parker's face saddened Campbell, and her tense posture greatly limited their body contact. Unsure what had bothered Parker so badly, Campbell tried to refocus on skiing, which wasn't easy.

The boys were tearing down the mountain, so Parker and Campbell took the easier route at a more leisurely pace. Campbell glanced over her shoulder a time or two and smiled as Parker followed exactly in her path, mimicking their practice sessions. As Campbell arced in wide, gentle turns, she took deep cleansing breaths, her body responding to a rhythm set by the mountain. They seemingly had the slopes all to themselves, a feeling they had grown used to. Once the resort opened, these precious, undisturbed moments would disappear quickly. Except for some early morning runs, before the public was admitted to the slopes for the day, they would have a lot more people to contend with over the next few months.

When they arrived back at the lift, the rest of the family joined them. Both of Janelle's children were bundled up and wiggling in their skis with anticipation.

"Hi, Campbell," Janelle's three-year-old son called as they approached.

"Hey, buddy. Are you going to ski?"

The child nodded vigorously. "I'm gonna go fast."

"Me, too, me, too," Noel chanted.

Irene and Janelle were talking to Emery and Greg about their afternoon plans. The adults decided to take turns with the kids, and Janelle offered to ski with her toddler first, sending Noel with Irene. Greg slowed the lift to allow the women to help the kids into the chair, and Parker and Campbell rode behind them.

"Can that little guy really ski?" Parker asked.

"Not on his own. He's still a little too young, but he played on the bunny slope a bit at the end of last season, so it won't be long before he takes off."

"You guys don't waste any time, do you?"

"Carson kids are born with skis on."

"Sounds painful for the Carson women," Parker teased.

Campbell laughed. "Really, we start skiing as soon as we can walk well enough to keep our balance. Janelle's boy is almost old enough for formal lessons. Noel is already a solid intermediate skier at five and will probably be able to ski black diamonds by her sixth birthday in March."

"You've got to be kidding. You'd let Noel go over the drop-off?"

"Well, I won't push her, but the kids actually take instruction a lot better than most adults. They go with the flow instead of fighting it."

Parker raised one eyebrow above the rim of her ski goggles. "Hmm, was that comment directed at me or you?"

Campbell pondered that question briefly as she skied along the slope. Was she fighting the flow with Parker? Was Parker fighting the flow of life on the mountain? Were they both headed for something neither of them had any real control over?

After everyone made it safely down the mountain, Noel squealed

"Ewwww," interrupting Campbell's inner wanderings and directing everyone's attention to her and her little brother. He had removed his glove and shoved his finger up his nose all the way to the second knuckle. Everyone laughed, except for the kid, who just grinned and kept picking his nose until Janelle pulled his hand away and wiped it with a tissue.

"Boys are icky," Noel said enthusiastically. "I like girls better."

"You get that from your cousin," Janelle teased, winking at Campbell.

"I like girls better, too," Sammy joked along with them.

"What about you, Uncle Emery?" Noel asked, pleased at the new game without realizing the nuances of the adults' answers.

"Well, girls only seem to get me into trouble," he said with a grin, no doubt alluding to his most recent divorce. Then, looking at the twins, he added, "I think I'll just stick with my boys for a while."

Noel frowned slightly at the fact that someone had chosen boys over girls, but quickly moved on. "Do you like boys or girls?" she asked Parker.

"What? Who? Me?" Parker stammered, her cheeks flushing.

Campbell wondered if she should step in and save her from possibly having to out herself. Parker wasn't likely to feel comfortable with the implications of her answer, but at this point it would raise suspicions not to play along with the children's silly game. Furthermore, everyone was waiting for the answer, and even if Campbell were to jump in, they would surely notice not only the lack of a response, but also who had rescued Parker, and she wasn't sure Parker wanted that either, so she didn't say anything.

"Well," Parker said slowly, "I'd have to say that I prefer girls."

A couple of the adults seemed surprised, and Campbell's parents shared a look she couldn't interpret, but Noel was oblivious to the fact that Parker had just outed herself. She began to chant, "Girls win, girls win," as she headed for the lift. Everyone took their cue to get back to the slopes, and for the rest of the day, no one said anything about anyone's boy/girl preferences. But the topic probably wouldn't be forgotten soon.

❖

Later that evening when Campbell and Sammy arrived home loaded with leftovers from the Carson family Thanksgiving celebration, they flopped onto the couch to watch the highlights from that afternoon's football games.

"Cam?" Sammy said, a few minutes into *SportsCenter*.

"What?" She was still focused on the TV.

"You did a good job teaching Parker to ski."

She stared at him. "How did you know?"

"You were two hours late getting home every night, I saw fresh tracks on the slopes every morning, and Parker follows you on the slopes like one of your little snow-school kids."

Campbell conceded they had been pretty obvious. "You think anyone else knows?"

Sammy shrugged. "Not much around here gets past Mom and Dad."

"You're probably right." Campbell nodded. "You won't say anything to Parker, will you?"

"You know I won't, and neither will Mom or Dad."

Sammy was obviously working up the nerve to say something more, most likely about her and Parker's shared sexual orientation, and she and Sammy would probably have several conversations on that topic during the next couple of days. But she didn't plan to make it easy for him.

"So I guess I don't have much of a chance with her," he finally mumbled.

"Probably not." She smiled. "Why, did you want one?"

"Nah, I won't have any problems finding someone else. Chicks dig me."

Campbell didn't know of any dates Sammy had been on lately, but now wasn't the time to mention that point.

Sammy became more serious. "You're my sister, so I'd rather not know too many details of your personal life. But if you ever want to have anyone over, I could make myself scarce."

Campbell blushed, equally uncomfortable about discussing this subject with her younger brother. "I don't think we have to worry about that."

"But Parker—"

"Geez, Sam. Just because we're both lesbians doesn't mean we're dating." Campbell fought to banish the memories of how it had felt to touch Parker's face, how she'd trembled when she was so near. Nothing good could come from letting herself think that way. "We're just friends."

"I know that." Now Sammy blushed. "But sometimes when she looks at you, I don't know. I mean, if things were different, I wouldn't mind her looking at me that way."

Campbell's voice caught. "What do you mean?"

Sammy shrugged. "Like she sees how special you are."

"Special." Campbell shoved him. "Now I know you're full of it."

"Fine, have it your way," he said, standing up and stretching. "I'm going to bed. Good night, Cam."

Then he was gone, leaving her with nothing to do but think about what he'd said. *As if I needed something else to keep me awake tonight.* Campbell's body was still on high alert from being so close to Parker all afternoon. Her skin had almost literally tingled every time they made contact on the ski lift's little bench, and the memory of their near kiss and Parker's soft, full lips sent Campbell's mind swimming. Aside from Parker's new love of skiing and their mutual occupations, they had nothing in common. They wanted different things out of life, had discordant values, and bickered about nearly everything. So why did this maddening pull between them keep drawing her ever nearer to Parker?

CHAPTER NINE

"B ear Run, Parker Riley speaking." Parker tilted her head so she could pin the phone between her ear and her shoulder, leaving her hands free to continue sorting through the paperwork on her desk.

"Yes, Ms. Riley, this is the Chicago Society Police. We have a warrant for your arrest on the charge of social suicide."

Parker chuckled. "Hi, Alexis."

"Don't 'hi, Alexis' me, darling. What are you doing at work at eight o'clock on a Saturday night? There'd better be a gorgeous woman under your desk."

"I wish." Parker laughed.

"It could be arranged."

"Do you ever think of anything other than sex?"

"Well, apparently I have to think about it enough for both of us, since you never do," Alexis teased, but she sounded concerned. "I know you work hard, but you have to play hard too in order to balance everything out."

"Balance has never been my strong suit," Parker said seriously. She'd been working full time before she even graduated from college.

"Well, admitting it is the first step."

"Admitting it is the only step for me right now. The women's ski clinics start right after New Year's and I've only started the advertising. I still have to set up radio spots, print ads, and the Web site. Of course, we're running the women's clinics on a trial basis. If they don't prove themselves quickly, they won't stay. That's the only way my boss could convince his older brother to agree to them."

The weekend had been a blur, with the onslaught of opening-day crowds. The mountain's population seemed to have multiplied by ten overnight. The building buzzed with activity, and out her windows Parker could see a steady stream of skiers riding up the mountain and zipping back down. She frequently longed to join them. Skiing had become an escape, and she loved its simple purity of thought and action.

Her thoughts about skiing with Campbell weren't that simple and certainly not as pure. She longed to be near her, to see that heartbreaking smile and those dazzlingly blue eyes. She missed the thrill that came from brushing up against her and the heat she felt in their closeness. She wanted to be out on the slopes with her right now, experiencing all of those sensations at once, but she simply had too much work to do.

"How are your conferences going?" Alexis asked, switching to her more official business voice.

"Slow," Parker answered, which was an understatement. There were a few returning conferences and retreats, but she hadn't booked a single new account. "Why?"

"What's your availability for January second through fifth?"

Parker grabbed her conference ledger and flipped to January, even though she already knew that the week after New Year's was the deadest week on the travel calendar. "We're completely open."

"Can you accommodate two hundred women?" Alexis asked, now in full business mode.

"Absolutely, that would be our largest booking of the year, but we have cabins and the lodge rooms to choose from. What kinds of meeting space would you need?"

"Not much. This retreat is for play and networking, but we'd need a place to mingle in the evening and booze, lots of booze."

Parker felt a slow smile spread across her face. "Are we talking about what I think we're talking about?"

"The Chicago Women's Democratic Caucus would like to reserve your services for our annual Blow-Off Bash." The bash was a raucous weekend where political workhorses blew off the steam of the campaign and congressional seasons as well as the stress of holiday event planning before they had to jump back into inauguration balls and the spring session. The women involved were rarely big-time politicians, but they were major players in the party, and they greatly enjoyed one of their few chances to escape the watchful eyes of their enemies and employers.

"You know this place isn't upscale," Parker warned. "I can hardly get a cell-phone signal most of the time."

"For a marketing executive, you sure know how to sell a place," Alexis responded dryly.

"I'm just being honest. It's beautiful and pristine, but it's not Vail," Parker said, rubbing her forehead. She wanted the booking, but she wanted it to be the right booking. "If you're doing this as a favor, you don't have to."

"Don't be silly. I love you, but I'd never make a business decision based on our friendship. We chose Bear Run because it's within driving distance from Chicago and close enough to Green Bay for those who want to fly. We also want to have a place to ourselves. This is a major networking event, and we don't want to be distracted by other functions in the area or prying eyes. We're willing to sacrifice some luxury for a little privacy," Alexis stated matter-of-factly.

"Well, we can certainly offer that." Parker began to frantically scribble notes on a scratch piece of paper.

"Don't go crazy right now. Just put us down for that weekend, and I'll fax you the details Monday."

Parker exhaled. "Alexis, thank you so much."

"Well, I began to worry that I'd never see you again. I can't believe you didn't come down for Thanksgiving. Whatever did you do there over the holiday? Please tell me you didn't work."

"No, I didn't. I slept practically all day. Well, until early afternoon. Then I went skiing with the whole Carson family, even the little kids."

"A typical holiday on Walton Mountain, eh?" Alexis didn't sound enthused about the event. It wasn't her type of fun, and to be honest it wouldn't have sounded like much to Parker a few months ago, but it had been enjoyable, in a different sort of way. Especially the time she spent with Campbell. "I guess your ski lessons paid off, then."

"Absolutely. Cam saved my ass, big time."

"I'm sure that's not all she wanted to do with that lovely ass of yours."

"Alexis," Parker snapped, "it's not like that."

"Oh, come on, darling. Nobody rides for free, right?"

"You're wicked." Parker laughed. "Campbell has no ulterior motives."

Alexis was obviously suspicious. "She gave you free private lessons every night for two weeks and didn't ask for anything in return?"

"Nothing," Parker replied. *Except for the kiss we almost blundered into.* But Campbell hadn't asked for that. In fact, she still wasn't sure what Campbell had felt about it. Then she began to feel guilty. She needed to do something to say thank you for the lessons, but what? How did you thank someone for saving both your job and your pride? "She's not like anyone I've ever met."

"Sounds like you're falling for her." Alexis's tone had turned serious.

"What? No. We're friends. Well, maybe a little more than that." At least she hoped Campbell considered her a friend. She hadn't seen her since Thanksgiving, and though it had been only two days, she had grown so used to spending their evenings together that she found herself feeling lonely despite the massive amount of work she'd had to do.

"Friends that spend hours together every day and invite each other to family events?"

"It's not what it sounds like. Everything around here is a family event," Parker said. "Work and family blend together. You can't separate the two. Her mother organizes the lessons, her dad runs the slopes, she and Sammy work under them. They keep me from being lonely."

"She sounds like your type," Alexis said, worry filling her voice.

Parker let the comment sink in, her stomach turning at Alexis's implication. "You don't know Campbell. She's nothing like Mia," she finally managed to say.

"You're right. I'm sure she's lovely. It's just that she lives at home with her brother and works with her parents, heir to the family business—"

"It's not the same. Mia did what her father told her to do. Cam does what she loves."

"If you say so, then I trust you," Alexis said, but her tone still held some doubt. "You just deserve someone who will put you first."

"Thank you, but Campbell and I really are just friends," Parker said. But did friends almost kiss the way she and Campbell had? None of her other friends made her feel the way Campbell did. Listing Campbell's noble qualities to Alexis had Parker wandering down a road she wasn't sure she wanted to take, but it was impossible not to notice what a catch Campbell would be for any woman.

"Whatever you say, my sweet, oblivious friend." Alexis chuckled. "I've got to run. I'll send that fax Monday."

"Alexis, thank you."

"Don't mention it. I'm just want to meet this mountain butch of yours."

"Good-bye, Alexis."

Parker sat back in her chair and smiled after she hung up the phone. She knew Alexis was merely being silly with her nobody-rides-for-free comment, but she'd been right about one thing. Campbell had been a great friend, and she had to find a way to thank her.

Several scenarios popped into her head at once—roses, candlelight dinners, sensual massages. Parker quickly shook them away, but not before she felt herself blush at the images. No, Campbell deserved better than her juvenile fantasies. She deserved a thanks worthy of the bond they had been building.

❖

The conversation at the staff meeting Monday afternoon flowed easily, and Parker doubted an avalanche could shake the Carsons' routine. She hoped they would take her big news in stride. After all, the clientele she had lined up for the first week of January wasn't remotely like any of the people who normally skied here.

"Parker looks like she's got big news," Sammy said, when there was a lull in the conversation.

"Actually, I do. I booked a major conference for right after New Year's."

"Well, I'll be damned," Emery said, running his fingers through his stylish new haircut. "Leave it to you to find business during dead week."

Parker grinned slightly at the compliment. "It's the Chicago Women's Democratic Caucus, which consists of about two hundred women. So this would be an all-hands-on-deck event."

"Wow," Sammy said, "two hundred women. Would it be inappropriate to tell you I love you?"

"Yes." Campbell punched him in the shoulder.

Parker laughed and continued. "Most of them would probably want to stay in the cabins, but we'd need to set up a central location here in the lodge for them to gather every evening. And there will definitely have to be a bar."

"We can set one up in the lounge area. That way they can sit by the fire. We'll pull in some chairs and tables to go along with the couches already in there," Janelle said. "What type of drinks do you want? Beer? Soda? Wine? Liquor?"

"All of the above, and we'll have to keep it coming. They're a classy bunch, so it won't be a kegger. These women are used to drinking with the big boys of old Chicago."

Greg sat amid the excitement like a grizzly bear. He usually didn't say much during these meetings, but when he did, everyone stopped to listen.

"I don't know about all this. It sounds good from a financial point of view, and I can respect that as much as the next guy, but is this really the direction we want the resort to take? We've always been a family-friendly resort, and this type of group will really change the feel of the place. The next thing you know, we'll be a playground for the rich and snooty."

"It's just one week, Greg." Irene placed a gentle hand on his shoulder.

"Just a week now, but what about when they tell all their friends in the big high-rises about the cute little resort that'll bow to their every whim if they flash around a little cash?"

"Greg, I made it clear to them this isn't Vail. They're coming here because of the peace and quiet. I didn't bill Bear Run as anything it's not," Parker said, trying to hide her frustration. How was she supposed to bring in new business if Greg didn't want anything to change?

"I know you're trying, Parker," Greg said in a patronizing tone, "but these types of people always want more than we feel comfortable giving. "First it's a bar, then it's fancy food. Next thing you know we won't be ski instructors. We'll be glorified bellhops."

"Dad," Campbell said softly. "It's good for business, and we *are* still in charge. We don't have to do anything we don't want to, and if they don't like that, they can leave. They're giving us a chance. Can't we at least do the same for them?"

Parker's heart swelled as she saw the tenderness pass from father to daughter. She knew Greg wished she'd never set foot on the mountain, but he obviously had a soft spot for Campbell, who in turn knew how to speak to him so he'd listen.

Greg raised his hands. "All right, Cam. I don't see as I have much choice, but if I catch one of them doing anything to upset the way this mountain functions, I'll personally put her on a bus back to Chicago."

"They aren't a destructive bunch, by any means, but they are used to being taken care of," Parker tried to assure him. "These are all good, hardworking women. I don't imagine we'll have any real problems, but they will be in definite need of constant attention. Some of them can be a little high maintenance."

Emery nodded. "Gotcha. We'll dot our *i*'s and cross our *t*'s."

"I hope this turns out like you all think it will," Greg told Parker as he left the meeting, obviously still not convinced. "If it doesn't, I'll be the first one to say I told you so."

Campbell was the only person left in the room after her dad left, and the corners of her mouth turned slightly upward.

"What?" Parker asked, flushing under the gaze of those bright blue eyes.

"This conference group, you used to be one of them, right?"

"Well, I—yes," she said, finally allowing herself to think about the fact that her past and her present worlds were about to collide. She had been so happy to have a major conference booking she hadn't thought about what it would mean for her personally.

"Who would have ever thought your political connections would pay off all the way up here in the black hole of civilization," Campbell said.

"Campbell, about that comment, it was just a friend joking. She teases me—"

"And will this friend be joining us for the conference?" she asked, a mischievous look flickering across her face.

"Yes, she will, and I'll personally thrash her if you'd like."

"No." Campbell smiled and shook her head. "We'll just have to do our best to prove to her that we're worthy of your presence. And to prove my dad wrong."

Parker stared at her, unsure of what to say. Finally she blurted, "Can I buy you dinner tonight?"

It was Campbell's turn to be surprised.

"You know, to thank you for teaching me to ski," Parker continued.

"I'd love to," Campbell answered slowly, "but I have to run the groomer all week from five till ten."

"Oh," Parker said, trying not to let her disappointment show. "Okay, I understand."

"But I do have to eat."

"Yeah, you do." Parker's spirits lifted as she thought about their options. "I could get some take-out, and you could show me how the groomer works."

"Hmm," Campbell pretended to mull over the idea, "dinner and a Sno-Cat tour of Bear Run. Sounds like a classy evening."

"It's the company that makes it classy." Parker laughed easily, pleased with herself for finding a way to spend more time with Campbell.

"All right. Should I pick you up here at the lodge around six?" Campbell asked.

"Sounds good."

"Then it's a date," Campbell said with a smile as she left.

Parker tried not to notice the subtle sway of her perfect hips. "It's a date" was just an expression, but this did feel kind of like a date. That thought was enough to place a silly smile of anticipation on her face for the rest of the day.

CHAPTER TEN

The sun had disappeared over the mountain, leaving only a thin pink strip of light along the horizon. The lifts had stopped running almost an hour earlier, and while a few employees were still at the lodge, the slopes were completely empty. Just as Campbell started up the steps of the back deck, Parker headed toward her. No matter how many times she saw her, Campbell still hadn't gotten used to Parker's striking beauty, and today was no exception. She wore a pair of black corduroy pants and a red turtleneck sweater, covered by a black peacoat unbuttoned halfway up the front. Her dark brown hair was tucked under a plain black stocking cap, and the ends tumbled over her shoulders, a few strands blowing in the snowy breeze.

"I take it that's our ride?" She nodded toward the Sno-Cat Campbell had just climbed down from. The machine resembled a bright yellow semi truck cab set atop tank treads.

"Sure is." Campbell tugged on the handle at the bottom of the door. As it swung open, she extended a hand to Parker as if she did it all the time. "Let me help you up."

Setting the bag of food she'd brought just inside the door, Parker put her gloved hand in Campbell's. "What's the best way to do this?"

"Like you're climbing a ladder. I'll hold you steady. Once you're up you can use that handle on the door frame to pull yourself in."

When Campbell got into the driver's spot, Parker had already settled into the passenger seat of the cab.

"I didn't know what kind of sandwiches you like, so I brought four different ones," she said. "Ham and Swiss on rye, turkey and cheddar on sourdough, roast beef and provolone on Italian, and veggies on wheat."

"Are you always this prepared?" Campbell chuckled, already knowing the answer.

"Whenever I can be," Parker replied seriously.

"All right, then, I'll have the turkey."

Parker pulled out the sandwich. "Mustard? Mayo? Ketchup?"

"Mayo, please." Campbell smiled as she watched Parker assemble their meal. Her overpreparation was just part of her personality, but Campbell would never be able to have a relationship with someone as anal retentive as Parker. At the same time she was touched that Parker had put so much thought into their evening together.

Campbell missed their ski lessons, and even though they hadn't talked about much beyond the skiing, she'd enjoyed spending time with Parker. She liked the way she laughed with her whole body when she was relaxed, loved the way Parker's eyes danced when she was pleased with herself, and craved the full-fledged smiles Parker sent her way when they fell into perfect rhythm on the slopes.

Now that Campbell hadn't experienced the joy of being close to Parker either physically or emotionally for several days, she was lonely. She wouldn't have thought it possible to feel that way at Bear Run, not when surrounded by the people she loved most in the world. Yet Parker's absence had left her wanting more. She was almost giddy when they had made plans to see each other again. In fact, she hadn't thought about anything else all afternoon.

"You're all set." Parker handed her the sandwich and a bottle of water.

"Then you'd better buckle up, 'cause you're in for a treat."

As the engine growled to life and the cab rattled and vibrated beneath them, Parker said, "There's no steering wheel. How are you turning this thing?"

Campbell explained how she using the two joysticks, exhilarated by Parker's nearness.

"It reminds me of the old Pac-Man arcade game controllers," Parker mused.

"That's a good comparison." Campbell bit into her sandwich as they rode in silence for a few minutes. She wanted to let Parker get used to the feel of the groomer and have time to appreciate the surreal, unique view. Parker's deep brown eyes made her feel as warm as if they were sitting by a fire instead of crunching over the snow at dusk.

"This is an impressive view," Parker said between bites of her sandwich.

Campbell smiled. It was so important to her that Parker be able to appreciate the mountain the way she did. It was one of the only tangible aspects of the growing connection between them. "I've been seeing it my entire life, and I haven't got tired of it yet."

"You must have led a charmed childhood, idyllic in a lot of ways, with the mountain, and the fresh air, and the freedom."

"Yes. I had a great family, a mountain, and plenty of adventures."

"Sounds like you had everything you wanted while growing up."

"Almost."

"Almost?" Parker asked. "What more could you ask for?"

Campbell paused. "A puppy."

Parker threw back her head and laughed. "Poor baby. They never let you have a puppy?"

"No." Campbell pretended to pout, but her heart was light with the knowledge that she'd made Parker laugh so easily. "Sammy and I begged and begged, but Dad said it was too cold to have a small dog around the slopes, and Mom didn't want a big dog messing up her nice house and yard."

"That's just tragic." Parker's eyes danced in the moonlight reflecting off the snow. "What about now?"

Campbell shrugged. "Guess that's just one of those things you let go of as you get older."

"Well, if it makes you feel better, I don't think you're too old for a puppy."

Campbell grinned. Her evening chores had never been so enjoyable as they were tonight. She always enjoyed the view, and the work was pleasant enough, but with Parker by her side she felt more alive than she had in months.

After some more time on the groomer, Campbell turned it toward the entrance of one of the steeper trails. She stopped at the edge, just before the slope took a drastic downward turn. "See that bar under the dash there?" She pointed to a metal bar just above the floor. "Put your feet up on it."

"Okay," Parker said. "What is it?"

Fighting to suppress a grin Campbell casually answered, "It's an 'oh-shit' bar."

"What's it for?" Parker asked suspiciously.

"I'll show you." She nudged the groomer forward over the steepest part of the run, causing the machine to move onto the slope at a sharp fifty-degree angle, the front of the cab pointing downward.

Parker, unprepared for the incline, threw her hands on the dash and muttered, "Oh, shit." She instantly locked her knees, bracing against the bar and pinning herself back against the seat.

Campbell gave a loud, body-shaking laugh. "You've got the hang of it."

"Jesus." Parker exhaled. "It feels like we're going to fall right over."

"Relax," Campbell said. "Really. I'll take good care of you." Without thinking, she placed a hand on Parker's shoulder and gently massaged the tense muscles with her fingertips. For a fleeting second she thought about telling her how absolutely stunning she was when she let down her guard, but she worried about opening herself up to Parker.

Parker's lips parted slightly in surprise. "I believe you."

Those deep brown eyes melted Campbell. Suddenly her throat went dry and her stomach clenched. She'd never seen such trust in Parker's expression before, and she felt inexplicably vulnerable for the first time in months. She didn't like the sensation. Vulnerably meant opening herself to pain, and she wasn't ready to take that chance again. Almost involuntarily she broke their contact, letting her hand fall onto the seat. Silence filled the cab as she turned the groomer around and headed back up the mountain, this time the incline forcing them back into their seats.

"So, Ms. Riley." If they were going to build a more meaningful connection, it was time to learn more about Parker. "What's a classy woman like you doing in Bear Run, Wisconsin?"

Parker laughed with only a hint of nervousness. "I wanted to get free ski lessons and Sno-Cat tours."

Campbell smiled at the clever attempt to dodge the question, but she didn't bite. "So you're not ready to talk about it?"

Parker gazed out the window into the darkness, and Campbell knew she would talk in her own time, not a minute sooner. She had probably been startled enough for one evening, so when they reached the top of the mountain, Campbell decided to go up only the steep grades and back down the gentler trails. They had just pulled onto the green trail they'd skied a few days early when Parker finally spoke.

"I was very good at getting people elected, selling a candidate to the voters, but I wasn't all that great at determining which of them were worthy of being elected in the first place." She paused and took a deep breath. "I worked for a man named Tim Brady and I thought he was the real deal."

Campbell nodded, hearing the pain just below the surface of Parker's steady tone. She knew a little about Tim Brady from the few news stories that made national headlines. As she recalled, he had been involved in some minor sex scandal with a woman who claimed she'd been sexually harassed, but most people seemed to have written off his accuser as a gold digger trying to make a buck off an up-and-coming politician.

"I thought he was different," Parker continued. "He had so much potential, and I helped him capitalize on it. I was entirely responsible for his senate campaign, from the media appearances, to fund-raising strategy, to staffing. I believed in him. I know that probably sounds silly—"

"Not at all," Campbell said softly. It didn't sound silly to her, at least not when Parker said it.

"Well, it was," Parker said resolutely. "He turned out to be just like the rest of them. He said whatever needed to be said whether he cared about the causes he was supporting or not, and obviously when it came to the most important issues, he did not."

Campbell sat silently. Parker was evidently reliving some painful memories, and while a part of her ached to alleviate that hurt, she knew enough to realize that kind of pain was personal.

"The establishment sided with him, of course. They didn't care what he believed as long as he did what they wanted. He was their golden boy, and they all rallied around him, but I just couldn't be a part of it anymore. And I knew if I stayed there I would be."

"So you got as far away as you could."

"I needed to be somewhere I could find my strength again, remember what really mattered, get my bearings, so to speak."

"And when you do, will you go back?" Campbell barely realized she was holding her breath while she waited for the answer, not looking at Parker, but out into the darkness.

"I don't know."

The tightening in Campbell's chest was almost too much to bear. She knew she was being stupid. Of course a woman like Parker would want more out of life than this little mountain could offer her, but still Campbell felt empty at the thought of her not being there. Lynn's voice echoed through her head. *I mean it. No self-respecting lesbian would ever settle for the life you're dreaming of.* Campbell was simply part of Parker's temporary retreat, and if she let herself dwell on that fact she would be undeniably hurt. But at the same time she wasn't likely to forget that reality anytime soon. Holding on to someone who wasn't holding on to you in return brought nothing but pain.

"Did I say something wrong again?" Parker asked softly.

"What?" Campbell realized she'd been lost in her own thoughts and the conversation had stopped. "No. What do you mean?"

"Campbell, you have a terrible poker face." Parker chuckled. "You just shut down completely, like you did when I mentioned going to Madison."

Campbell winced, and the tightness in her throat prevented her from answering right away. Parker couldn't possibly know the comparison she'd just made between her and Campbell's past, but the connection was unsetting nonetheless. Had she reacted to the thought of Parker's leaving the same way she did when she thought of losing Lynn? This wasn't the first time the similarity between Parker and Lynn had been mentioned. Sammy had said basically the same thing not too long ago, and Campbell was even more disconcerted this time around.

"I'm sorry if I did." Campbell forced a weak smile. "I certainly didn't mean to."

Parker gently covered Campbell's hand with her own, and the touch sparked a chain reaction that shot though Campbell's body, igniting a heat that did more than comfort her. "I didn't mean to either, but obviously something about Madison upsets you. Even hearing the word seems to hurt you."

"Just your usual youthful indiscretions." Campbell tried to shrug off the inquiry.

"Now who's dodging questions?"

Campbell considered the remark. Parker had answered her

honestly. She at least deserved the same. "I fell in love there, for the first time, the only time, really."

"Oh." Parker's expression gave no indication of what she was thinking.

"Lynn was amazing, like no one I'd ever met, which ended up being the problem. We wanted different things from life. We were too different to make it work. So she built a life I didn't fit into, and I came back home where I belonged." Campbell could still hear Lynn shouting the day she'd pronounced the ultimatum, forcing Campbell to choose between her lover and her family. *You can't have it both ways, Campbell. While I'm gone, decide whether you want to be a dyke or play heterosexual homemaker at Bear Run.*

Campbell shook her head, trying to wipe away the memory. Without realizing it she had threaded her fingers through Parker's, finding the simple gesture both comforting and exciting. "Bear Run isn't what most power lesbians want for their future, but for me it's home. My family is my past and my future. I bet that sounds silly."

"It might to anyone who doesn't know your family," Parker admitted. "I know they're more than special to you."

"Lynn saw what she wanted to see." Campbell sighed. "But in the end the choice was mine."

"Well, I'm glad you made it." Parker squeezed her hand gently.

"Yeah?" Campbell's spirits began to rise.

"I can't imagine you anywhere else."

"It is pretty amazing, isn't it?" Campbell asked, stopping the groomer on top of the mountain. Moonlight cast an incandescent glow over the entire resort, and the snow shimmered with the reflecting light.

"Absolutely." Parker sounded almost wistful as she stared out at the stunning view. "Every time I think I'm really getting to know this place, you show me something new about it. You deserve to be happy, Campbell, and I'm sure someday the right woman will come along and share your dreams."

Campbell smiled at the sentiment, but her heart ached at the implications of what was left unspoken. Parker was wishing her the best, but she certainly wasn't offering to fill the role of "the right woman."

CHAPTER ELEVEN

Parker was spending far too much time staring out the window and not nearly enough preparing for the major conference that was now little more than a month away. She pretended she had no idea why she was so distracted, but then she would see Campbell on the slopes and remember the feel of their interlocking fingers or the soft touch of a hand on her shoulder or the heat of their near kiss. Or she would recall the sadness in Campbell's voice when she spoke about her first love. To think about someone hurting Campbell, and her still mourning the loss of a woman who so obviously didn't deserve her, disturbed Parker.

Since Parker had arrived seven weeks earlier in October, she'd gone from being single-mindedly obsessed with her job to wanting to play on the slopes all day, and Campbell had been responsible for that change in attitude. Though Parker knew she shouldn't, she lingered a little longer at the window, watching Campbell take her after-school group, mostly six- and seven-year-olds, down the mountain and around an obstacle course of orange traffic cones. Parker couldn't hear her, but every now and then all of the kids would alter the position of their skis at exactly the same time, and she knew Campbell had just called out either "pizza" or "French fries."

Parker hadn't skied during the week since Thanksgiving, and that needed to change. Not only was it important to practice her new skills, but she also needed to relax and get out of the office. Turning back to her work, she told herself that if she stayed late tonight and got some work done, she might take tomorrow off to hit the slopes. It would probably be a good day for it, since she'd overheard Emery tell some guests that they were supposed to get several inches of new snow overnight. So she forced herself to focus on preparing for the conference.

She wasn't sure how long she'd been working when she noticed the snow falling outside her window. Even through the clouds it was easy to tell that the sunlight had faded and evening had set in, so it had to be after five o'clock, but she had no idea how long it had been snowing. The flakes were large and seemed to be coming down consistently, but they weren't heavy. She fought the urge to peek outside. If she allowed herself to be distracted once again, she might never get back on track.

Parker didn't stop until a dull thud on her window got her attention. Unsure of what had made the sound, she listened carefully to see if it would happen again. After a minute passed, she began to convince herself that she'd imagined it and was just about to return to her paperwork when a snowball hit the window, rattling it ever so slightly as some of the snow stuck to the glass. She peered through the portion of the window that wasn't plastered with snow. Campbell stood below her bundled up in her coat and gloves, with a scarf around her neck and her stocking cap pulled down over her ears so that only her mouth and sparkling blue eyes showed. Her clothing was covered with the rapidly falling snow, and the massive yellow Sno-Cat was barely visible about thirty yards behind her.

Parker slid open the heavily framed pane of glass, then the smaller storm window, and the frigid air rushed in past her face. The temperature had dropped considerably since this morning, and she shivered.

"If you're trying to start a snowball fight, I think the odds are in your favor," she called down to Campbell.

"I wish we had time to play." Campbell smiled that broad easy smile that came so naturally to her, and Parker felt awash with pleasure that she was able to engender such a response. A faint flutter unsettled her stomach. "But I came to let you know it's turning into a real blizzard out here," Campbell continued. "You should head home."

It hadn't occurred to Parker that the weather might be dangerous, but as she considered the heavily falling snow, she realized that if it had been coming down like this for several hours, they had likely already received several inches, and it didn't appear to be letting up. "Thanks for the warning bulletin. I'll be on my way soon."

"You better go now," Campbell said more seriously, her voice raised to be heard over the increasing wind. "If I'd seen your light on, I'd have come up earlier."

"Okay. What about you?"

"I'm in the groomer. I'll be fine. You just be careful."

"You, too, and stay warm," Parker called before closing the window. She was touched that Campbell had been concerned enough to stop by, but she wondered if she wasn't being overprotective. The thought of having Campbell there to protect her was nice, though. She wrapped up her tasks for the evening, taking only a few more minutes to finish some of the items she'd been working on before she packed the rest to take home with her. If she got snowed in, she wanted to have something to do.

Almost half an hour later she waded across the parking lot to her little Volvo C70. At least five or six more inches of snow were piled on the hood and windshield, and it took her another fifteen minutes to scrape it all off. When she pulled out onto the road that led around the resort and past her apartment complex, she wished she'd left sooner. If the snowplows had been through, she couldn't tell. She couldn't see the road at all, but she simply tried to keep an equal distance between the rows of trees on either side of her vehicle. To make matters worse, the snow was pelting down on a collision course with her windshield. Her headlights illuminated the swiftly blowing flakes, making it appear as through she were making the jump to light speed in the old space movies she used to watch as a kid.

Although she was driving only ten miles an hour, her tires began to slip and she gasped as she started to slide sideway across the road. If anyone else was foolish enough to be driving from the other way, she would be directly in their path. Trying to avoid any sudden moves, she attempted to adjust the steering wheel in order to correct her trajectory, but the change in angle did nothing for her traction. She skidded back the other way. As she neared what she perceived to be the edge of the road, she tried to turn in the other direction once again, but failed. Tapping the brakes, she couldn't stop the Volvo's momentum and slid off the shoulder of the road into a snowbank.

After Parker caught her breath, she scanned her surroundings. The entire passenger side of the car was covered by snow, and the driver's-side tires seemed to be several yards off the road. Though she knew it was probably useless, she gave the engine a little gas and turned the steering wheel, hoping the tires would catch enough traction to move the car. Instead they spun in place, no doubt digging her in deeper. She shifted into reverse and tried again with the same results.

Cursing quietly, she opened her door and stepped out of the car. Snow immediately covered the top of her short snow boots and seeped into her socks, mocking her for choosing fashion over functionality. She trudged to the back of the car and checked to make sure her tailpipe was clear, then scooped some snow away from the tailpipe, the cold penetrating her gloves and freezing her fingertips. Satisfied she would be safe from carbon monoxide for a while, she climbed back into the driver's seat, trying to shake off the snow and cold.

Parker dug through the leather shoulder bag she carried back and forth to work and fished out her cell phone. Flipping it open, she held it in every imaginable position trying to get a signal, but she knew she was only deluding herself. She rarely got a strong signal on this side of the mountain even in the best of conditions. In a blizzard the phone was totally useless.

"Okay, Parker," she said aloud, "don't panic. You can do this. Just think."

She mulled over her options. She could try to make it to the lodge on foot, since she was less than a mile from the main building. But the snow and the cold were a strong deterrent, and without her headlights she wouldn't be able to see more than a few feet in front of her. She'd already stumbled just getting to the back of the car. The thought of trudging all the way back to the lodge was just too much to bear. She was probably closer to Campbell and Sammy's house, and she knew that either of them would be willing and able to help her, but she'd have to climb halfway up the mountain, and on the slippery road she wasn't sure she'd make it in one piece—if she could even find the road to get there.

Or she could stay put and hope that someone would come along soon and find her. In theory the snowplows should clear this road soon, but since it wasn't a main thoroughfare, they might have to wait until the major roads were accessible. With the snow still falling, no one might come by for hours. Her windshield was already covered, and in an hour or so she would have to get out and check the tailpipe again. Not liking any of the possibilities, she turned up the heat, closed her eyes, and rested her head on the steering wheel. She needed to make a decision soon, but not until she warmed up a bit.

❖

Campbell turned up the windshield wipers on the groomer, and the massive blades snapped back and forth across the large panes of the glass that made up the front of the cab. The thick, wet snow had been coming down hard for hours. After a storm like this they would be able to open all the slopes, even the ones they hadn't been able to make much snow on. A major storm during the first weekend in December was good for business, and now that Parker had finally gone home, Campbell could enjoy the weather more.

Parker hadn't been far from her thoughts all week. When they'd almost kissed, they crossed a line from casual company to something more. Parker obviously hadn't given her the full story about why she fled Chicago. She had probably only skimmed the surface, but at least now Campbell understood that Parker was shaken. It must have been so hard for her to have misjudged Tim Brady's character like that. Parker definitely took a lot of pride in her work, so spending all her efforts on someone so unworthy would have devastated her. No wonder she'd thrown herself into her new job with such intensity. She wasn't a workaholic. She was simply trying to prove to herself that she could do something right.

As Campbell throttled down the groomer, nearing the base of one of the mountain's main trails, she glimpsed lights just beyond the single line of trees that marked the resort's boundary. Normally she wouldn't have thought anything of it, but something about their angle made her slow the groomer and look again. She could barely see through the driving snow, but the light obviously wasn't a street lamp. It was much too close to the ground in an otherwise dark area. Then she realized she was seeing headlight beams, coming from something buried on the far side of the snowbank.

"Damn," she muttered, realizing that whoever had slid off the road probably needed help. She pulled the parking brake to anchor the groomer and zipped up her coat. A cold blast of air hit her the second she opened the door and hopped out. She pulled down her hat, trying to protect her ears from the biting wind, and trudged toward the lights.

The snowbank was at least six feet high and not easy to scale. Campbell sank up to her knees with every step. As she crawled over the pile of snow several feet away from where the headlights appeared to start, she slipped several times. She was glad she hadn't changed out of her weatherproof ski clothes. She was freezing already and didn't want to be damp also.

As she slid down the other side of the snow bank and planted her feet on more solid ground, she first caught sight of the car. It was Parker's black Volvo, half buried in the bank and completely covered in a layer of freshly fallen snow.

"Oh, my God," she gasped, stumbling to the driver's side as quickly as possible. Brushing the snow from the window, she saw Parker slumped over the steering wheel, not moving. Her stomach clenched and she fought the urge to vomit at the prospect that she was hurt, or worse.

"Parker," she yelled, and quickly whipped open the door.

Parker jumped, looking shocked and staring. "Campbell?"

"Where are you hurt?" Campbell knelt next to the car, trying not to cry with relief. At least Parker was conscious.

"Holy shit," Parker shouted. "You scared the crap out of me."

"I scared *you*?" Campbell shouted back. "I thought you were unconscious or—" She choked on the last word, unable to speak her worst fear.

"I'm sorry." Parker's voice softened. "I'm fine. I was just catching my breath."

"You're not hurt?" Campbell reached in and touched Parker's thigh, but that wasn't enough. She was still upset. She needed to feel her, touch her, hold her close. Campbell's racing pulse wouldn't return to normal until she was completely convinced that Parker was safe.

"I'm fine. I just slid off the road and couldn't get any traction. I was trying to decide what to do."

Campbell sighed in relief, the knots in her stomach starting to loosen. She stood up and examined the car again. It wasn't going anywhere tonight. Parker got out of the car and stared at it, too.

"We'll have to leave it here for now," Campbell said, "but I can tow it out tomorrow. It'll be okay."

Parker nodded, and Campbell realized that while she wasn't hurt, she was overwhelmed. Her pants were soaked from the knee down, and her long, dark hair was tangled from the wind and the snow. She needed to get Parker someplace safe and warm before the shock wore off and she crashed from exhaustion. "Come on." She wrapped her arm around Parker's shoulders. "Let's get you out of here."

It wouldn't be easy to get Parker back over the snowbank, but the groomer was the closest thing to comfort. So Campbell plotted the easiest path, then steadied Parker on her way up, both of them stumbling and falling. They were covered in wet, clinging snow but Parker didn't have weather-resistant apparel, and she was shivering heavily as they slipped down the other side and waded to the groomer. Campbell placed her hands on Parker's hips, only briefly noticing the subtle curve of skin beneath her fingers as she lifted Parker onto the tread and into the cab. She mentally chastised herself for noticing Parker's body at a time like this, but she couldn't stop the tingle that raced through her.

As soon as she had the groomer's heater running full blast, she slipped off her coat and wrapped it around Parker's shaking shoulders. At first she seemed as though she might refuse the coat, but then she merely mumbled, "Thank you."

"Just hang on," Campbell said. "We'll be home in a minute."

Firing up the groomer and taking the most direct route to her house, she didn't want to think about the fact that she had just referred to her home as though it were Parker's as well. Just a slip of the tongue, or perhaps something more Freudian?

After she stopped outside the small, two-story cabin less than ten yards from the edge of the trail, she hopped out and struggled through the snow to help Parker down. Each threaded an arm around the other's waist and they stumbled up to the porch. When Campbell pushed open the door, the warmth rushed out to greet them. She kicked off her own boots as she went, then removed her coat from Parker's shoulders on the way across the living room. "Upstairs," she muttered as they headed for her bathroom.

She turned on the water as hot as possible and put the stopper in the tub. "Get out of those wet clothes."

Parker flushed. "Campbell, I think I can take it from here."

Campbell blushed when she realized she had basically ordered Parker to strip in her presence. An image of Parker's naked body flashed across her mind, and before she could stop it, her pulse quickened. "Right," she stammered. "I'll go get you some dry clothes and put them outside the door. Call me if you need anything," she said, then turned to leave.

"Campbell?"

"Yeah?"

The clouds of shock in Parker's eyes had disappeared, replaced by a raw softness that made Campbell light-headed. Parker closed the distance between them and wrapped her arms around Campbell's waist, pulling her close and resting her head on Campbell's chest. The move caught her off guard because Parker didn't seem to be the hugging type. But this felt so right, and Parker's body fit so snugly into her own. She pulled Parker to her and shivered at how good it felt to hold her.

"Thank you for rescuing me," Parker whispered.

"Anytime." Parker had worked her way into Campbell's heart, and after feeling the length of her body against her own, it wasn't a sensation she'd soon forget.

CHAPTER TWELVE

When Parker finally emerged from the bathroom half an hour later, she felt infinitely better. The warm water had eradicated the bitter cold from her body, and Campbell's steady presence had helped calm her mind. While Parker was in the bathtub, Campbell had changed into pajamas—an old pair of flannel pants and a ribbed, long-sleeved shirt. The sweatpants she had left for Parker were a few inches too long, but she'd snugged up the drawstring so they stayed firmly above her hips. Parker also wore a long-sleeved T-shirt with a Wisconsin Badger on it. She chuckled at the choice. Campbell had used up any brownie points she'd garnered during the rescue by picking that shirt.

"Thanks for the clothes," Parker said, a bit sarcastically.

"It suits you," Campbell teased back. "Why don't you just keep it? I've got plenty more where that came from."

"Maybe I will." Parker grinned. "I could wear it to paint in, or dust with."

Campbell threw back her head and laughed, and Parker was relieved they were back to their familiar banter. The shock and cold that had quieted Parker on the way to the cabin was beginning to wear off, but now she felt exhausted.

Campbell must have read her body language because she started for the door. "You must be pretty tired after all the excitement today. I've changed the sheets on the bed and I'll be right downstairs if you need—"

"Absolutely not. I'll take the couch. You've done more than you should have already."

"No." Campbell shook her head as she yawned. "Sammy will be up before five tomorrow morning to go groom the rest of the slopes, and I may have to help. You need to get some sleep, and you won't be able to do that with the two of us moving around downstairs."

Parker studied Campbell. She seemed exhausted, too, the lids of her piercing blue eyes getting very droopy. "I'm really not that tired."

"You will be soon. Why don't you get in bed? I bet you'll crash right away. I'm always asleep before my head hits the pillow."

"I doubt it," Parker said with a shiver. "Every time I closed my eyes in the shower I could still feel myself slipping and sliding on that road."

Parker wondered if Campbell could sense how terrified she'd been during the wreck. Surely she knew Parker didn't cope well with losing control.

Finally Campbell smiled at her reassuringly. Her lips looked so full and soft that Parker wondered what they would have felt like brushing against her own if Campbell had followed through on the near kiss a week earlier. "Okay, how about this? Why don't you get in bed, and I'll sit with you until you fall asleep? I'll help you keep your mind off things."

Parker wanted to refuse the unaccustomed help, but something about Campbell's offer seemed so genuine and not the least bit condescending that she couldn't say no. Instead she nodded and climbed into the double bed, snuggling under the sheets, but propping up on her elbow and a pillow.

Parker thought she heard Campbell's breath catch when Parker motioned for her to join her on the bed, but she shook off any further thoughts about the reaction. Campbell was just going to help her get to sleep, and then she was going downstairs. She even reclined on the other side of the bed without putting her body under the covers where she might touch Parker, which was probably for the best. If they touched again she might not be able to let Campbell leave.

"Your house is lovely," Parker said, trying to take her mind off the nearness of Campbell's body. Campbell's room reflected her personality—clean, comfortable, and completely unaffected. The walls were a non-descript cream color, but the woodwork was all original and well kept. The decorations, while simple and mostly family pictures, gave the space a homey feel. The room was on the second story, and the large windows in front of them provided a view of the slope that ran along the back of the house.

"Thanks. It's one of the ones my grandfather built. It's become a sort of halfway house for his children and grandchildren. I think every one of his kids lived here at some point, and I'm sure someday Emery's twins and Janelle's kids will get their turn, too."

"So you'll stay here until you start a family of your own?"

"That's the plan. I want to build my own place at some point. I even have the spot picked out, but my dad doesn't want me to build anything new on the resort property. He's a little resistant to change."

"Yeah, I've noticed that," Parker said, "but I'm sure you'll find the perfect place for your and your future family."

"I'll work something out with my dad eventually, but whether that will be for a family or not"—Campbell shrugged, her eyes heavy, as she attempted unsuccessfully to stifle another yawn—"only time will tell."

A hint of sadness mixed with the weariness in Campbell's face, and Parker thought back to their conversation in the groomer earlier that week. Perhaps Campbell was thinking about her first love again. Parker could hardly bear to watch the subtle hints of pain that creased Campbell's gorgeous features but didn't know how to ease them, so she lay back and stared at the ceiling. Surely Campbell hadn't given up on the idea of a future just because it hadn't happened on her first try. The silence stretched between them as she tried to think of something to say to help Campbell. Finally she said the only thing that felt right. "I'm sure someone will snatch you up before long. You're too special for them not to."

When Campbell didn't respond, Parker began to worry that she'd said too much. Had she made her uncomfortable, or hurt her further? When she finally got up the nerve to sneak a peek at Campbell, her worry disappeared. Campbell's eyes were closed, her breathing soft and steady as she slept. She looked so innocent, almost cherubic. Parker quickly pulled the covers up over Campbell and switched off the bedside lamp, then studied the darkness and waited for sleep. She refused to think about how much the sight of Campbell asleep stirred her.

❖

When Campbell awoke, the soft light of dawn was beginning to show through her window. The snow had stopped, and outside the sounds of morning spread across the mountain. She felt wonderful, better than she had all year, but it took her a moment to realize what made this day so different. The answer was right in front of her or, more accurately, pressed against her. Sometime in the night she had curled herself around Parker, her front to Parker's back, spooning perfectly. Her arm wrapped around Parker, and her hand rested on the flat plane of Parker's stomach, slightly under her shirt.

Campbell lay very still for fear of waking her. She tried to control her breathing as her sleepy comfort gave way to arousal. When she breathed in their combined scents, her body betrayed her further and her nipples hardened. She fought to keep from pulling Parker tighter. Shocked at her response to their nearness, she tried to remember the last time she'd felt like this. Not since Lynn had she been so aroused, and even then her reaction wasn't this sudden or strong. Sure, she had been attracted to women. She had a pulse, but it hadn't raced like it did for Parker. Her reaction was specific to *this* woman, and the feeling was downright dangerous. If she needed merely a physical touch, she could deal with that, but having that need directed at Parker was simply too much. She was too close, the feelings too complicated.

Campbell carefully withdrew from Parker's waist. Struggling not to groan at the emptiness she felt, she edged off the bed. She pulled on a pair of jeans and quietly closed the bedroom door behind her, then tiptoed downstairs. Sammy, in his ski clothes and a stocking cap, sat at the bar between the kitchen and the living room sipping coffee and watching the muted weather report on TV. Wordlessly, Campbell poured herself a cup.

"I saw the groomer out back. Did you break it?" Sammy asked, absentmindedly.

"No, I just left it there after I brought Parker here last night." That got his attention.

He quickly flipped off the TV and faced her, grinning wickedly. "That was fast."

"She ran her car off the road last night. Got it stuck in a snowbank." Campbell ignored his innuendo.

"Is she okay?"

"She was cold and a little shaken up, but she'll be fine."

"So she stayed in your room." Sammy's voice took on a more suggestive tone again. "Not on the couch?"

"It's not what you think, Sam." She wanted him to know that the joking was inappropriate, but then she sighed. How she felt when she woke up with her arms wrapped around Parker was probably closer to Sammy's suggestiveness than she cared to admit. "We fell asleep while we were talking."

Sammy appeared skeptical but stopped teasing her. "Okay, then why don't I finish grooming this slope? You should be here when she wakes up."

Campbell shook her head. "I'll do it. I need to stop by Mom and Dad's anyway and have them help tow her car over here so she can go home when she wakes up."

Sammy shrugged. "Whatever you say. I'll hang out here until you get back."

"Thanks," she said on her way out the door. She wasn't ready to face Parker yet, but she hoped some space and some fresh air would help clear her head and, more important, calm her body.

❖

Parker slowly stretched out and, during her gradual awakening, sensed an emptiness she couldn't name. She rubbed her eyes, attempting to focus on her surroundings. This wasn't her bedroom, but it felt like home. Slowly she remembered she was in Campbell's home, Campbell's bed, and had, up until a short while ago, been in Campbell's arms. She flushed at the image that was half memory, half dream of sleeping soundly, wrapped in the safety and warmth of Campbell's embrace. She had expected to sleep fitfully, given the stress of the evening and the unfamiliar setting, but in the unguarded moments of sleep, she surrendered herself to the innocent intimacy of Campbell's touch. She sat up suddenly. She wasn't thinking of some random woman, some stranger to seek solace in. This was Campbell—strong, sweet, sexy Campbell—with her sharp blue eyes, knee-weakening smiles, and firm muscles. Her entire body tightened in arousal.

Parker knew that Campbell was gone. Even in her sleep she'd felt the shift of their bodies separating, and the emptiness that she'd awoken with was tempered by relief at not having to face the woman who'd held her all night. She wasn't ready to see in her in the soft light of morning. The myriad feelings that washed over her every time she recalled the feel of Campbell's body lightly pressed against hers were too much to let herself dwell on, so she decided to put some distance between herself and the memory.

She smelled coffee the minute she opened the bedroom door and instinctively headed toward it. In the kitchen Sammy sat on a stool watching an infomercial for a product that promised to make food in half the time, even though it came out slightly deformed. He smiled when she approached. "Good morning, Parker. How do you take your coffee?"

"Hi, Sammy." She returned his smile, which was nearly as contagious as his sister's. "One cream, one sugar."

He offered his stool to Parker before hurrying around to the kitchen. "Cam said you had a little scare last night. How are you feeling?"

"Much better now, thanks to Campbell." She said the words before she realized their double meaning.

If Sammy noticed the blush rise in Parker's face, he didn't show it. "Good to hear. She went to have your car dug out, but she should be home before too long." He set a steaming mug of coffee in front of her, then hesitated as though he wanted to say more but was unsure whether he should. "I'm biased, but you know she's pretty special, right?"

Parker stopped, her mug poised in midair. The question was serious, and the fact that Sammy had asked it carried a lot of weight. "Sammy, you *are* biased," she smiled, "but anyone who's been around Campbell for more than a few minutes can tell she's special. I may not know her like you do, but I realize she's one of a kind."

"Good." He nodded, seeming relieved at her answer, and added more nervously, "Then I'll save us both the awkwardness of asking what your intentions are with her."

"Sammy, I don't know what you think happened last night…" Even as Parker began the denial, she felt herself leaning back into the comfort of Campbell's arms and hoped her face wasn't her giving away.

"I know," Sammy said. "Campbell told me it was completely innocent, but I like you, and I love her, so I thought you should know that if anything ever were to happen somewhere down the line, you should know that she's been hurt pretty badly."

"Lynn?"

"Yes. And that's all I'm going to say. She'd hate for me to be the one to tell you about it. Just be careful, okay? I'll have your head if you hurt my sister." Sammy shuffled his feet, visibly uncomfortable with the topic and probably jittery about having threatened her. He ran his hand through his sandy brown hair in a gesture with an uncanny resemblance to his sister when she was nervous.

Parker opened her mouth, but the sound of the front door opening stopped her. What had Sammy hesitated to tell her about Lynn?

"Good morning," Campbell said as she rounded the corner, windblown and flushed from the cold.

"Good morning." Campbell was stunning enough before last night, but now Parker wondered if she would ever be able to see her again without remembering what it felt like to be held by her. She almost wished she had made more of the contact between them and slid her hands over her finely muscled torso, run her fingers through those golden locks, maybe even finished that kiss they'd never quite gotten to last week.

"Dad and I got your car pulled out of the snowbank. It's outside," Campbell said calmly, giving no indication that she was rattled by the time they'd spent in each other's arms. Was Parker reading too much into it? "It's not too bad—pretty dirty and the paint roughed up a little, but no dents or engine trouble that I could tell."

"Thank you so much, Campbell. You're a lifesaver."

Campbell blushed. "You don't have to thank me. I'm glad I was there for you."

"Me, too," Parker said seriously, and she meant it. In only a few hours, she had experienced relief, security, comfort, arousal, and emptiness, all tied to Campbell. Campbell was deeply wounded from her past with Lynn, but Sammy was right. She was special. Steady, dependable, and so giving of herself, she was also a strong, sexy woman, and that combination was enough to send both Parker's mind and body in directions she wasn't sure either of them could control.

CHAPTER THIRTEEN

Parker looked up from the paperwork she was scanning before the staff meeting started and flashed a full-fledged smile. She wore khakis and a black sweater, and a single ruby hung from a delicate silver chain around her neck. Her long dark hair was pulled back loosely, revealing simple, elegant earrings to match her necklace. She gave the impression of being poised yet approachable, the epitome of class. A twinge of arousal hit Campbell again when she thought about last night, and in a brief moment of panic, she heard the familiar refrain. *What could a woman like that possibly see in someone like you?*

Then Parker spoke and wiped away that sliver of doubt. "Campbell, you're just the person I've been waiting for."

Campbell was sure that everyone in the room could sense her inordinate pleasure. "Why? Did you find another snowbank?"

Parker laughed and shoved her gently. They rarely shared playful physical contact, but it seemed natural now. "No, I just haven't been skiing in over two weeks."

"Well, there's a ski hill right outside your office." Campbell settled into their comfortable banter.

"So I've been told," Parker said. "I've also heard that I can't really market it effectively unless I experience it."

"That does make sense."

"I just can't seem to tear myself away from all my paperwork and business meetings, and since Christmas is only two week away I'm only getting busier."

Campbell nodded, repressing a grin. "Perhaps you haven't had the right motivation."

Parker played along. "And what do you suggest?"

"Maybe you need to have one of those business meetings out on the slopes."

"Well," Parker pretended to mull the idea over, "I really should review some of the details for the ski instruction, just to make sure everyone's on the same page for our big upcoming conference."

"I could probably pencil you in for a three o'clock appointment. We could run through some of your concerns between my lessons." Campbell felt a surge of joy at the thought of being back on the slopes with Parker. Any excuse to see her would be wonderful, but skiing together seemed perfect.

"That sounds great." Parker wrote down the time in her date book. "Where should I meet you?"

"I wouldn't worry about that. Just head out onto the mountain. I'll find you."

"Great," Sammy interjected. "Now that's settled, what else do you need from the rest of us?"

A hint of color rose in Parker's face, and Campbell realized everyone had just overheard their flirting. *Flirting? Is that what that was? Surely not.* She must be imagining things. Their relationship had definitely taken on a new tone, but she reasoned that waking up in each other's arms, no matter how inadvertently, would do that to a friendship. Still, their banter had been friendly, nothing more, or so she tried to convince herself. It had been a long time since she'd flirted with anyone, and even if she decided to start now, remembering that Parker was way out of her league was enough to kill that mood.

Parker flipped through her notes, a move Campbell thought was probably more a habit than a necessity. "I'm sure no one needs to be told how busy next month will be, but we're right on track for the big events of New Year's Eve and the Blow-Off Bash. We're at over ninety percent occupancy for both, and I've arranged the same DJ for New Year's Eve and the last night of the conference."

"Do you think they could DJ the employee Christmas party, too?" Irene asked.

"I didn't know we were having one."

"Every year we throw a little get-together a few days before the Christmas rush gets out of hand," Janelle explained. "It's a way for us to all hang out, have some fun, and meet the new staff."

Greg chuckled. "Some of us enjoy getting out of the office to have fun once in a while."

"Gotcha." Parker nodded as she took down the information, choosing to ignore the dig from Greg. "What's the date? I'll call the DJ."

"What about the Thursday before Christmas?" Emery said, without even glancing at his calendar. "That's before the rush begins, and it gives us plenty of time to recover before New Year's Eve."

"Sounds good," Parker said. "Anything else I can help with?"

"I've got the food covered." Janelle ticked through her own mental checklist for the upcoming events. "We'll just do snacks for the Christmas party to keep it casual. New Year's Eve will be simple but a little classier, with some hors d'oeuvres and champagne for the midnight toast. The conference will have something different each night, but we've already bought enough alcohol to keep a small fleet of sailors plied with liquor for a week."

"And all the reservations are set. We'll just need to stay on our toes as far as special requests go," Emery confirmed.

Campbell sat back and watched the dynamics of the room. Parker was obviously running the show, as was to be expected since she was the point person on both the New Year's Eve Party and Blow-Off Bash. She seemed at ease with the free-flowing style of the group and had adapted a much more casual approach since her first meeting almost two months earlier. She still hadn't overcome her addiction to her day planner, but she appeared much more comfortable with the back-and-forth, conversational style in which business was done at Bear Run.

Campbell would like to see Parker as part of the family, but she would never fit in here. She was too independent, too goal-oriented, and still too uptight. Besides, the continuing clash between her father and Parker was making everyone uncomfortable. Campbell once again remembered how miserable she would make herself if she even considered the possibility that someone like Parker might want to be with someone like her. Hadn't her five-year-long mistake with Lynn taught her anything? She needed to forget about women like Lynn and Parker and focus on the ski business and life with her family. She would make a great old-maid cousin, and eventually an outstanding old-maid aunt to Sammy's kids. That was the life she had chosen.

People began shuffling to their feet, a clear sign that Campbell had missed the end of the meeting. "So I'll see you at three?" she asked Parker as she slipped on her coat.

"I wouldn't miss it," Parker confirmed with another megawatt smile.

Try as she might, Campbell couldn't focus on the fact that falling for Parker was a sure-fire way to get hurt again. Every time she looked into those stunning brown eyes, she fell a little farther out of her comfort zone. Rather than try to find her voice through the faint flutter in her chest, she simply nodded and tried to exit gracefully, but she didn't miss the look her parents shared as she left. She couldn't read their expression as easily as usual. It might have been curiosity, amusement, or apprehension, and at that moment all three were justified.

❖

Parker was giddy at the thought of hitting the slopes with Campbell, though she tried to pretend she was excited about the skiing rather than the company. She stopped by the ski-rental booth and picked up her gear, then headed for the base of the mountain. It was a weekday, so the crowd was thin, most of the skiers either local college students or those who had likely taken off work early to beat the after-school rush.

As she clicked her boots into her skis, she admitted Campbell had been right. That click was quickly becoming one of her favorite sounds. She used her poles to push herself to the lift, and in a matter of seconds she was whisked up the mountain. Despite the slightly gray condition of the sky, the snow was smooth and pure white, interrupted only by the evergreen of the pine trees that served as natural barriers between various trails.

She scanned the slopes, searching for Campbell, which she did every time she glanced out her office windows. She spotted several red jackets, the color that the ski instructors favored, but she couldn't make out much beyond that. Instead, she focused on the impending dismount from the lift, executing the once-treacherous move with ease.

She wondered whether she should wait there and catch Campbell exiting the lift, but then she remembered Campbell's promise to find her. That prospect, coupled with the allure of the slopes, was too hard to resist, so she started down the familiar green trail she'd skied with the Carsons on Thanksgiving.

Beginning her descent, she swiveled her skis from French fries to pizza a couple of times to make sure she still had a feel for the terrain. She made a mental note to tighten her right boot when she got a chance and then began to practice some turns. It felt so wonderful to be out on the mountain with the cold air invigorating her and the gentle slope pushing her to go faster. Energy surged through her, giving her a rush as she cut smoothly from one side to the other, flowing with her surroundings.

Parker didn't feel rusty at all, but in tune with her body and energized by the freedom of being out from behind her desk. She wanted to push harder and began to understand how Campbell and Sammy could take off at dangerous speeds around hairpin turns. Without much thought she leaned left and pointed the tips of her skis toward an intermediate slope that intersected several of the mountain's main thoroughfares in a path toward the main lodge. Her speed increased noticeably with the steeper grade and more firmly packed surface, but she stayed in control, measuring each turn carefully and reacting almost instinctively to the little dips and rises of the trail. She flew past beautiful scenery, virtually untouched except for the occasional signs marking the intersection of another trail or pointing to various lifts and landmarks. Her body moved naturally, her toned muscles flexing and retracting with each pull of the mountain. Skiing could become an addiction, with the runners' high she already felt.

Suddenly another skier flashed into her field of vision, his path set to collide with hers as he hurtled down the mountain on a slope running above hers. She barely had time to react or consciously register the fact that skiers downhill were supposed to have the right of way. But the other skier didn't appear to see her, judging by his full-throttle approach. She made an instinctual decision, out of fear and inexperience, and threw her skis into the sideway position she'd seen Campbell and the other Carsons use to instantly halt their forward progress. However, instead of skillfully throwing a wave of snow and stopping gracefully, she managed only to plant her feet, leaving one ski behind as she hurtled forward.

Her shoulder hit the snow first, immediately followed by the rest of her body. The impact knocked both of her poles from her grip, and the momentum kept her rolling, limbs flopping like a rag doll's. Her vision blurred from the rapid movement, and her mind was too jumbled to focus on any action other than tucking into a ball. She rolled for what seemed like an eternity until slowly she came to rest in a small rise of snow at the edge of the trail.

As she lay there panting, she began to take inventory of her extremities, first wiggling each finger, then each toe to make sure everything functioned without pain. Once convinced all of her body parts were still attached properly, she sat up and surveyed her surroundings. She was off to the side of the trail, resting in the softer snow that the groomer hadn't packed solid. One ski and pole were lying near her, but she couldn't see the others. Then Campbell appeared, carrying her missing equipment.

She could have been a classic advertisement for a mountain adventure. Her ski clothes, which would have appeared bulky and awkward on most people, were like a second skin on her. Her hair peeked out from under her cap, and her ski goggles did little to dim the sparkling blue of her eyes.

"Ah, my knight in shining ski clothes," Parker said when Campbell stopped next to her. She was at once embarrassed and relieved.

Campbell chuckled. "So I take it you're okay?"

Parker rose clumsily to her feet and trudged through the snow and back onto the trail. "Yeah, my pride is a little injured, but everything else seems to be working."

"Sometimes pride is harder to mend than a broken bone," Campbell said softly. Parker wondered which of them the statement was directed to. Perhaps it rang true for them both.

"But that wreck wasn't entirely your fault. This ski popped off too easily," Campbell continued. "Why are you still using beginner skis when you're obviously set on tackling blue slopes?"

"I just go to the rental counter and grab one in my size. I didn't know there was a difference."

Campbell smiled and shook her head. "Skis tuned for beginners pop right off when you do more advanced moves like you tried back there. They help avoid injuries but don't exactly win you any style points."

"I wasn't trying to win any style points," Parker said seriously. "I was trying to not get hit."

"Well, let's make another run, and maybe we can manage to not get hit with style."

Parker shook her head. "I'm not trying that again anytime soon."

"Sure you are. We'll just take it at an even speed and stay more alert. When these trails merge, you have to take some extra care. You never know who you might run into," Campbell said with a wink.

Did she just wink at me? Parker couldn't hide a smile as she clicked back into her skis and followed Campbell down the rest of the trail. How did Campbell make anything seem possible? She was good-looking, good-natured, and good to have around. She was just all-around good. Parker wasn't sure she would survive another fall like she'd just taken, but with Campbell in the lead, she would take the risk. But only on the slopes.

She would never follow anyone's lead, especially someone like Campbell, who would be happy with her only if she turned into a Carson clone. While she was beginning to like most of the Carsons and respected the business they ran, Parker had larger ambitions than spending the rest of her life on a remote mountain in Wisconsin. She planned to be here only long enough to get herself together. She'd find another job that suited her ambitions and inclinations better. One that would allow her to make a difference in the world.

Campbell and Parker barely paused before catching the lift back up the mountain.

"Do you really want to discuss something about the women's conference? I'm sorry my dad gave you a hard time about it at first. As I told you, he doesn't do well with change."

"No." Parker remembered the charade they'd used as an excuse to ski together in the middle of a workday. "We're all set. And your dad is pretty typical. I can handle him."

"Are you nervous about seeing your old colleagues?" Campbell sounded hesitant, as if she understood how complex that question was for Parker.

Parker was silent for a few seconds, considering her response. She took in the pristine setting once more, enjoying the now-familiar sights and sounds. The drone of a snowmobile, the gentle sway of the lift, and the brightly colored snowsuits on the skiers that passed below her made the resort seem so idyllic. "Honestly, I've been so busy preparing the resort that I haven't thought much about preparing myself. I suppose the business side of the event has given me a convenient excuse to avoid the personal aspects."

Campbell didn't say anything.

"If I were completely honest I'd have to say that I am a little nervous, but I'm not completely sure why." For the first time Parker let herself dwell on the fact that in a few short weeks her new world would be invaded by the world she used to inhabit, the world she had had to leave. She would no doubt enjoy certain aspects of the meeting, chief among them the chance to spend some time with Alexis. Still, she wasn't sure she was ready to face other parts of that realm. Everyone there would know every detail of her most devastating failure.

"I guess I'll just have to deal with that when I have to," Parker said as they prepared to exit the lift. She hoped she sounded more confident than she felt.

Campbell simply nodded. If she sensed Parker's self-doubt, she chose not to acknowledge it. "You know I'll be right here if you need someone to talk to."

"I'll remember that. Thanks."

Then Campbell changed the subject entirely. "Let's take the same run you did last time, this time without the fall."

Campbell's matter-of-fact suggestion comforted Parker. Actually, she felt comfortable with almost everything about Campbell—her steady presence, her easygoing attitude, her eagerness to help in any situation. These qualities helped reassure Parker when she felt uncertain of her own place on the mountain. Only the way her heart beat a little faster every time Campbell got too close made Parker uncomfortable. She couldn't ignore the attraction and wasn't sure she wanted to, but she wasn't prepared for the risks involved in acting on it.

Campbell had become a good friend, and given Parker's track record with past relationships, she wasn't sure it was wise to make that leap to something more. But bridging that gap from friends to lovers would also have definite rewards. Her heartbeat registered somewhere distinctly lower than her chest when she thought of just how enticing those rewards were.

Parker quickly pushed that thought from her mind. She certainly didn't need to be distracted on the slopes. She would have her hands full on this run even if she remained fully focused. As they started out, Campbell swung to the far side of the trail, and Parker followed without question. They kept a controlled speed so that when they crossed onto the steeper trail, they were moving just fast enough to experience a thrill but feel no fear. This time Parker was prepared for the intersection and scanned the crossing slope in advance. A few skiers were uphill, but she quickly gauged their speed and realized none of them would pose a risk. She and Campbell flew over the most challenging section of the trail with ease, and her tension gave way to relief.

There was only one more big drop. This time she didn't hold back. The slope was wide, with plenty of room at the bottom to burn off excess speed. Parker pulled even with Campbell, and they took the exhilarating finish side by side.

"That was amazing," Parker said, breathing heavily from the exertion and excitement.

Campbell smiled one of her broad, easy smiles. "You're becoming a real speedster. I'll be signing you up for our race team soon."

"I don't think so." Parker laughed, but she was pleased with the compliment. "I'll never be able to keep up with skiers like you."

"You'll be able to do anything you set your mind to," Campbell said, suddenly serious, and Parker suspected they weren't talking just about skiing anymore.

"I don't know where you'd get an idea like that. You always have to come to my rescue. First you save me from hunters, then you pull me out of a snowdrift, and now you appear out of nowhere to get me back on my skis. You're a real-life Prince Charming, or Princess Charming, whichever you prefer."

"Nah." Campbell blushed. "You're no helpless maiden, and Prince Charming always gets the girl. What you say doesn't mesh with my track record at all. I'm just a regular, everyday ski bum who has to get back to her lessons."

As the familiar cloud settled over Campbell's features, Parker suspected that her comments had once again triggered memories of Lynn, and her heart ached at the sadness she saw. Campbell's wounds obviously hadn't healed fully. "Well, then, I'll let you go, but only if you promise to come save me again if I get into any more trouble."

Campbell smiled weakly. "It would be my pleasure to rescue you anytime you need it."

"Thanks." As Campbell walked away, Parker whispered, "But who will rescue you?" How had Lynn wounded her so deeply?

CHAPTER FOURTEEN

Campbell stomped the snow from her boots as she entered the main lodge. The low hum of conversation floating out from the large lounge at the back of the building told her that the employee Christmas party was in full swing. College students only around for a winter or two milled around talking to seasoned groomers and maintenance staff who had made a life on the mountain. The common thread among them was the Carson family, and they were all there.

Janelle was setting out another bowl of chips and dip while Sammy talked to one of the new ski instructors by the punch bowl. Emery and his twins stood by a group of Sno-Cat drivers, and Greg was laughing at something one of the kitchen staffers was saying. Campbell's mother sat by one the large windows that overlooked the slopes.

Irene Carson was petite and seemed even smaller in a crowd. While she was as much a member of the family as those who shared the bloodline, she was by nature more of an observer than her husband and children. She always seemed to stand just to the side of most family gatherings, watching with amusement in her sparkling blue eyes, which Campbell had inherited.

Campbell strolled across the room, greeting people as she went. She bent down and kissed her mother on the cheek, then sat next to her.

"Hi, sweetheart," Irene said. "Did you just get done with the groomer?"

"Yeah, for tonight anyway. What did I miss here? Has anyone been dancing on the tables or wearing the punch bowl on their head yet?"

Irene chuckled. "No, your brother is making a bit of a fool of himself chasing after that new ski instructor, but other than that it's been pretty quiet."

"Sam's always had a thing for blondes." Sammy was clearly attempting to lay on the charm, but he was obviously nervous, and the blonde looked bored. "Poor guy."

"I'm not worried about him. The right girl will come along eventually."

Campbell nodded. Her brother would make a great husband and father. Some woman would see past his silly boyishness and recognize him for the man he was becoming, and Sammy would appreciate her like she deserved. Relationships still worked like that. If not for her, then at least for people like her parents and Sammy. She was likely destined to continue falling for women out of her league.

As if on cue, Parker entered the room, carrying a tray of food and talking with Janelle as she worked. She wore a maroon sweater and blue jeans, with her dark hair pulled back from her face and secured with a simple silver clip. Her attire wasn't all that special, but somehow it seemed elegant. Try as she might, Campbell couldn't help feeling breathless every time she saw Parker Riley.

Parker flashed her a brilliant smile. She was stunning, and when she smiled like that, Campbell wondered what it would be like to see her the first thing in the morning, every morning. It wasn't healthy, this obsession she was developing for Parker. It opened old wounds. Parker was too perfect, too good to be true, or at least too good for her. Campbell kept telling herself that she needed to put some distance between them in order to protect her heart, but then Parker smiled and her resolve faded.

"Why don't you go on over and talk to her?" Irene asked.

"What?" Campbell realized she'd been caught staring.

Her mother laughed softly. "Honey, don't take this the wrong way, but you've got to get out more."

Campbell shifted nervously in her seat. Her mother wasn't kidding. "I thought you were happy to have me home."

"I am, but more than anything I want you to be happy."

"That's why I'm here, with the people I love. That makes me happy."

"And we all love you. You know that, but you're young and

beautiful, and full of life. You have so much to offer a woman, and you're wasting it all sitting here with your mother when someone just across the room looks at you the same way you do at her."

Campbell wondered if everyone could tell she was falling for Parker. "How did you know?"

Irene smiled as she stood up, then kissed the top of Campbell's head. "I'm your mother. Mothers know everything."

After setting the platter of cold cuts on the table, Parker scanned the room one more time. She wasn't searching for Campbell. At least she hadn't realized she was until she saw her, engrossed in what appeared to be a serious conversation with her mother.

Campbell certainly resembled her father, with similar coloring, facial features, and mannerisms. But she and Irene shared a tendency to nurture with quiet intensity and to reflect on their surrounding and on other people, characteristics that set them apart from the men in their lives. Parker wasn't sure what they were talking about, but the love and understanding that passed between them was apparent. She had a strong urge to join them, to be included, to have Campbell show her that much unguarded faith and trust.

Parker shook her head. What was going on with her? Her connection to Campbell was becoming almost magnetic. She was drawn to her in ways that were hard to ignore and needed to restrain this attraction before it got out of control. She had to focus on work, on getting her life back together, on moving up and on to bigger things. She didn't need to fall for a colleague. She needed to pull herself together, so she quietly stepped outside, hoping the cool air would clear her mind.

The mountain was dark, but the warm glow from the lodge softly illuminated the deck and cast gray shadows onto the snow. However, she didn't need the light to examine her feelings for Campbell, which had moved far beyond friendship and well into the realm of attraction. Not just physical attraction, although that was certainly part of it. The way she smiled, the way her blue eyes danced when she was happy, the warmth and firmness of her body as they pressed against one another in bed. Parker gasped. It was hard enough to keep from being distracted without listing Campbell's finer physical qualities. She was already preoccupied enough simply thinking about their enjoyable times together, Campbell's childlike exuberance on the slopes, and her ability to always be there at just the right moment.

Parker sighed. She'd been down this road before. Sure, Campbell seemed perfect now, in this time and place, but mixing business with romance was rarely worth the risk. Her last relationship should have taught her the old adage about mixing business with pleasure was true, but none of the fixed rules seemed to apply here. The Carsons didn't seem to distinguish between the two, enforced no boundaries between work and family. But she wasn't one of them, not really.

She was getting ahead of herself. Even if she were ready to date again, and even if she were willing to accept the risks associated with a relationship, she had no reason to believe Campbell felt the same way. "So it's a moot point," she said aloud.

"What is?"

"Oh, shit!" Parker spun around and saw Campbell grinning at her. "You have got to stop scaring me like that."

"Sorry." Campbell propped herself against the porch railing next to Parker. "I didn't mean to interrupt the conversation you were having with yourself."

Parker shoved her playfully. "Are you making fun of me?"

"Not at all." Campbell's expression turned serious. "I saw you come out here and was scared you were leaving."

"I wouldn't leave without saying good-bye."

"Good. Then what were you doing? Other than talking to yourself, that is."

"Just getting some fresh air." Parker turned away, not wanting Campbell to see the emotions she was afraid were evident in her expression.

"Hmm, are you sure you weren't snooping for your Christmas present?"

"Is it here?" Parker asked, glancing around.

Campbell nodded. "I didn't think I'd see you again before you went home for the holidays, so I brought it with me." She disappeared around the corner, and when she returned a few seconds later, she carried a pair of skis fully outfitted with bindings and boots, and strapped together with the ski poles.

As she got closer, Parker could tell that the skis and boots were

Rossignols, the brand Campbell used. Giddy, she clasped her hands together. "Campbell, they're wonderful."

Campbell blushed and Parker immediately ran her fingers along the edges from the tips to the bindings. These were so much nicer than her rentals.

"I tuned them especially for you, and the bindings are set to intermediate resistance so they won't pop off next time you skid to a stop," Campbell said.

"You tuned them yourself?" Parker was touched that Campbell had put so much thought into such a personal present.

"Of course," Campbell replied quickly, then hesitated. "I wouldn't trust just anyone to know what you need."

Parker's breath caught at the truth of the statement and all it implied. "Thank you."

"Do you really like them?"

"Oh, Campbell, yes. I can't believe you did this. It really is too much." Parker answered sincerely, then with a mischievous smile said, "I got you something, too."

"You did?" Campbell grinned. "When did you plan to tell me?"

"Well, I wasn't sure if I'd say anything at all," Parker murmured, deciding honesty was her best option. "I was afraid I'd gone overboard and you'd think it was too much."

Campbell laughed. "Now you're just teasing me. Where is it?"

"At my apartment. We can go get it now if you want to come home with me." Parker didn't realize how much that sounded like a come-on until the words had already left her mouth. Thankfully, if Campbell noticed the innuendo, she chose not to acknowledge it.

❖

Campbell pulled into Parker's driveway a few minutes later. Her mind had been racing during the short ride. She hadn't even been able to respond when Parker casually mentioned going home with her. Though the comment was completely innocent, she immediately took it into the proverbial gutter. Her attraction to Parker was tainting her view of everything. Sometimes she and Parker had such a natural connection, and it was becoming easy to just relax around her, but if she didn't keep up her guard she'd be in trouble.

While she could fall hard for someone such as Parker, women like Parker weren't usually happy with someone like her for long. She was small-time compared to the flash and excitement their high-paced jobs and social lives offered them. Campbell wanted to run the family business and carry it into the future with a family of her own. Parker wanted to return to the world of power and prestige. Campbell needed to keep that difference in mind or she might get hurt again. Still, it was harder to remember her resolution each time she looked into those deep brown eyes.

"Wait here for a second," Parker said when Campbell met her on the porch of her ground-level apartment. She disappeared and shut the door behind her.

Campbell smiled at the care she was taking with the Christmas present and wondered briefly what it could be, but soon Parker reopened the door and extended her arms. She held out a large ball of brown-and-white fuzz.

"Oh, my God, it's a puppy," Campbell exclaimed, taking the dog and pulling him to her chest. He was obviously a St. Bernard and was a lot heavier than he appeared, at least fifteen pounds, with beautiful markings and fur so soft she couldn't resist hugging him. She rested her chin on his head. "You got me a puppy."

Parker nodded tentatively. "I know you aren't supposed to buy pets for people, but you said you always wanted one…Do you like him?"

Campbell choked up, touched that Parker had remembered their conversation. "I love him."

A look of relief washed over Parker's face and was replaced by a genuine smile. "Good. I was getting pretty attached to him, but he'd be much happier at your place than mine."

"Oh, yeah, you are definitely a ski dog, and Sammy's going to go crazy over you too," Campbell told the pup. "What's his name?"

"That's up to you." Parker smiled. "I've been calling him Wildcat."

Campbell laughed at the mention of Parker's college mascot. "Oh, no, you're much more of a Wisconsin Badger, don't you think?" The dog whimpered in response and tried to burrow farther into her coat.

Parker shook her head playfully. "I think I'm outnumbered." Then she patted the puppy's head. "Okay, Badger it is."

"When did you get him?" Campbell still marveled at the thoughtfulness of Parker's gift. The puppy was so perfect, so personal, so much more than just a present.

"After we skied yesterday. I'd been thinking about it before, but after you saved me on the slopes once again I couldn't resist. Since St. Bernards are search-and-rescue dogs, and since I've gotten very attached to my rescuer, I decided you should have one, too."

Campbell's chest ached as emotions welled up in her. If Parker kept saying things like that, Campbell would never remember why falling for her was a bad idea. The moment was so perfect that she didn't know what to say, so she did the only thing that felt natural and moved toward Parker. Still holding the puppy in the crook of her arm, she lowered her head and brushed her lips across Parker's cheek. "Thank you," she whispered in her ear.

She meant to leave it at that. She hadn't intended to take it further, but after she felt the soft warmth of Parker's skin, her pulse accelerated. She broke the contact and searched the depths of Parker's eyes. She was waiting for a reaction, a warning, any indication that she shouldn't do what she was about to. Instead, she saw only an invitation. With little more than a breath between them, she couldn't bear to pull away, so she neared once more.

This time her lips skimmed the corner of Parker's mouth and then she shifted, searching for more until their lips came fully together. She barely had time to register what she had done before she realized that not only was she kissing Parker, but Parker was kissing her back.

The kiss was slow, tentative, as though neither of them was completely certain it was actually happening. Gradually their lips parted and the kiss deepened. Campbell thought briefly that she was falling, floating. Any doubt she had left evaporated as she surrendered completely to the wave of warmth that surged through her entire body.

Aching for more, she reached up with her free hand and curled it around the back of Parker's neck, pulling her closer, but the puppy blocked their connection and wriggled and whimpered in protest, so they broke apart.

"Wow," Parker murmured.

"Yeah." Campbell was unsure of any other way to convey the gravity of what had just occurred. "Wow."

"Do you want to come inside?" Parker asked, resting her back against the door as if trying to regain her balance. She seemed as unsteady as Campbell felt.

"Yes, I want that very much," Campbell said honestly as her body cried out, every nerve ending buzzing with arousal, "and that's why I'd better not."

Parker gave a reluctant sigh. "You're probably right."

"I'll see you when you get back from Chicago?" Campbell couldn't imagine waiting that long to feel Parker's mouth on her own again.

Parker nodded, and her sweet smile melted Campbell's heart. If she didn't leave immediately she'd end up doing something she couldn't undo. Parker was smart, and sexy, and oh so alluring standing there in the doorway. It would be so easy to give in to the urge to take her in her arms and take her bed, but Campbell knew there would be hell to pay afterward.

Parker clearly wasn't interested in sharing the life Campbell dreamed of, and Campbell knew too well the heartache that came from turning her back on everything she cared about to attempt to please a woman. She could try to be someone else, but in the end she'd always fall short, leaving them both unhappy.

So as hard as it was to turn down Parker's invitation, Campbell summoned all the strength left in her and got in her truck.

Just before she closed the door, Parker called out, "Have a merry Christmas."

Campbell couldn't help but say, "I already have."

Chapter Fifteen

Every detail of the elegant interior of the Lockwood restaurant said old money, from the plush upholstery to the crystal chandeliers to the impeccably dressed clientele. The restaurant was located in the Palmer House, one of the most luxurious hotels in the heart of Chicago's Loop district. Parker was spending Christmas morning having brunch with Alexis before she went to a formal gathering of her parents' business associates and Alexis attended a political function at the governor's private residence on the lakeshore.

The opulence of her surroundings constantly reminded her how far she was from the rustic lodge at Bear Run, and Parker wondered what it was all worth in the grand scheme of things. Were the people in this restaurant happier than the people at Bear Run? Did they lead better lives? Did they leave a legacy any more powerful than the ones the Carsons left their children? It was difficult to imagine any of them enjoying their holiday more than she had during those few moments she and Campbell exchanged gifts. The skis weren't the biggest or most expensive present she'd ever received, but she couldn't think of any that had been more precious.

"Merry Christmas, darling," Alexis said, raising her crystal champagne flute and bringing Parker out of her philosophical musing. Parker's best friend was stunning, a blonde with hypnotic green eyes that stood out against her porcelain skin. Her voice carried the slight lilt so common among Chicago's North Shore elite. Her black slacks, cream-colored blouse, and sling-back heels held labels that read like a who's who of the world's most prestigious designers. She would easily be mistaken for a debutante or trophy wife, except for the wicked wit and sharp tongue she exercised on anyone who dared make such an assumption.

"Merry Christmas, Alexis." Parker sipped her mimosa.

"Oh, God, I have missed you," Alexis said dramatically. "You really are the only person in my life who's neither an idiot nor a bore. Everyone else I know is either proficient or fun, but never both."

"I find that hard to believe." Parker laughed. "You know every major player in Chicago's business, government, and fashion industries."

"Yes, and business is boring, fashion is dim-witted, and politics is, well, let's just say that it has certainly made for the strangest of bedfellows lately."

"Oh, no." Parker leaned a little closer. "Whose wife have you been sleeping with lately?"

"No one's wife." Alexis pretended to be offended, then cracked a mischievous grin. "Now, the deputy mayor's mistress, on the other hand…"

"Seriously?" Parker asked, though she wasn't surprised. "She has legs that go up to here." She indicated her chin.

"And they are absolutely divine," Alexis agreed. "However, I'm not sure they are worth the bitter divorce and political fallout that the deputy mayor is most certainly headed for."

"He'll bounce back. The men always do," Parker said, feeling more sadness than venom.

"Hmm." Alexis nodded reflectively. They were likely thinking of the same man, the one responsible for Parker's career change and all the transformations that were coming about because of it.

Parker wasn't surprised that being back in Chicago brought all her misgivings about her former occupation back to the surface. Old demons seemed to lurk around every corner. She had yet to run into any of her old acquaintances who weren't tied to her political downfall in one way or other, and the afternoon gathering at her parents' house was likely to offer more of the same.

"Anyway," Alexis waved dismissively, "enough of that. It's Christmas. We should be celebrating."

"Right," Parker said resolutely. "Happy topics."

"I'm dying to see this little mountain of yours," Alexis said, referencing the Blow-Off Bash that would have Chicago and Bear Run colliding in just over a week.

"It'll be a little surreal to have everyone from here, up there," Parker admitted.

"You sound nervous."

"I guess I am. The last time I saw most of those women was before the whole ordeal," Parker said, referring to the unhappy topic they had just agreed to avoid.

"No one blames you for what happened," Alexis said softly.

"Maybe not for what happened, but they certainly think I overreacted to the whole thing." Strangely, the people with all the details about what had happened—who knew about every underhanded move and dirty trick—still thought she was out of her mind to give up a prime campaign slot when Campbell, who didn't even know the half of it, seemed to accept her decision as though it were the most logical and sane thing possible. Alexis was the only other person she knew who supported her.

"Well, some people don't share your moral caliber, but I say fuck 'em." Alexis grinned. "And to one in particular, good riddance to bad trash."

"Alexis, let it go. I know Mia will probably be there, and I'm fine with that." She noted the hint of resignation that had replaced the sadness she used to feel when she mentioned her ex. "Really, I've moved on."

"Right, we've moved on to a mountain that comes complete with its own lesbian ski instructor."

Parker flushed involuntarily and tried to hide her reaction by focusing on her eggs Benedict.

"Please tell me there's something about the mountain that just made you blush," Alexis said seriously, "because if it was the mere mention of your ski instructor, you've failed to tell me something, and I know you wouldn't keep any juicy details from your best friend."

"It's probably nothing," Parker answered. At least it might not have meant anything to Campbell, she told herself. She, on the other hand, hadn't been able to think of anything else for the past few days. Even now the dull throb of arousal pulsed though her when she remembered the kiss they'd shared. She knew it was a bad idea to let herself fall for Campbell, even temporarily. It would complicate matters both at work and in relation to her long-term plans. She didn't want to be pinned down, at least not metaphorically. She had a sudden mental image of Campbell holding her down on the bed while she did all sorts of delicious things to her, and her body reacted accordingly. She shook her head in a futile attempt to clear it and said, "I mean it. It's nothing."

"What, may I ask then, is this 'nothing' you're referring to?"

"We just gave each other our Christmas presents, and she kissed me, and then she went home and I came here." Parker rattled off the abbreviated sequence of events, trying not to put too much emphasis on the kiss, despite the fact that she could still feel Campbell's lips claim hers. Just thinking about it sent goose bumps up her arms. Why couldn't she get Campbell out of her head? All they'd done was kiss.

"She kissed you where?" Alexis asked coolly.

"On the mouth," Parker answered. "Well, on the cheek, and then on the mouth."

"I should hope it was on the mouth, dear. I meant where were you when this happened?"

"Oh." Parker flushed again. "We were standing outside my apartment."

"And then she dragged your sexy ass inside and had her way with you?" Alexis asked expectantly.

"No, then she said Merry Christmas and left."

"She's sexy, right?"

"God, yes," Parker almost gushed. "She's got this gorgeous mane of golden-brown hair that curls up at the ends, and blue eyes you could drown in."

"Tight body? Firm ass?" Alexis prodded.

"Uh-huh."

"And kisses like a wet dream?"

Parker let out an exasperated sigh. "Yes, are you trying to torture me?"

"Just trying to get a visual here so I can understand why the hell you didn't invite her inside and rip her clothes off."

"I did," Parker exclaimed, a bit too loudly, attracting the attention of a few other patrons. She lowered her voice. "I mean we didn't, but not for lack of trying on my part. I asked her to come in, but she said no."

Alexis's eyebrows shot up. "Are you sure she's really a lesbian?"

"Yes, I'm sure. All other evidence aside, there's no way a straight woman could kiss like that."

"Okay, okay." Alexis took another sip of her champagne. "I just can't think of another logical reason why any hot-blooded lesbian wouldn't jump at the chance to ravish that sexy body of yours."

"Oh, she wanted to." Parker smiled at the memory of the way Campbell's breath caught when their lips met, and the anguish in her eyes when she turned to leave. Yes, Campbell had wanted it as badly as Parker had. She was almost certain of that, which made it even harder to focus on anything else. "Trust me, we both wanted to."

"And yet, no sex was had, darling. Something isn't adding up here."

"Yes, it is. It all adds up, Alexis." Parker sighed. "She's been hurt, and so have I. We both need to work through a lot of things. She's my colleague. I'm not sure what I want from life in the future, and she isn't likely to trust anyone with her heart anytime soon. If anything's going to happen, and that's a big *if*, it won't be a quick roll in the hay. She's not like that. She's, well, she's a gentleman."

"And are you seriously thinking about sticking around to play Waltons Mountain with your own little lesbian family man?" Alexis asked seriously.

"To be honest with you," Parker replied, "I know it sounds crazy, but I haven't been able to think of anything else since the moment her lips touched mine."

Alexis studied her for a moment, then said, "Well, then, this is something I'm simply going to have to see to believe."

Campbell slowed the lift as a father and his young daughter approached. The girl was about six years old and was obviously breaking in her Christmas present, a brand-new bright purple snowboard. The mountain was full of people just like them, families decked out in new gear and giddy with the excitement of the holiday. Christmas was a big day at Bear Run with all the locals itching to try out their newest toys. A fair number of vacationers were also making use of the inn and cabins for their Christmas getaways. While the entire Carson family spent the afternoon working in order to give some of the staff the flexibility to be with their own families, they also made the most of their time off the slopes.

A traditional Carson Christmas consisted of Christmas Eve with the entire extended family attending church, something Campbell had missed over the past few years. While not particularly religious, she loved the golden candlelight and familiar hymns that accompanied the service. After church everyone congregated at her parents' house to exchange presents. Lynn had never wanted to spend the night, so it had been a while since Campbell had seen her cousins open the gifts she bought them. This year she made up for all those missed holidays by giving them several years' worth of presents, but the fun she'd had playing with the kids was worth it.

Christmas morning was more intimate, spent with Sammy and her parents before the slopes opened at noon. They shared a big breakfast of decadent pastries and hot chocolate while checking out their stockings and a few extra gifts always labeled "from Santa" even after they passed into adulthood. This was the only part of the ritual she had been present for lately, and while Lynn had conceded that sliver of the holiday with her family, Campbell had been tense knowing that Lynn didn't really want to be there.

This year Campbell allowed herself to relax and savor every minute of those family traditions. She was home for Christmas, in the place she loved, surrounded by the people she loved. It had been everything she'd wanted it to be, everything she'd longed for during those years away, and everything she'd looked forward to when she finally returned home. The holiday had been virtually perfect, so why was she sitting at the base of the lift thinking about the one thing that was missing?

"Hey, Cam," Sammy called as he slid to a stop next to her. He was on his snowboard and wearing a new coat and boots that he'd gotten the night before. His head was uncovered, his sandy brown hair a windblown mess.

"Hi, Sam. What's up?"

He nodded toward the lift. "It's closing time. Go ahead and shut her down."

Campbell glanced at her watch. She'd been so lost in thought she hadn't noticed the sun dropping below the horizon. No matter how hard she tried, she hadn't been able to get Parker off her mind all day, or all week for that matter. She had mentally replayed that kiss ever since it happened, but that hadn't done anything to lessen the effect the memory had on her. Just thinking about it now made her warm all over.

She absentmindedly powered down the lift and locked the control booth, then whistled for Badger, who had fallen asleep under a tree a few yards away. The pup immediately woke and looked up at her, then yawned and stretched before flopping back into the snow. Campbell and Sammy both went over to pet him.

"Parker sure did a good job picking him out," Sammy said as they started up the hill toward home. Sammy had fallen in love with Badger immediately, and the pup spent as many hours following Sammy as he did Campbell. They were taking turns letting him out between their classes, and Badger had ridden in the groomer with one of them every night that week. "He's the perfect little ski-patrol dog."

"Yeah." Campbell smiled. "He certainly loves being out in the snow."

"So have you heard from Parker since she left?" he asked nonchalantly.

"No. Why would I?" Campbell tried not to sound jumpy. She hadn't told Sammy about the kiss, but she sensed that he knew something was up.

"No reason." He shrugged. "I just thought that maybe, I don't know, you guys have been getting pretty close lately."

You have no idea, Campbell thought. It wasn't that she didn't want to talk to Sammy. She just didn't know what to say. She wasn't sure where her relationship with Parker stood. At least now she knew their attraction wasn't one-sided, judging from the way Parker returned the kiss—but attraction didn't mean the same thing to everyone.

"Anyway," Sammy continued when Campbell didn't respond, "I just wondered when she was coming home."

Home? Was this home to Parker? Campbell wasn't about to let herself assume that, as much as she liked the idea. "I don't know exactly when she'll be back." *We were too busy making out to talk about that before she left.*

"Before New Year's Eve, though, for sure, right?" They had arrived at their house and were removing their outer layers of clothing at the door.

"Yeah, she'll be here for that whole weekend, I'm sure." Campbell regarded him suspiciously. "Why?"

"I was just wondering if you were going to go to the party together."

"Sammy, are you trying to play matchmaker again?"

"I'm just saying, it is New Year's Eve, you don't have a date, she doesn't have a date—"

"You don't have a date."

Sammy laughed. "Hey, if I thought I was her type, I'd ask her myself, believe me, but since you're the Carson with the equipment she prefers, you might as well make the most of it."

"Come on, Sam." The phone rang.

Sammy picked up the cordless receiver. "Hello?" A big grin spread across his face. "Merry Christmas, Parker," he said with exaggerated enthusiasm, "Campbell and I were just talking about you."

"Give me that." Campbell lunged for the phone, but Sammy moved swiftly to the opposite side of the couch. "Oh, we were discussing which one of us you would rather go out with on New Year's Eve."

"Sammy, I swear if you don't hand it over right now..." she said through gritted teeth.

Sammy threw back his head and laughed at Parker's response, and Campbell lunged again. "I sure am glad you called. I haven't seen my big sister's face this red since she was fourteen and I caught her and Linda Watson down by the—"

"Samuel Michael Carson," Campbell said sternly, stopping him in mid-sentence.

"Oh, hey, Parker, I think Cam wants to talk to you," he stammered as he stared at her. "Enjoy the rest of your Christmas."

Campbell snatched the phone from him. "Hi," she said into the handset, still glowering at Sammy, who wisely left the room.

Parker's laughter came across the line, rich and clear, and Campbell's anger immediately dissipated. "Sorry about that. Sammy still behaves like he's twelve years old sometimes."

"He's your younger brother," Parker said, her laughter subsiding. "He's supposed to tease you about the Linda Watsons in your life."

"Yeah." Campbell grinned. "I guess I did make his life pretty hard when I caught him and her little sister doing the same thing."

Parker chuckled. "See, it goes both ways."

"I guess so." Campbell felt awkward. She wasn't sure where she stood with Parker after their kiss, but she was too nervous to broach the subject. "Are you having a good trip?"

"It's been nice," Parker answered, but she sounded ambivalent.

"I've spent some time with Alexis, I got to hang out with my brother and his wife a little bit, and now I'm at my parents' house."

"That sounds like fun." Campbell flopped down onto the couch and drew her knees up to her chest. Parker's voice was comforting, even if it did remind her how much she missed having her there.

"It really isn't," Parker said. "All their colleagues are over. It's a pretty stuffy crowd, and my father's business partner has had too many cocktails and is pretending to be interested in talking about my job so he can keep staring at my chest. Ugh, I don't know how I ever managed to attend events like these several times a week. It all seems so contrived now. I can't wait to get out of here. I just hope I can before any of the guys try to get handsy."

Campbell cringed at the image of Parker dodging their attention. "I'm sorry."

"It's okay. I'm just realizing that I don't care for holidays with my family nearly as much as I enjoy spending time with you."

Campbell's breath caught at the sincerity of the statement. Again Parker had gotten her to let down her guard, and without thinking she said, "I missed you today."

"I've missed you all weekend."

A shudder ran through Campbell's body at the intimacy in Parker's tone. "When are you coming back?"

"Two more days."

"Can I see you?" Campbell held her breath, afraid she sounded desperate.

"I'd like that very much. I should be around the office in the afternoon."

"I have lessons." Campbell rubbed her forehead as she tried to think of a way to see Parker immediately. She didn't want to wait any longer than she had to. "We'll be swamped since the schools are all out, but I could try to come in between classes."

"No, just stay on the slopes," Parker said. "I'll find you this time."

"Sounds good. See you then."

Campbell hung up and headed upstairs, smiling. Neither of them had mentioned their kiss, and she still wasn't sure where she and Parker were headed, but she had to admit she was enjoying the ride.

CHAPTER SIXTEEN

Parker stopped at her condo only long enough to change and pick up her new skis before she headed to Bear Run. It didn't matter that she got on the road at six o'clock that morning, or that she hadn't checked her e-mail or voice mail. She didn't even go to her office, but headed directly for the beginners' lift. Campbell was most likely conducting lessons on the bunny trails. Parker didn't make any excuses for being on the slopes. She was there to see Campbell, and admitting that made the trip seem that much sweeter.

The day was stunning, and while the snow was more manufactured than natural, she didn't mind. In fact, she was proud to be able to tell the difference between the thicker base that the snowguns cranked out and the lighter top coating that blew in on its own. She shuffled her skis back and forth for a few seconds, then rocked from side to side in her bindings to get a feel for her new equipment. Not surprisingly, everything felt wonderful. Campbell had tuned and sized every piece to perfection, knowing her needs better than Parker knew them herself. She smiled and wondered briefly if the same would hold true in other areas.

Slow down, Parker. Let's take this one step of at a time, she admonished herself gently as she boarded the lift.

When she exited the chair she turned right and spotted one skier in a red coat standing at least a foot taller than anyone else around, which was probably Campbell with a class of kids. As she got closer, she realized the kids were winding through an obstacle course of traffic cones and plastic flags. Campbell still had her back to her, calling out instructions as her students progressed.

Feeling like an exuberant child, Parker slid into line behind the last student and followed him around the obstacles.

"What's this?" Campbell said loudly. "That has got to be the tallest ten-year-old I've ever seen."

The kids all laughed as Parker stopped and grinned. "Come on, Coach. I wanna be on the ski team."

"Well, then," Campbell motioned for her to continue, "let's see what you've got."

Parker wound slowly around one of the cones, then made the turn toward the farthest flag. She moved her skis parallel to one another and moved faster through the last two turns and across the finish line, where everyone waited for her.

She flopped down into the snow with all the children, pretending to be exhausted, and asked, "Well, Coach, how did I do?"

"I don't know. What do you guys think? Can Parker come ski with us from now on?" The kids all shouted out a course of yeses, giggling. "All right, then," Campbell said. "We'll do this all again tomorrow, and Parker can come too if she wants."

The group erupted again, and Parker gave several of them high fives.

Campbell dismissed the class and watched them ski over to the deck, where her mother waited to lead them back into the daycare room. When she was certain they were all accounted for and supervised by another adult, she turned to Parker, who still sat on the ground.

Parker grinned at the amusement and pleasure on her face, and when Campbell offered her hand to help her up, she gladly took it. She allowed herself to be pulled back onto her skis but didn't have time to dig in and establish her balance fully before she began to slide downhill. Without thinking, she latched on to Campbell, throwing one arm around her neck and the other around her waist. Campbell held steady, every bit as grounded on skis as she was when standing flat-footed. She merely placed her hands on Parker's hips to stabilize her.

"Thanks," Parker said, staring up into those crystal blue eyes, and didn't move immediately to break their contact. She wouldn't have thought it possible to get turned on with so many layers of clothing between them, but she grew warm and knew she had to be blushing. However, she also detected the slightest hint of pink creep into Campbell's already cold cheeks.

"Uh, how was your vacation?" Campbell asked, clearly thrown off guard by the unexpected embrace.

"Not nearly as enjoyable or relaxing as being here," Parker answered, and realized that was true. She had always liked what she did for a living and found her work fulfilling, even exhilarating, but she would never have called it fun, and certainly not relaxing. "It was good to see my family and Alexis, but I'm glad to be back."

"I'm glad you're back, too." Campbell lightly kissed Parker's lips.

"Ahem." Someone coughed and a snowboard ground to a slow stop beside them. Parker broke her contact with Campbell and pushed off clumsily on her skis, putting a respectable distance between them.

"Don't mind me," Sammy continued, making a big show of pretending not to look at them, "but I thought Campbell might like to know her one o'clock lesson group is suiting up."

"Right." Campbell exhaled slowly. "Thanks."

"You're welcome," he said, then added, "glad you're back, Parker."

"Thanks, Sammy," she said through her embarrassment.

"I take it you don't need a date on New Year's Eve after all, huh?" Sammy teased.

"We actually hadn't gotten that far." Leave it to Sammy to keep things moving.

"Well, sis, you'd better get to asking, or somebody might just beat you to it."

"I'm working on it, Sam."

"I'll leave you to it, then." With that he pointed his snowboard downhill and left them alone.

"So, I know we'll all kind of be working on New Year's Eve," Campbell started, then paused, as if searching for the right words.

Parker nodded. She knew what Campbell was getting at, and she was giddy.

"Well, if you get a free minute or two at the party could you spend them with me?"

Parker hadn't been asked out on a date in years and didn't think she'd ever received such a sweet invitation. "Campbell, there isn't anyone I'd rather bring in the new year with."

❖

Campbell stood in front of her closet, pushing the hangers back and forth, glancing at each item of clothing only briefly before she dismissed it and moved on to the next.

"I don't have anything to wear," she told Badger, who lay on the end of her bed watching her. Perhaps more accurately, she had nothing appropriate to wear. She had several pairs of jeans, even a few without holes in them, but they didn't seem appropriate for a date, and the pair of nice slacks that went with a suit coat she'd bought to wear to formal events in college seemed too stuffy for an event at a ski lodge. That left her one pair of khakis, so she settled on them. All her shirts were dull. She had a few button-downs and some sweaters, but nothing seemed worthy of her first official night out with Parker. When she finally got tired of trying to choose, she grabbed one of each and pulled on a navy blue V-neck sweater over a starched white long-sleeve shirt.

"What do you think?" she asked the pup, who yipped in support. She glanced in the mirror one more time to survey the outfit. It wasn't terribly formal, but hopefully it was nice enough for their first date.

A date? Am I really going on a date? The idea seemed daunting. The only woman she'd ever dated was Lynn, and then she'd been so inexperienced and unaware of the risk that she hadn't given much thought to what was happening. She had let herself be swept away completely in the moment, so drunk on being in love she hadn't been able to imagine the devastation she was opening herself up to.

That thought made her a little queasy, so she tried to push it from her mind. She wasn't nineteen anymore. She'd learned from her mistakes, hadn't she? Though that's what she wanted to believe, she couldn't shake the suspicion that she was headed down a similar path again. Parker was exactly the type of woman she had always been drawn to—smart, self-possessed, driven, and devastatingly good-looking. The kind of woman who could have or do anything she wanted in life. The sort of woman who was ultimately bound for bigger things in life than Campbell could offer her at Bear Run. Parker didn't want to live on the mountain forever, she didn't care for the big family events Campbell relished so much, and while she was learning not to be so uptight all the time, she still wasn't likely to be content with the easygoing way of life Campbell strove for.

"Stop that. It's just one date. I'm not asking her to marry me, right?" Campbell mumbled, and Badger to perked up his ears. She smiled at his attentiveness and patted his head before she headed out the door.

She continued to talk to herself as she drove toward the lodge. They were two adults who enjoyed each other's company very much, she reasoned, two grown women with a mutual attraction who had both been alone for far too many months. There was nothing wrong with spending time together and exploring some possibilities. She didn't have to go overboard. She could take it slow and just have a pleasant evening with Parker. By the time Campbell got to the main lounge of the lodge, she had herself talked into believing she was in complete control of her emotions.

Then, across the large room, she saw Parker.

She wore a simple black evening dress and her long hair spilled down her back. She spotted Campbell at the same time and flashed a brilliantly unguarded smile, her eyes shimmering with delight. That look, that smile sent Campbell over the drop-off, and without making the conscious effort to move, she was drawn to her.

All the memories of past mistakes disappeared. The fear and the pain faded, replaced by the image of Parker watching her like she was the only other person in the room. The sound of her own rapidly beating heart drowned out all her self-warnings about not getting carried away. As she moved helplessly toward Parker, all she could think was, *Here I go again.*

Their date wasn't conventional. The party was an all-hands-on-deck event for the Bear Run staff, so whenever the snacks needed refreshing or the fire needed stoking, Parker and Campbell were on duty. Emery, Greg, and Sammy performed miscellaneous tasks necessary to keep things running smoothly, and Janelle and Irene kept the child-care kids entertained with games and movies in a nearby room. Not many couples had their first date where they worked and with their entire extended family in the room, but Campbell thought it seemed fitting. This was her life, the life she chose to return to, and Parker had chosen it, too, at least for now.

Parker was stunning and gracious, and even when they weren't together, Campbell couldn't take her eyes off her. Campbell loved the way she moved around the room talking to staff and guests. She could make everyone feel welcome and important, and must have been amazing on the campaign trail. The men and a few of the women blatantly appraised her physical features, several asking for dances or offering to buy her drinks. Parker declined each one with such charm that the admirer hardly noticed the rebuff.

In between social chores and hostess duties, Parker always returned to Campbell's side, even if only for a few minutes. A smile or a brief caress constantly reminded Campbell that tonight wasn't just another social function at work. Tonight they weren't just colleagues. They weren't just friends. They were a couple, and while it wasn't clear when they crossed that line, evidently they had.

Where were all the warnings she had given herself? Wasn't Parker still destined to break her heart? Wasn't Campbell still dedicated to a life Parker wanted little part of? Were they both headed down a dead end? The answer was still yes, so why couldn't Campbell stop feeling awestruck every time Parker looked at her with those big brown eyes?

As midnight approached, Campbell stood pouring flutes of champagne when her uncle Emery tapped her on the shoulder. "What can I do for you?" she asked, opening a bottle of sparkling wine.

"Let me do that while you go ask that young lady to dance." He nodded toward Parker, who was just leaving the kitchen.

Campbell paused, listening to the slow song pouring through the DJ's speakers. "I don't know if our clientele is ready to see two girls slow-dance."

Emery regarded her seriously. "This isn't just a business, Cam. This is the Carsons' family home. Last time I checked, your last name was Carson, and unless I've misread the way you two have been making eyes at each other all night, you and Parker are headed in a direction that I, for one, am very happy about."

Campbell nodded and glanced over at Parker, who returned her attention with one of those brilliant smiles.

"Thanks, Uncle Emery," she said before she strolled over to Parker. "Would you like to dance with me?" She felt a little awkward and hoped she didn't sound too much like an eighth grader at her first school dance.

Parker nodded. "I was beginning to think you wouldn't ask."

Campbell took her hand and led her a few feet to the dance floor. Still holding Parker's hand in her palm, she slipped her other arm around Parker's waist and gently pulled her near. Campbell was only slightly taller than Parker, who looked up into her eyes, the corners of her mouth turned up slightly. "You feel good," she whispered.

"You do, too." They swayed back and forth to the music. Campbell inhaled the scent of Parker's perfume, which was subtle and sweet, and her body warred between comfort and arousal.

"I'm having a good time tonight," Parker said, resting her cheek on Campbell's shoulder.

"What's your favorite part, the work or having my whole family along for the ride?" Campbell asked playfully.

Parker chuckled. "That's a tough choice, but I think this is my favorite part."

"Well, that's good to know. I'd hate to play second fiddle to the snack table." Though Campbell joked, there was nothing funny about the way Parker's body felt against hers. She was turned on, and she didn't try to explain her reaction away any longer. It wasn't merely physical or the result of being alone for too long. Parker was one sexy woman.

Parker rested her hand on Campbell's chest, just above her right breast, and Campbell covered it with her own, hoping Parker couldn't feel her body tighten in response to her touch. She wanted this woman so badly it was becoming exponentially harder to stay focused on simple conversation. Though she tried to remind herself her heart was at stake, her body was taking control. For the first time she wished she could separate making love from falling in love, but knew she couldn't.

And even if she could have sex with a woman merely to fulfill some baser instinct, that woman couldn't be Parker. Their connection involved more than simple sexual attraction. It would be easier if she was just gorgeous, but she was smart, fun, and so easy to be with. Campbell couldn't possibly resist her, but if she wasn't careful, the attraction could consume her.

"Less than one minute to midnight," the DJ announced.

"Come on, let's get some champagne." Parker stepped back but didn't let go of Campbell's hand. Campbell was happy to follow so long as she could enjoy the touch of Parker's skin against her own.

The countdown began just as Parker passed her one of the champagne flutes she'd filled a few minutes earlier. "Ten, nine, eight." Campbell gazed at Parker, then down at their intertwined fingers, and tried to remind herself not to get too used to that feeling. Parker would move on and leave her alone, wouldn't she? She struggled to remember why it was a bad idea to fall for this woman who seemed so perfect.

"Seven, six, five." She was going to start the new year surrounded by her family, in the place she loved more than any other, with an amazing woman by her side. Wasn't that what she'd always dreamed of? What did it matter what things were like a year from now? Why shouldn't she enjoy what she had right now? Suddenly the past and future lacked importance compared to her yearning for Parker right now.

"Four, three, two." While family conflicts and business deals and future plans were bound to catch up with them eventually, right now the only thing between them was caring, understanding, and an abundance of sexual tension. Why was she trying to resist? What more was she waiting for? The ideal woman stood next to her, and every move Parker made all night indicated that she was offering herself fully to Campbell. Now Campbell just had to find the courage to accept.

"One."

At the stroke of midnight, nothing seemed more natural than to kiss Campbell. Parker wasn't sure when she came to expect and even crave physical contact between them, but in that moment their lips came together so perfectly that she didn't care about anything else. This kiss, like the others, started slowly, sweetly, Campbell's tenderness so complete that it almost overwhelmed Parker. But then something changed. Her lips parted and Campbell's tongue slipped inside, caressing hers. The hunger behind this kiss hadn't been so apparent in the others. Whatever restraint Campbell had been clinging to had broken. And Parker was far beyond resisting. If she had been open to the possibility of making love to Campbell before, now her body begged for it. If Parker hadn't held a glass of champagne, she would have drawn her in closer.

Finally, Campbell broke the kiss, pulling back only far enough for her bright blue eyes to meet Parker's. They held no questions, only need. Parker wanted desperately to fill that void, recognizing it as the twin to hers.

"We should stay and help close the lodge," Campbell said, as though she had no intention of doing so.

"Yes, we should." Parker took a sip of her drink before she set it resolutely on the table. She refused to let such a perfect moment pass. "Take me home with you."

Campbell's eyes darkened with desire. She had obviously swallowed the last of her reservations. Then without a word she turned and headed for the door, leading Parker.

The ride to Campbell's cabin was a blur. Parker could think of nothing but the want that burned inside her. She craved to reach across the cab of the truck and take Campbell right there, but knew they both deserved better. So she waited until they entered the cabin's front door before she kissed her again. This time, with both hands free, she sank one of them into the thick locks of golden hair at the base of Campbell's neck and snaked the other around her waist. Their bodies fused as if a dam had broken inside each of them, releasing months of passion.

Campbell deepened the kiss with her tongue as she ran her thumb along Parker's jaw. They slowly worked their way across the room, Campbell's fingers inching down the curve of Parker's neck and tracing her collarbone, gently caressing every exposed inch of skin along the way. They broke their kiss long enough to safely climb the stairs, then resumed with even more fervor when they reached the landing. Campbell walked her backward down the hall, their bodies still pressed together, as though miming the tango.

Thankfully, when they entered the bedroom Campbell switched on the bedside lamp. Parker wanted so badly to see the woman who was making her experience all these intoxicating sensations. In fact, she couldn't wait a second longer to see more of her, so she stopped just long enough to clutch the hem of Campbell's sweater and lift it over her head. She then brought their mouths back together as she fingered the buckle on Campbell's belt. Campbell groaned into her mouth as Parker undid the button on her khakis, which she took as encouragement to continue. As she slid Campbell's zipper down, her knuckles grazed bare skin, and now she moaned. Never before had such a small hint of things to come stirred her so thoroughly. Just one brush against the taut flesh of Campbell's abdomen almost made her melt.

Campbell took advantage of her lust-induced haze to turn her around and pull her close again, now placing kisses along the back of her shoulders and neck. She unhooked the clasp on Parker's dress, then drew the zipper slowly down the length of her back. Parker shuddered and bit her lip as Campbell slipped the straps from her shoulders and the dress fell free from her body into a pool at her feet. Campbell then turned her around so that they once more faced each other and, cradling the back of her head tenderly, lowered her to the bed.

Parker grabbed a fist full of Campbell's shirt and pulled her down with her. Then she rolled them over so she was on top of Campbell, straddling her waist. The lust in Campbell's eyes only made Parker want her more, so she planted a deep but brief kiss on her lips before gliding down Campbell's neck and chest. She slowly undid each button of her shirt, placing a kiss under each one as she went. Then she trailed her mouth across the tightly muscled torso, reveling in the feel of bare skin on her lips. Campbell wasn't wearing a bra, so when Parker reached the last button she pushed the shirt off her shoulders, leaving her naked from the waist up. Not wanting to stop there, she hooked her hands into the waist of Campbell's boxers and in one motion removed them and the khakis.

Parker took in the exquisite body beneath her. Campbell was everything she expected her to be and so much more. Her dark complexion lightened only slightly where she wasn't tanned, and her entire body was smoothly muscled. Below her small, firm breasts, the lightly rippled plain of her stomach descended into soft golden curls at the apex of her thighs. "God, you're gorgeous," Parker whispered, awed.

Campbell sat up and wrapped her arms around Parker's back, then pressed her cheek to her chest. Parker held her close, Campbell's breath on her skin followed by her mouth. Campbell kissed a line across the top of her bra while she ran her fingers under the bottom of the lace cups, teasing the underside of her breasts. Her hands slid to her back and unclasped the bra, then drew the fabric away from her breasts. She leaned back only long enough to look at Parker's body and mumble, "So beautiful," before pressing close again.

Parker gasped and threw her head back as Campbell's mouth connected with one of her breasts, while the other was cradled in one of her hands. She began to wonder how long she could wait before losing control and didn't want to let go until she felt Campbell. So, still sitting on her lap, Parker slipped her hand between their bodies. She worked her fingers in circles along Campbell's chest, caressing the soft skin of her breasts and grazing her nipples, which were firm to begin with but grew even harder at her touch. When Campbell moaned her approval, Parker paused to give them extra attention, but the vibrations from the sound sent a bolt of pleasure through her own body, reminding her once again how close she was to coming.

It would be so easy to succumb to ecstasy, but the feel of Campbell's body beneath her was too exquisite to ignore. She moved her hand farther down against her abs and stomach into those soft golden curls where she found Campbell wet and waiting for her. When she parted the delicate folds and ran her fingers across the hardness beneath them, Campbell's hips jerked and she clutched Parker's back tighter.

"Oh, God, Parker," Campbell said into her chest. "That feels so good." Parker continued to circle her fingers, deliberately increasing the pressure. Campbell's breathing became erratic, and her hips rocked in a steady rhythm with her hand.

"I can't take any more," Campbell panted. "I'm going to lose it."

"Go, baby," Parker whispered. "Let go."

"No." Campbell practically choked on the word, clutching Parker with both her arms and rolling her over slowly onto her back and propping herself up on one arm above her. "I want to be inside you when I come."

The statement was so raw with intensity and need that Parker almost exploded, but she willed herself to stay focused on this amazing woman gazing down at her. Campbell ran her hand up Parker's thigh and slid first one finger, then two inside her, her thumb brushing her clit as she pushed deeper. Parker cried out on the verge of orgasm and pulled Campbell's body flush against her own. With one hand still between them, she continued to stroke Campbell in rhythm with the thrusts of her own body. She wouldn't last much longer. Her muscles were already beginning to shake as she arched up to meet Campbell. She forced her eyes open, not wanting to miss a second of the connection she felt when her gaze locked with Campbell's blues eyes, now dark with lust but filled with so much tenderness. The deep, intense emotion there, when paired with the physical sensations, sent her tumbling into ecstasy.

"Campbell," she sobbed as her body contracted. Somewhere through the roar of her own heartbeat pulsing through her ears, Campbell called out to her, and the muscles beneath Parker's fingertips tightened. Their bodies shuddered in unison, and the realization that Campbell was coming with her made another burst of pleasure consume Parker.

As they both descended from their orgasms, Campbell rested her cheek on Parker's chest, her breathing beginning to return to normal. Parker wondered if Campbell could hear how hard her heart was still beating. Every nerve ending in her body still buzzed, but even as the physical high began to subside, her emotions continued to rise. Campbell had touched her with such reverence, such tenderness. She felt both desired and cherished. What had just happened was so much more than sex. They had made love.

Chapter Seventeen

Campbell awoke to the wonderful realization that Parker's head was resting on her chest. She was asleep, her breathing slow and even. Campbell lay in the silence, soaking up the pleasure of having her arm around Parker, holding her close. Skin-to-skin contact was something she had resigned herself to living without. Now she reveled in the luxuriousness. She didn't know what the events of the last few hours meant to Parker, and part of her was afraid to find out. Still, if it had been a one-night stand, Campbell wouldn't trade it for anything.

"Happy New Year," Parker said sleepily as she opened her eyes.

"Yes, it is a very happy new year." Campbell placed a kiss on Parker's forehead.

"I'm glad you think so." Parker snuggled a little closer.

"What about you? Are you happy about how we started the year?" Campbell asked hesitantly. She wasn't sure she was ready to hear the answer, but she needed to know where they stood.

Parker searched her expression as if trying to gauge the seriousness of the question. "You don't know how I feel?"

Campbell shrugged. "I don't want to assume anything. I made that mistake once, and I don't want to go through that pain again."

Parker cupped Campbell's face with one hand and looked into her eyes. "Campbell Carson, you're sweet and sexy and one amazing lover. Any woman who wouldn't be thrilled to be where I am right now is a fool."

Campbell flushed at the compliment, but had trouble internalizing it. The way Parker made her feel only reminded her of how special

Parker was, too special to be happy in a little slope-side cabin for long.

Parker propped herself up on one elbow and ran her other hand through Campbell's hair. "You don't believe me?"

"I never said that." Campbell wondered how Parker read her so easily.

"You didn't have to. It's there in your beautiful blue eyes." Parker kissed her temple to accentuate her point. "You're already shutting me out. Don't put that wall back up, not after tonight. Tell me what you're thinking."

"I'm thinking," Campbell started, then swallowed, trying to force a tremor from her voice, "that you're out of my league." Parker started to protest, but Campbell silenced her with a kiss. "I know you're happy right now, but you're used to having more than I'll ever be able to give you. You're passionate, intelligent, and stunning, and you're accustomed to all the power and prestige that come with that."

"You're all of those things, too, and you're happy here."

Campbell pondered that logic for a second, then remembered the conversation they'd had in the Sno-Cat earlier that season. "But you told me once that you wouldn't be able to stay out of politics unless you got away from the city. When you regain your confidence, you'll miss all the things that can come with it."

"Maybe you're right." Parker lay back and stared at the ceiling. "I will miss it after a while. Sometimes I already do."

An ache began to throb in Campbell's chest, but she refused to voice her pain. If Parker wanted to go, she wouldn't do anything to stop her. She would never again hold on to something that didn't want to be held.

"But," Parker continued after a second, "I wasn't in politics because I got a kick out of it. I was in politics because I felt guilty."

"Guilty?" Campbell sat up in bed. "What do you have to feel guilty about?"

"I was born rich and white on the lakeshore while people less than a mile away were born into pain and poverty. I've had the whole world laid at my feet, and people who are every bit as deserving are denied access to health care, a living wage, or an education because of where they live, how they talk, or who their parents are. What kind of person would I be if I didn't try to change that system?"

The anguish in Parker's voice made Campbell pull her close once again. "That's so much weight to put on yourself."

"I know. I bet it sounds pretty stupid." Parker shrugged. "I should be grateful that I was one of the lucky ones and enjoy all the privileges of my upbringing, right?"

"No, not at all." Campbell hugged her a little tighter. "I know exactly what you mean. When I was in Madison I worked for a YMCA program for underprivileged kids, and I saw exactly what you're talking about. The contrast in how I was raised and what they had to deal with was overwhelming. I couldn't imagine making a difference."

"I used to believe politics was the answer, but I'm not sure that's the case anymore. I wasn't making a difference, and I wasn't happy. Here with you, on this mountain, I've found peace I didn't know I was capable of."

Campbell felt a sort of guarded elation to hear Parker say she was happy at Bear Run. That alone set her apart from the problems she had experienced with Lynn. But she knew better than to assume that because they were happy now they always would be. "You might change your mind. You didn't stop caring about the poor and disenfranchised. What if that need to effect change resurfaces in a few months, or even years?"

"And what if you fall on the slopes tomorrow and break your neck or I get hit by a snowplow next weekend?" Parker said. "I want to be with you, and right now there's nothing I want more. I can't tell you that nothing about our lives will ever change, and you wouldn't believe me if I did."

"I know that." Campbell leaned back against the headboard and closed her eyes. "I just need to know I'm not the only one feeling this way."

"Feeling what way?" Parker ran a finger down the center of Campbell's chest.

A shiver ran over Campbell's body and she opened her eyes to Parker's mischievous grin. "Like I'll explode every time you look at me."

Parker nodded and began to place kisses at random intervals along Campbell's throat and shoulders. "What else?"

Campbell felt the edges of arousal stir. "Like I don't want you to ever stop doing what you're doing."

Parker moved lower, dragging her tongue across Campbell's breasts, abdomen, and stomach until she was between her hips. Campbell parted her thighs as Parker rested her body between them. When Parker's breath warmed her clit, every muscle in her body coiled with anticipation.

"And now?" Parker's teasing lilt suggested that she knew the answer but wanted to make her say it anyway.

"Like I want—" Campbell choked on her own excitement. "I want you to make me come."

Parker's only reply was the broad strokes of her tongue at Campbell's very center. Campbell's breathing immediately grew quick and shallow, and she clutched the sheets to steady her body as she arched up to meet Parker's mouth. Her pleasure built quickly despite the fact that she had already come once that evening, and she rocked her hips with the insistent strokes of Parker's tongue. In less than a minute the only sound she heard was the roar of her own throbbing pulse. She wanted to make the feeling last, but her control crumbled under Parker's persistent caresses.

Closing her eyes, Campbell surrendered fully to Parker, opening herself as the first tremors of her climax rushed over her. She rode the excruciatingly beautiful sensation to its peak and exhaled slowly as the high subsided.

Parker returned to her side and whispered, "Now what are you feeling?"

"Satisfied." Campbell slipped her arm around Parker's shoulder and drew her close.

"Well, then," Parker said playfully, "I can honestly say you're not the only one who feels that way."

❖

"Campbell." Parker sat up in bed. "We overslept."

"What?" Campbell asked frantically as if trying to understand what had happened. "What time is it? I was supposed to be in the groomer at five o'clock."

"It's almost nine." Parker jumped out of bed, searching for her clothes as she mentally ran through her to-do list. "We've got a staff meeting."

"Oh, God." Campbell grabbed a pair of jeans off the floor and pulled them on in one motion as she stood.

"I've got to get home to shower and change," Parker thought aloud. "Where's my bra?"

Campbell found the bra under the comforter that had been pushed to the floor during their lovemaking, then opened her closet and picked a long-sleeved polo at random. "You don't have time. The meeting is in ten minutes. Wear something of mine."

Parker stopped to consider the idea. Campbell's clothing would be too big for her, but it could work. She'd never make it if she went home first, and since she was supposed to run the meeting, being late wasn't an option. "All right. Do you have any slacks?"

"Sure." Campbell pulled a pair of black slacks off a hanger and then sized up several of her tops. "This maroon one should fit you best." She handed Parker a cable-knit sweater.

Parker hastily pulled on the clothes, then ran her hands through her hair before turning to the mirror. The pants were too long, but with her high heels from the night before, they were passable. The sweater was a bit too big in the shoulders and small across the chest, but it would to have to do until later.

"You're beautiful," Campbell said, making eye contact with Parker in the mirror. She had tucked her hair behind her ears and covered it with a U of W baseball cap. She was smiling, and her blue eyes sparkled. In the chaos of the last few minutes, Parker had almost forgotten that she'd woken up in Campbell's bed, but staring at their reflection, she felt a rush of happiness. They made a beautiful couple.

"Let's do this better tomorrow, okay?" Parker kissed Campbell on the lips. "I want to take the time to wake you up right."

"That sounds nice," Campbell murmured, then returned the kiss. "Let's go back to bed and do it now?"

"I'd love to," Parker laughed, "but we've got a meeting with your entire family in less than five minutes." They headed for the door.

As they entered the part of the lodge that held the offices and meeting spaces, they kissed each other thoroughly one more time. A few feet from the open door to the conference room Parker overheard Janelle say, "They were awfully cozy when they left last night."

"And Parker's car was still in the parking lot this morning," Emery added.

"Hush," Irene said. "Maybe Parker came to work early."

Parker flushed as realized they were debating whether she and Campbell had spent the night together. Campbell appeared to be genuinely embarrassed and was so cute that Parker gave her a reassuring smile. She couldn't have Campbell without including the entire Carson family, and she didn't know if that prospect was charming or irritating.

Reluctantly, she let go of Campbell's hand as they entered the room. Everyone stood to greet them and wish them a happy new year. She was surprised that when she reached Irene, she hugged her. The Carson matriarch had always seemed to respect Parker's personal space, but as she released her she gave Parker a conspiratorial smile and said, "That sweater is lovely on you."

When everyone settled down, Parker took her seat next to Campbell and whispered, "Did your mother get you this sweater?"

Campbell's expression was quizzical. "Yeah, for Christmas last year. Why?"

"We've been caught," Parker said, mildly embarrassed. She rested her hand above Campbell's knee under the table reassuringly. She wasn't ashamed to have made love to Campbell, and while she wouldn't have chosen to broadcast her love life to the entire mountain, she wouldn't deny it either.

Suddenly she noticed Greg scowling at her from across the table. Perhaps her relief had come too soon. The one downside to the Carson family was her ongoing conflict with Campbell's father. Now she wasn't just tied to him through business, but also through her relationship with his daughter. His quiet disdain was an unsettling contrast to the reception she'd received from the rest of the family. She understood why he would be protective of his daughter, but this wasn't a typical doting-father reaction. He looked like he wanted to strangle her. Parker wondered what she had done to evoke such loathing.

"We should get started." Parker collected herself and focused on the meeting. She opened a binder she'd grabbed out of her office on the way in and scanned the event itinerary. "Members of the Chicago Women's Democratic Caucus should arrive tomorrow afternoon. We'll have an informal reception that night. Then we get into the full conference schedule the next day, with lessons every two hours. We'll offer light dining options and a bar in the lounge until one in the morning. That's the standard schedule for the next three days, with bulk checkout on Friday afternoon." Parker finished the schedule review. "How does everybody feel about that?"

The Carsons assured her everything was taken care of, and she didn't doubt that it was. The Carson family, for all their casualness, rarely missed a detail. Whether their attention to minutiae came from living where they worked, or loving what they did, Parker didn't worry about their meeting the needs of their guests. In fact, if anyone had anything to be anxious about, it was her, but her concerns weren't related to her job.

As the conversations went on around her, she considered the fact that in one day she would have to face the people who had witnessed her biggest failure. Alexis would be here, of course, but so would other staffers who had seen her fall from grace. So would the woman who had shaken her foundation. One day after allowing herself to open up to the possibility of intimacy again, she would confront the ultimate reminder of what could happen when she believed in someone else. A wave of nausea swept over her. Mia was coming to Bear Run.

"Parker?" A question from Emery brought her back to the meeting. "Do you need anything else from us?"

"No," Parker replied absentmindedly. "Everything will work out just fine." She wasn't sure if that comment was meant to reassure her or the others, but she hoped it sounded more convincing to them than it did to her.

With the official business out of the way, the meeting wrapped quickly. Holidays were busy on the slopes, and everyone except Greg rushed off. He sat quietly, glaring at her.

Parker had hoped to put off a confrontation with him until after the conference, but the tension in the room was too much for her to bear. She snapped, "What's the matter now, Greg? You don't like the conference schedule? You don't like the way I do my job? Or you just don't like me?"

"I don't like the way you and my daughter look at each other," Greg stated flatly, his eyes full of anger. "You're just like the last woman who broke her heart, and I won't stand by and let that happen again."

Parker was shocked at the force of his statement. "I have no idea what you mean, but I would never intentionally hurt Campbell."

"The first time she brought Lynn home, I knew she was trouble.

She spent her whole time here complaining about not having a cell-phone signal and made Campbell leave early so she could get back to her fax machine. We weren't good enough for her. Our home wasn't good enough for her. Every visit after that got shorter until they stopped coming home altogether. Campbell missed holidays and birthdays and football games because Lynn wanted her all to herself. She couldn't take it that Campbell cared for something other than her. By the end she had her convinced that she had to choose between being loved and being with her family. I don't know why, but I think she still feels that way, like she doesn't deserve both."

"I'm sorry for all the hurt she caused Campbell," Parker said sincerely. "She wouldn't be Campbell if she wasn't on this mountain. Anyone who loved her would understand that."

"I'm glad you realize it, but forgive me if I don't trust you to do right by her. You've made it clear you see our family and our way of life as beneath you, just like Lynn did. We're just some temporary safe haven for you, yet you still dragged my daughter into something with no intention of sharing your life with her. I don't like it, and I want you to leave her alone."

"Now, wait a minute." Parker could understand a protective father, but she wasn't about to give up her relationship with Campbell. "Your daughter is a grown woman, and so am I. I didn't drag Campbell into anything, and I'll be damned if you're going to rule my life."

"So you're just going to use her while it's convenient and drop her when you find something better?" Greg was now speaking through clenched teeth. "Do you expect me to sit by and watch you hurt my child?"

"I expect you to show Campbell and me a little respect," Parker shouted, "and let us navigate our relationship in whatever direction we decide."

Campbell ran back into the room. "What's going on? I could hear you two yelling all the way down the hall."

"You heard Parker yelling," Greg said. "I never raised my voice."

"No, you just told me to stay away from your daughter." Parker paced around her side of the conference table, too furious to stand still.

"Dad? Please tell me you didn't."

Greg sighed. "I don't want to see you hurt again, and I told her that."

Campbell sighed. "I appreciate that—"

"Appreciate it?" Parker could hardly believe her ears. Campbell was agreeing with him. "You appreciate him telling me off?"

Campbell raised her hand. "You didn't let me finish. I appreciate that he loves me and wants to protect me, but I knew what I was getting into. Dad, Parker has never misled me about her intentions."

"Thanks for the ringing endorsement," Parker mumbled.

"Come on, you're both important to me," Campbell told her. "Dad, can't you make some kind of peace?"

"I don't like this, Cam," Greg said, but his tone had softened.

"I'm not asking you to. I'm just asking you to let me make this decision for myself. Can you do that?"

"Of course I can," Greg said. "I can't stop worrying about you, but I'll try to worry more quietly from now on, okay?"

"Deal." Campbell smiled at him, then turned to Parker.

"Deal," she said tersely, once again marveling at the way Campbell could calm her father.

Greg left the room, and Campbell gave Parker her full attention. "Are you okay?"

"Yeah, I'm fine." Parker exhaled slowly, trying to gather her thoughts as she put loose papers back into her conference binder.

"Are you sure?" Campbell sounded uncertain. "I know my family can be—"

"No, baby, not your family. Just your father. I like most of your family. He's the only one I can't stand."

Hurt flashed across Campbell's face. "I know he can be gruff, but he's still my father."

"I realize that, but you don't have to agree with him all the time." Parker was pouting, but she couldn't get over the way Greg had attacked their relationship.

"I didn't agree with him. I conceded a few of his points, but ultimately I agreed with yours, too."

Campbell's levelheadedness frustrated Parker. "Why do you have to be so diplomatic? Why don't you just tell him to butt out of your life?"

"What part of 'he's my father' don't you understand?" Campbell snapped.

Parker was taken aback by the anger in Campbell's voice. She was obviously more upset than she had let on, and Parker's sulking hadn't helped the situation. "Hey, let's just table this for now. We've both had a long night."

At that, Campbell's expression softened noticeably.

Parker continued. "We've got a big day ahead of us, too, and this argument won't be resolved now anyway, so let's save it for later."

"That's probably for the best." Campbell still seemed frazzled, but the tension was starting to fade from her expression.

Parker hooked a finger through the belt loop in Campbell's jeans and tugged her close. "I know this conflict is far from over, but no matter what happens with anyone else, just remember one thing."

"What's that?"

Parker kissed Campbell on the lips, lingering a bit longer than she intended to before saying, "I adore you."

Campbell felt like she could fall asleep standing up by the time she parked the groomer and climbed into her pickup. She had gotten only three hours of sleep the night before and worked without a break all day. She should go home and get some sleep. Still, she wasn't surprised when she pulled into the parking lot of Parker's condo complex.

She hesitated at Parker's door. It was eleven o'clock, and Parker might be asleep. Then again, after the fight with her father, Parker might not want to see her even if she was awake. Campbell knocked softly and held her breath, listening for a response from inside. Immediately the door swung open and Parker stood smiling in the doorway. She wore a pair of gray sweatpants and a NWU T-shirt, and her dark hair was slightly damp, as though she had recently gotten out of the shower. Campbell's pulse quickened.

"I was hoping you'd come over when you got off the slopes." Parker led her inside. "Let me take your coat."

"That's a warmer welcome than I expected." Campbell stood still while Parker removed her ski jacket and tossed it over the back of the love seat.

Parker sighed. "I have to admit I was pretty frustrated with you this morning,"

"But you're not now?"

"I'm still fuming at your father's attempt to come between us, and honestly I'm frustrated at your lack of outrage, but somehow having you so close does something to my short-term memory."

"Why's that?" Campbell asked hopefully.

"Because I'm having a hard time remembering why I should be mad at you, but I remember what you did to me last night very clearly."

Campbell smiled at the lust that clouded Parker's eyes.

"Don't give me that rakish little grin," Parker warned. "You're not off the hook just because you've temporarily distracted me with your firm ass in those sexy ski pants."

"I'm sure I'll pay dearly later," Campbell said with mock seriousness, but she knew that was probably true. There would be consequences for her recklessness with Parker, and her heart would pay the price, but that would come later. Now was not the time to think of the future, or about the wedge their relationship was driving between her and her father.

Campbell enveloped Parker in an embrace and inhaled her scent, a simple pleasure she hadn't realized she missed until that moment. "I'm exhausted. We've both got a lot on our minds, and I didn't come over here to rehash all of that. I just wanted to see you."

"I'm glad you did." Parker kissed her slowly, deeply. "I've been thinking about you all day."

"Me, too." Campbell slipped her hands under the hem of Parker's shirt, and the feel of bare skin kicked her libido into overdrive. She moved her fingers slowly upward, massaging Parker's torso as she went. Their kiss grew more passionate with each second. When she realized Parker wasn't wearing a bra, Campbell groaned into her mouth. She broke the kiss immediately and swiftly removed Parker's shirt like a woman possessed. She had denied her need too long.

She hadn't meant for this to happen, at least not this quickly. She had intended for them to talk first. She wanted to know how Parker was feeling. She'd expected to talk about her father. She'd planned to ask about the conference. She was going to make sure Parker wasn't nervous about seeing all her old colleagues again or uncomfortable about where their relationship was headed. She'd had the best of intentions when she walked through the door, but they all left her mind the minute she skimmed across the bare skin of Parker's breasts.

She laced her fingers through Parker's long hair and drew her close once again, this time kissing along her jaw and down her throat. Parker threw back her head, exposing the slender curve of her neck for Campbell to nip and suck. Campbell let her mouth travel lower along her collarbone and then dipped to take one of Parker's nipples between her lips and run her tongue across the tip. Parker moaned her approval and swayed slightly.

Encouraged by the reaction of Parker's body, Campbell worked her free hand beneath the waistband of Parker's sweatpants and between her legs. The wetness she found broke the last bit of restraint she had clung to. She backed Parker against the wall and steadied her with an arm around the waist and a knee between her thighs. While Campbell continued to taste Parker's breasts, she moved her fingers directly to Parker's clit. She started quickly and then increased her pace. There was a time for patience, a time to tease, a time to take things slowly. Now was not that time.

"Oh, God." Parker panted and let her head drop onto Campbell's shoulder.

Campbell continued to stroke her, bearing her weight on her own weakening knees. It was as if a dam had broken inside her. During all the months of pretending she didn't want this, refusing to let herself even wish for it, her quiet energy had gathered. Now she allowed all the storm of her need to rumble to the surface. She couldn't even hope to temper it. She could only ride the wave of passion. Blind with lust, she barely registered the feel of Parker's nails digging into her back. Parker grew hard under her fingertips. "Come for me, baby," she whispered, barely able to speak because of her desire.

"Inside me," Parker begged between ragged breaths. "Please… need you…inside."

The raw intensity of the request almost made Campbell come without being touched, but she held on to her composure and pushed into Parker with a single thrust. Parker hooked one leg over Campbell's hip and rode her erratic movements, rocking forward and pushing back each time Campbell lunged into her.

Campbell leaned her weight into Parker, pinning them both to the wall. Parker contracted around her fingers, then shook. She called out, an undistinguishable sound muffled by the press of Parker's mouth against her shoulder. Campbell lifted her completely off the ground with one final push, and Parker went limp in her arms.

Campbell held Parker steady while she regained her composure. She kissed the top of her head and stroked her thick, dark hair, wishing she could touch every inch of her at once. It felt wonderful to hold her, and Campbell wanted to soak up every sensation she could. She knew they were most likely headed for disaster. Their avoidance of any serious discussion regarding what they were doing, where they were headed, and how it would ultimately affect their lives only delayed the inevitable. The consequences of their actions would catch up to them eventually, but until they did, Campbell was content to enjoy what little reprieve they'd been given.

CHAPTER EIGHTEEN

"It must be nice to spend the busiest day of your year staring out the window." Alexis chuckled.

"Alexis." Parker jumped out of her chair to hug her. "You're early."

"Not really, darling. It's after three o'clock." Alexis did a fine job of hiding her surprise at the outdated and underwhelming décor of Parker's office. In her cream silk blouse, navy slacks, and matching blazer, with her platinum blond hair clipped loosely in the back before cascading down across her shoulders, she stood out against the dingy office decor. "I expected you to have a scotch on the rocks for me."

"I planned on it," Parker admitted with a yawn. "I lost track of time." She opened her desk drawer and produced a bottle of Crown Royal. "How about straight up?"

"How rustic." Alexis took the offered glass, then pointed to the bottle of liquor. "You must have needed that every day."

Parker laughed. "No, I don't drink at work. I picked it up for you."

"Whatever you need to tell yourself, darling." Alexis laughed softly as she took a seat across from Parker and kicked her Manolos onto the desk. "Now tell me what's made you look as though you might nod off any minute. I know that it isn't too much sex or—" Something must have flickered across Parker's face to make Alexis stop in mid-sentence like that. She regarded Parker carefully and took a sip of her scotch. After a long pause she said, "Your mountain dyke, I assume?"

She wasn't sure how Alexis figured it out without her saying a word. Was it that easy to see the effect Campbell had on her? "It just happened."

"I'm waiting." Alexis motioned for her to continue.

"On New Year's Eve," Parker started, then smiled. "And New Year's morning, and last night."

Alexis raised an eyebrow.

"Okay, and this morning, too." Parker buried her face in her hands. "God, Alexis, I don't know what's come over me. We're like teenagers. She makes me crazy. She can be wonderfully tender, then at other times the urge is overpowering. I mean, last night she took me right up against the wall."

Alexis held up a hand to cut her off. She drained her scotch, then grabbed the bottle and poured herself another glass. Seeming to read Parker's surprise at the move, she said, "Why not? Apparently we've thrown moderation out the window."

"I know. This isn't like me, but I can't help myself," Parker gushed.

"What are we talking about?" Alexis asked seriously. "Fucking? An affair? Friends with benefits?"

"Alexis, I think I might be falling in—"

"Christ. You'd better not have been about to say what I think you were."

"I'm not sure, but it feels real, unlike anything I've ever felt before."

"Come off it. You're a serial monogamist. You're indulging your lesbian urge to merge. It'll pass."

"I don't think so. This is more than good sex and polite conversations. She makes me feel like I'll come unglued, like she knows what I need and exactly how to give it to me." Alexis cracked a wicked grin, prompting Parker to clarify herself. "I'm not talking about the sex here. That's only part of it. She's easy to talk to and sensitive to my moods. She can see through all the walls I put up, and she understands what drives me, and she doesn't think I'm silly for believing in the things I believe in."

"What ever happened to your independence? Taking it easy for a while? Clearing your head and getting back on your feet again? Remember all those reasons you came here?"

"She's not inhibiting that. She's helped make it all happen for me.

When I'm with her, I'm comfortable in my own skin. I'm relaxed. I have fun. You'd hardly recognize me."

"If that's true, I'm happy for you, darling. You know I am," Alexis said. The teasing was gone from her voice, but the skepticism remained.

"But?" Parker asked.

"I don't want you to get hurt again. You tend to jump into these things too quickly, and I saw what happened last time. I'm worried about you, and don't tell me not to. As your best friend that's my right."

Parker didn't know what to say. Alexis had a point. She was the only person who knew what Mia's betrayal had cost her. She couldn't blame Alexis for being suspicious of Campbell, but she also wanted to convey to her how different Campbell was from anyone in their social or business circles. She was searching for some way to reassure Alexis when someone knocked on the door.

Campbell peeked into the office, beaming with unguarded affection at Parker. Her smile faded when she glanced at Alexis with her feet up and a drink in her hand. "I'm sorry. I didn't know you had company."

Alexis immediately rose to greet her. "Please tell me this is the divine creature who's kept you up all night."

Campbell was in her usual winter attire, ski pants and snow boots, but she'd removed her coat to reveal a tight black turtleneck that showcased her lean torso and the subtle curve of her breast. Alexis's eyes flickered over Campbell in a blatant appraisal of her features. She made no secret of her approval as she extended both her hand and smile. "Alexis Reynolds."

A brief flicker of recognition flashed over Campbell's face as she took Alexis's hand and shook it firmly. "Campbell Carson. Welcome to the black hole of civilization."

Alexis threw back her head and laughed. "I like a woman who doesn't pull any punches. Come have a drink with us."

Campbell glanced at Parker as if trying to gauge her welcome. Parker was once again reminded how attuned Campbell was to her moods. "Please," she said. "I've missed you today."

The corners of Campbell's mouth hinted at a grin, but she didn't break into a full smile. Parker remembered how guarded Campbell could be around someone new, especially someone like Alexis, whose background and demeanor were likely to remind her of Lynn. The smiles that lit up Campbell's entire face appeared only in the presence of people she trusted. Parker felt honored to have received so many of them over the past few days.

"So, Campbell, you're a ski instructor?" Alexis poured her a drink.

Alexis was probing for more information and Parker was sure Campbell knew it, too, but they acted as though the conversation was simply small talk between two new acquaintances.

"I am. Do you ski?" Campbell's tone was level, conversational.

Alexis nodded. "I have a time or two."

"Forgive me if I'm a little skeptical. I've heard that from other people in this room."

Alexis chuckled, and Parker gave Campbell a light shove. "Geez, you tell one little white lie and can never live it down."

"Perhaps I should lie and say I'm a first-timer to get some free individual instruction," Alexis said coyly. "Are you in the habit of doing such things?"

"Only once." Campbell leaned against Parker's desk, her arms folded loosely across her chest. The gently defiant stance was tremendously sexy. Parker's worries had been unwarranted. Campbell could obviously hold her own.

"Then you don't usually seduce women on the slopes?" Alexis pushed further, but Campbell didn't even flinch.

"Actually, I haven't seduced her on the slopes yet, but if she gives me a little more time, I'll make sure to do so."

Parker flushed. "I'm right here."

"I see that, darling," Alexis said. "I was trying to discern if your paramour would be interested in giving me some private instruction tomorrow, and if so what that would entail."

"I thought you were trying to discern if I was worthy of your best friend's affections." A flicker of mischief flashed in Campbell's eyes.

"Your directness is endearing. Parker and I don't get that often in our line of work."

"Actually, Parker gets it plenty in her new job," Campbell answered quickly. "I believe that's one of the reasons she took it."

Alexis pursed her lips, but there was still amusement in her eyes. "I forget sometimes that Parker has defected. I think of her as merely being on sabbatical."

A muscle in Campbell's jaw twitched and Parker knew Alexis had struck a nerve. Alexis had certainly seen it, too, but before she could jump in, Alexis continued. "Anyway, what do you say, Campbell? Interested in assessing my skills, maybe offer me a few pointers?"

Parker felt a twinge of jealousy at the thought of Campbell giving lessons to Alexis while she was stuck in her office.

"I'd love to, Alexis," Campbell said jovially, then turned to Parker. "Why don't you come, too?"

"Well played," Alexis mumbled.

Parker kissed Campbell on the cheek. "I'd love to hit the slopes with my two favorite people."

"Good." Campbell kissed her back, this time on the lips. Parker liked the possessiveness of the move. "I'd better get back to work."

"Will you come over tonight?" Parker asked.

"I wouldn't miss it," Campbell replied.

"Wow," Alexis said once Campbell was out of earshot. She pretended to fan herself with her hand. "She's hot enough to make your teeth sweat."

Parker laughed, but didn't disagree.

"And oh so taken with you."

"Do you think so?" The idea made Parker giddy.

Alexis regarded her over the rim of the scotch class she had raised to her lips. "Don't tell me you haven't noticed that she looks at you like you're the only woman she can see. I know she melts that romantic little heart of yours."

Parker noted the grudging acceptance in Alexis's voice. "Does this mean she passed muster?"

"It pains me to admit it, but I do think she's everything you made her out to be." Alexis downed the remainder of her drink and stood up. "Now all that's left to be seen is how long she will be enough to hold your attention."

❖

Campbell slept soundly, luxuriating in the feel of Parker's body curled into hers, and woke refreshed. That new energy made her and Parker spend some extra time together in the shower, and they barely made it to the lodge for the first round of lessons.

She stood on the back deck of the lodge and rested one ski-booted foot on the lowest porch railing as she surveyed the base area of the mountain. Lift traffic had increased with the majority of the conference guests on the slopes. Sammy was off to one side, corralling a group of young women on snowboards. Since she and Parker had begun to spend their nights together Campbell hadn't had time to talk with him, but judging by the way the women were crowding around him, Sammy would also be busy pursuing a few interests of his own in the upcoming days.

Campbell heard the sounds of boots on the deck behind her and felt two arms slide around her. "Excuse me, ma'am, but where would someone go for an extra-special private lesson?" Parker whispered, her lips brushing Campbell's ear.

A shudder ran through Campbell's body at the thought of what she'd do with Parker if they were in private, and she turned around. Parker wore a white jacket and gray pants with her new boots. Her dark hair was in a loose ponytail beneath a white ski cap. "That depends on what type of lesson you want—skiing, snowboard, or perhaps something else?"

"Christ." Alexis rolled her eyes. "Please tell me I won't be subjected to this drivel all morning."

Campbell laughed and loosened her hold on Parker, but didn't let go completely. "Good morning, Alexis. Parker and I were warming up for your lesson."

"How's a woman supposed to focus on skiing with you sexy beasts going at it like that? I thought I was here for some expert instruction."

"I aim to please, Ms. Reynolds. If it's skiing tips you're after, that's what you'll get," Campbell said cheerfully. She liked Alexis, though she wasn't sure why. She was cocky and superior, but she cared for Parker. That gave her credibility with Campbell.

"If all your services were available, I'm not sure I'd waste my time skiing, but since your other skills are currently monopolized"— she flashed a sly grin at Parker—"I'll have to take what I can get."

"Yes, you will," Parker gave Campbell one more squeeze before she broke the contact between them, "because I can't wait to hit the slopes with you two."

"How about adding a third?" a woman Campbell didn't recognize said as she approached them. She wore a fur-lined ski coat and matching pants that had apparently just come out of the box, and her brand-new skis retailed for an absurdly expensive price. Her looks were equally polished, her deep complexion flawless and her jet-black hair perfectly drawn back and tied with a silk ribbon. Her dark brown eyes were almost black, and Campbell didn't care for how they were currently taking in Parker with a knowing gaze.

"Mia," Parker said flatly, looking slightly surprised at the greeting, but beyond that she gave no indication of her relationship to the newcomer. Alexis, on the other hand, emitted a low noise that sounded almost like a growl.

"I haven't seen you in months, and all I get is 'Mia'?" The woman kissed Parker on the cheek, and Campbell felt a possessive anger well up. "What do you say? Care if I join your little group lesson?"

"This is an intermediate lesson, Mia. I didn't think you skied." Parker sounded unsure.

"I skied a time or two in prep school. I'm sure I'll be able to keep up with you." Mia smiled what seemed to Campbell a practiced smile. "I'm sure your instructor won't mind, if I promise to tip her well."

Parker's eyes were filled with questions and the hint of an apology, but Campbell couldn't tell if she wanted her approval or her help getting out of the situation. Either way there was more to the story than either Mia or Parker let on. Campbell resented having to read Parker's mind. Her first instinct was to rebuff Mia's request, but her curiosity overruled it. "If it's all right with Parker, it's all right with me."

"Great." She extended her hand, fingers pointed down as though Campbell should kiss it rather than shake it. "I'm Mia."

"Campbell." She tried to force a smile. "Let's go ahead and take the lift up and make a run down so I can see where everyone is skill-wise. Then we'll take it from there."

"All right," Campbell said, when they were next in line for the double chairlift that ran up the center of the mountain. "Alexis, why don't you ride with Mia?"

"There's no chance in hell of that happening," Alexis said tersely.

Campbell stared at her for a moment, considering the comment. Parker didn't volunteer to ride with her either, and she couldn't decide if that was because she didn't want to or she didn't want to say so in front of Campbell. "Fine. Alexis and Parker go up first. Mia and I will be right behind you."

Alexis and Parker got on the lift ahead of them, and Campbell barely acknowledged Mia as she skied into place. As the lift swung around, they both sat down. Mia hit the seat a little hard, but she settled in and quickly lowered the safety bar. That was odd since Campbell didn't know anyone who actually used the bar, at least not any adults.

"Wow, these lifts are small. I've only been on the four- and five-people kinds," Mia said.

"We're a small place. We don't have any quads here." Ahead, it was clear from their posture that Alexis and Parker were having a tense conversation, but Campbell couldn't hear what they were saying.

"It's all so quaint," Mia said, a hint of condescension in her voice. "Parker didn't seem bothered by it, though. She got on the lift like she does this all the time."

"She does." Campbell didn't mean to sound rude, but the way this woman rattled on about Parker made her uncomfortable. She'd hoped to talk to Parker on the ride up. Instead, she was left trying to fit together pieces of a puzzle she wasn't sure she wanted to see the big picture of.

"Leave it to Parker to make the most out of any situation. She never does anything halfway." Mia's tone held intimacy and innuendo that made Campbell sick to her stomach. Mia was oblivious to her discomfort and seemed to think they were having a conversation. "I appreciate you letting me join the lesson. I've been looking forward to this weekend. It'll be great to spend time with Parker. You don't mind if I ride with her next time, right?"

"I'll leave that up to Parker." Campbell lifted the safety bar as they neared the top.

"There'll be a nice gratuity in it for you if you help make it happen."

Campbell stared at her blankly, not sure if Mia understood how offensive she sounded. Even if she weren't in a relationship with Parker, she would have wanted to tell her to take her tip and shove it, but professionalism restrained her, so she simply said, "Turn to the right up here."

She stood as the lift reached the dismount ramp. Leaning forward slowly, she let gravity glide her down the ramp to where Parker and Alexis waited. The move was second nature to anyone who skied, so she didn't think about it until she heard the lift grind to a stop behind her. She turned around in time to see Mia go around the turnstile, still in her seat. Thankfully her skis caught the emergency stop gate at the end of the lift, which caused it to halt automatically. She hadn't made the turn to head back down the hill, but she was no longer over the ramp, which left her three feet above ground.

"That's a first. Whoever knew Mia to have a hard time getting off," Alexis mumbled sarcastically.

"Shut up, Alexis," Parker snapped.

Campbell skied over to the lift, hoping Mia couldn't see her roll her eyes under her ski goggles. "Maybe I should have been more specific. You get off the lift when it comes to the ramp, and then you turn right."

"Back it up," Mia said curtly.

Campbell tried not to laugh. "Sorry. The lift doesn't go in reverse. You need to drop from there. Slide off the edge. It's not that far."

Mia took a big breath as if steeling herself for a rough drop. She then hung awkwardly, her arms holding her on the lift while she scooted her butt over the edge of the seat. Then she let go. The minute her skis hit the snow, they went out from under her, and her backside hit the ground with a thud. Alexis released a hearty laugh, and Campbell tried to stifle one of her own. Parker, on the other hand, skied over and offered to help Campbell pull Mia back onto her feet.

"Are you okay?" Parker asked.

"Of course I am." Mia brushed herself off and straightened her shoulders. "I'm used to having more room to work with."

Campbell didn't buy that excuse. "Are you sure you're ready for an intermediate lesson? I can get you in a beginner group."

"I'm fine, just a little rusty. Let's go."

She had to give the woman credit for her resilience. A fall like that would bruise more than her ego. "Okay, then, follow me." Campbell pushed off with her poles and wound her way over to a blue trail. The grade at the top was steep, but the turns were gentle, and skiers had the opportunity to burn off some speed in the middle of the slope before it dropped into the main basin. It offered the perfect variety for her to assess Alexis's skill level, which was what she intended to do with this lesson.

When they reached the start of the trail, she edged up where the terrain dipped sharply. "I want you guys to go first, and I'll follow so I can see your form."

"You want us to go down this trail?" Mia's bravado started to crack.

"Yes, why don't you start us off?" Campbell motioned her forward.

Mia hesitated before inching her skis toward the drop-in. "Okay, I can do this," Campbell heard her whisper. She then leaned forward and moved onto the slope. For a second she acted like she might go through with it, but she quickly fell to the ground with a shriek.

"That's the Mia I know. When things get tough, go down on something," Alexis muttered loud enough for all of them to hear.

Campbell sighed loudly and moved up to offer Mia a hand, but instead of accepting it, Mia stayed planted on her butt and began to scoot down the hill. "I'll do this until it levels out."

Campbell almost felt bad for her. "Mia, it's a long way down. Why don't you try again?"

Mia ignored the suggestion and kept scooting. "Is this a green?" She referred to the color designation for beginner trails.

"No, this is a blue slope. I thought it was clear when I said this was an intermediate lesson that we'd be on intermediate trails." Campbell tried not to lose her patience with the fact that Mia had drastically overstated her skill level.

"I thought we'd try a green trail first. I didn't know we'd jump right onto a blue. Doesn't it seem fast to skip to a blue without doing a green first?"

"What does it matter if you do them like that?" Alexis called. "They're all green if you go down on your ass."

Campbell couldn't help but laugh. Her distrust of Alexis had faded. She'd liked her before, but now it was clear why. She didn't suffer fools, and Mia was certainly being foolish sliding down the slope.

"Okay, then," Campbell finally said. "Mia, you keep doing what you're doing. Alexis and Parker, you can take another run or two. Mia and I will meet you at the bottom."

"Sounds good to me." Alexis took off, cutting a beautiful path down the slope. If Mia had overstated her skiing abilities, Alexis had understated hers. She had the form of someone who could ski any black diamond slope at Bear Run.

Parker wasn't as quick to go. She seemed embarrassed about leaving Campbell with Mia, but also eager to be away from the awkward situation. Campbell thought she deserved an explanation, but neither the situation nor the setting was conducive to personal conversation, so she would have to wait. "Go have fun with Alexis. We'll be fine."

"Thank you," she said, her face filled with gratitude, and left Campbell to supervise Mia's snail crawl down the slope.

It took nearly half an hour to make it back to the lodge. Mia skied only a small portion on the run and scooted the rest. Campbell had never seen anything so painstakingly annoying, and she vowed not to take anyone else at their word for the rest of the conference, at least not when it came to skiing skills.

By the time they reached the end of the trail, she was exhausted and Mia was soaked, the fur lining of her coat matted to her skin with melting snow. "You better take a break," she told her as more of a command than anything else, when they joined the others. "Alexis, I need to check in with the ski school, then I'll restart your lesson."

"No problem, darling. After that display of sainthood you need a stiff drink, and Parker had better get back to work. We'll try again tomorrow."

"That sounds great," Campbell said appreciatively as Alexis left. Mia had obviously missed the fact that she'd been dismissed, or perhaps she was waiting for Campbell to leave so she could be alone with Parker. Campbell refused to let that happen until she got some explanations. "Was there something else, Mia?"

"Should I pay you now?"

Campbell shook her head. "That hardly qualified as a lesson."

"Then something for your time?" Mia unzipped her coat and pulled out a coin purse.

Parker finally cut in. "Mia, you don't tip the proprietor."

"The proprietor?" Mia was obviously confused.

"Campbell is a Carson. Her family owns the resort," Parker snapped. "She was being gracious. The time you wasted was worth much more than whatever you were about to insult her with."

Parker had been uncharacteristically quiet throughout the entire ordeal, and it surprised Campbell to hear her voice tinged with such venom.

"I had no idea," Mia stammered.

"Now you do, so you'll understand why we both have to get back to work." Parker's expression showed no mercy. Campbell, on the other hand, was feeling a wonderful mix of smugness at Parker's praise and sympathy for Mia, whose face was red with embarrassment.

"Right. I'm sorry," Mia said, then turned to Campbell and reiterated, "I'm sorry."

When Mia was gone, Parker said, "I'm sorry, too. I should have warned you about her, and I know I owe you a better explanation than that, but I'm supposed to check in with Janelle in fifteen minutes, and I have to stop by the office and—"

"It's fine," Campbell said, the look of guilt on Parker's face melting her anger. "We'll just add this to the long list of unresolved issues we need to discuss later. You go ahead."

"That list is getting awfully long, isn't it?"

Campbell nodded gravely.

"Have I told you lately how much I adore you?"

"You have, but you can remind me again tonight," Campbell said wearily.

"I will."

But would that be enough to get them through? Campbell wondered.

CHAPTER NINETEEN

Parker took a deep breath, straightened her shoulders, and entered the main lounge of the lodge. The lighting and music were low. A makeshift bar stretched the length of one wall. A ring of couches surrounded the large double-sided stone fireplace, and many smaller tables were scattered around the large room, nearly all of which were occupied by the women of Chicago's Democratic Caucus. Parker knew most of them by sight and many of them by name. They'd been her colleagues, her peers, even her friends. Now she had to summon all her strength to face them.

Everywhere she turned, old memories sprang forward to send her head reeling. The woman who'd given Parker her first job stood by the fireplace, talking to the woman who'd recruited her to join Tim Brady's campaign. Sammy entertained two of her old staffers at the bar. Several of the Cook County party officers were in an animated conversation near the DJ table. Women from the fund-raising board she had served on were talking with Janelle over at the snack table.

She wanted to run away, but her sense of professionalism wouldn't let her. As point person for the conference, she was obligated to make an appearance. The Carsons and the CWDC expected it.

Parker walked across the room purposefully, without looking at anyone directly, and signaled to Sammy at the bar. "Hi, Sam. Can I get an amaretto on the rocks?"

"Sure thing." Sammy wore his trademark grin as he poured her drink. "You sure did a great job with this event. Beautiful women, good booze, and little competition. This is my kind of party."

Parker had to smile at his youthful exuberance. He was only three years younger than her own twenty-nine years, yet he projected the image of the proverbial kid in a candy store. "I'm glad you like it."

"What about you?" He seemed to notice her less-than-enthusiastic demeanor. "You should have some fun, too."

"She will. She just needs a nudge in the right direction," Alexis said as she approached them. She examined Sammy up and down. "How about a scotch on the rocks, handsome?"

Sammy's cheeks turned pink under her gaze, but he managed to keep his tongue in his mouth. "You got it."

"Be nice to him. He's Campbell's brother." Parker chuckled. Sometimes Alexis didn't know how her beauty and demeanor affected both men and women. Then again, sometimes she knew exactly the effect she had on people and simply chose to enjoy it.

When Sammy returned with Alexis's drink, she winked and said, "So you're one of those gorgeous creatures known as the Carsons?"

"Yes. Yes, I am. Sammy Carson," he stuttered.

"Nice to meet you, Sammy Carson. You aren't my variety of Carson, and that devilishly good-looking sister of yours seems to be taken, too." She glanced briefly at Parker. "Please tell me there's another available Carson woman you could introduce me to."

Sammy appeared deflated as he thought about the question, but he still managed to flash her a smile as he said, "Sorry, the next girl in the Carson line is only five."

Alexis laughed. "Well, that won't do, but we shouldn't waste that amazing smile of yours simply because it doesn't suit my tastes." She scanned the room and her eyes settled on a group of women down the bar. One of them was an intern from the mayor's office and another was the governor's undersecretary. "Ladies, this is Sam Carson, one of the heirs to this lovely castle."

The women introduced themselves to Sammy, who acted like he might die of happiness. "You all play nice while I go try to steal his sister from my best friend," Alexis said.

Sammy mouthed "Thank you" as Alexis took Parker's hand and led her away from the bar.

"See, I'm not totally heartless." She steered them toward the fireplace.

"No, it was sweet of you to make some well-timed introductions for him," Parker admitted.

"I'm glad you see it that way, darling, because I'm about to do the same for you." Alexis tapped on the arm of a stunning African American woman who stood near the edge of a circle of women in the center of the room. "Alderwoman Nadia Baker, I'd like you to meet Parker Riley. She's our event liaison for the retreat."

Parker barely had time to process what Alexis was doing before the woman in front of them extended her hand. "Ms. Riley, of course. I'm glad to meet you."

"Likewise, Alderwoman Baker." Parker took in her statuesque frame and dark coffee complexion. She was stunning, and her grip was firm as they shook hands. She was obviously a woman who could command an audience, which wasn't surprising given her elected position. Parker was immediately impressed, and that said a lot, considering her jaded view of Chicago politics.

"Please call me Nadia. I'm not much on formalities."

"Thank you, Nadia, and I'm Parker, please. We don't stand much on formalities around here either."

"Now that we've got that out of the way," Nadia smiled broadly, "tell me about this lovely resort that stole you away from my fair city."

"Nadia, I imagine you know exactly why I left Chicago, and while the resort is lovely, I didn't come here for the scenery." Parker didn't sugarcoat the situation. She didn't need pity or someone to make excuses for her failures, and that was certainly what caused her to flee her hometown, a failure.

Nadia nodded appreciatively and took a sip of the drink she held in her hand. "All right, I do know why you came here, and I don't care about that. I care about what you've found to keep you here."

Parker was confused by that statement, but she knew Alexis hadn't introduced the two of them for social purposes. She glanced around the room to buy time while she considered her answer. That was when she saw Campbell coming toward them, her blue eyes reflecting the flickering light of the fire, lines of apprehension creasing her forehead.

"Honestly," Parker focused her attention back on Nadia, "there are a lot of reasons I've chosen not to return to Chicago yet. For one, the company I've found here is even more alluring than the scenery."

Nadia and Alexis both followed Parker's line of sight as Campbell approached them. She wanted to kiss her but Campbell seemed tense, so she contented herself with sliding an arm loosely around her waist. Even with the stress of their incident involving Mia still between them, Parker felt calmer with Campbell by her side. "Nadia, this is Campbell Carson. Cam, this is Alderwoman Nadia Baker."

Nadia regarded them both with a warm smile. "Campbell, it is truly a pleasure to meet you."

When the conversation stalled, Campbell said, "I hope I didn't interrupt something."

"Actually, I was about to invite Parker to dinner at my cabin tomorrow. I'm having a little get-together to talk about a pet project of mine, and I'd love to hear her take on it. It'll be casual. I would be honored to have you both join me."

"I'll defer to Parker on that one," Campbell said gracefully, but Parker wondered if she was simply leaving the decision to her or whether she was still angry over Mia and uninterested in whatever Parker did.

Parker almost declined outright. She was just beginning to feel secure and content with her new life, and she had no desire to realign herself with a Chicago politician. Still, Nadia Baker didn't seem to be a woman who was easily dissuaded, and the fact that Alexis had introduced them meant a lot.

As if reading her mind, Nadia reassured her. "I wouldn't ask you if I didn't think you would get as much out of it as I will. There's no obligation to stay. If you could stop by for a little while, I'd appreciate it."

"I'll think about it," Parker said noncommittally. She would have to quiz Alexis for more information before she agreed to anything.

"That's all I ask," Nadia said, then excused herself from their company.

"What was that about?" Campbell asked suspiciously.

"I have no idea," Parker answered, then pointed at Alexis, who was still close by. "What are you up to?"

Alexis raised her hands and started back toward the bar. "Don't shoot the socialite, darling. I'm going to get another drink. Need one? No? Okay, I'll be over there. You two make yourselves cozy."

Campbell chuckled at Alexis's fast retreat and hesitantly kissed Parker on the cheek. "Cozy sounds nice."

"Yes, it does." Parker took her hand, their fingers intertwining as they made their way to a table at the edge of the room. "Still mad at me?"

"Not really. I haven't had time. Some of your old colleagues can be a little high maintenance."

That was the understatement of the weekend. Parker had spent her afternoon fielding requests for everything from use of her fax machine to copper-bottom cookware for one of the cabins to low-carb, vegan options on the menu at the lodge. She was prepared to cater to the whims of these women, but the Carsons had probably never seen a group quite like this before, and she looked forward to hearing their reactions after it was all over. Suddenly Campbell's features darkened. Parker followed her gaze and saw Mia headed toward them.

Mia smiled as she approached. She was dressed perfectly for the situation in designer jeans and Kenneth Cole calf-length boots and a black turtleneck, probably Christian Dior or Chanel. The ensemble had likely cost a fortune at some boutique, since Mia never bought anything off-rack despite the fact that she could have purchased something similar at any mall in America. Still, the outfit achieved its goal of accentuating Mia's finer features, namely her legs and her breasts, without flaunting them.

"I'm glad I found you two." Mia grabbed a chair and situated herself between Campbell and Parker without being invited.

"I wanted to apologize again for this morning. It's a reminder of how far Parker and I have drifted apart, and I hope to change that this weekend." Mia directed her comments to Parker, then glanced at Campbell. "When you introduced yourself as Campbell Carson, I didn't know the Carsons owned the resort. I'm sure if Parker and I had talked more over the past few months she would have told me more about you."

"I don't know about that," Campbell said dryly. "She hasn't told me anything about you."

Parker winced at the remark. She'd hoped to avoid this conversation with Campbell in a public place, but since Mia seemed determined to force the issue, Parker wanted to be the one to explain. "Mia and I were together for two years when I lived in Chicago."

Mia sat back and smiled. "I'm glad you remember. You've been so quiet since I got here. I worried that you had forgotten all about us. Honestly, sometimes you're hard to read."

"I remember," Parker assured her. She did recall a few good times before she realized that they had come to the same end by different means. What she remembered most vividly, though, was her devastation when she finally accepted how badly she had misjudged Mia's character for so long. She could still feel the disappointment that overwhelmed her when she faced the fact that "loyalty" and "ethics" were words Mia knew only from stump speeches and not anything she practiced when it wasn't convenient for her.

"Good, because I've missed you. Mother and Daddy send their love, too. You know Daddy was always proud of you."

"Mia's father is the chairman of the Chicago Democratic Party," Parker clarified for Campbell. "And he wasn't proud of me the day I submitted my resignation from his golden boy's senatorial campaign."

"All that ugliness is over now. All's forgiven, water under the bridge." Mia gave a wave of her hand as if she could, with the flick of her wrist, brush away the most devastating event in Parker's past.

"How magnanimous," Parker said through gritted teeth. She wanted to ask what exactly she'd been forgiven for since she was the one who'd been betrayed, but rehashing that argument would only drag her back into something she had worked hard to leave behind.

Mia, who'd obviously misread Parker's tone, continued talking. "We were all upset when you left, but I think this little hiatus was probably the best thing for everyone."

Parker felt Campbell tense at the word "hiatus," the same way she'd reacted when Alexis used the word "sabbatical." Parker had to stop that line of thought and make it clear to both Campbell and Mia that she wasn't interested in reconnecting with her ex-girlfriend in any way. "Mia, I'm sorry if I led you to believe you should wait for me. I've moved on, both in my career and in my personal life."

Mia pursed her lips in what Parker recognized as an attempt to control her temper. It was only a momentary lapse in her otherwise perfect façade, and in a second her practiced smile was plastered back across her face. "Of course you have. I didn't expect you to be a nun while you were away. Lord knows I haven't been. I realize you have needs. I assumed we would both see other people while we were separated."

"Mia, I wouldn't fill those needs with someone else if I thought you and I might reconcile. The fact that you would even suggest that possibility shows how little you know me." Parker was shocked that she had to break off their tragic excuse of a relationship a second time. "I'm only interested in one woman at a time, and right now I'm with Campbell."

Mia's mouth fell open and she gave her full attention to Campbell for the first time all day. "You two are dating? How embarrassing. Here I am talking to Parker like…I can't believe I've managed to be offensive yet again." Mia pushed her hands through her long black hair as if trying to collect herself. "Really, though, how could I have known? I mean, you're hardly her type. She's outgoing and driven. Who would've thought she could fall for the strong, silent type? Then again, who would've thought she'd last a month out here? She thrives on the high life." Mia stopped rambling and stood. "I have sufficiently embarrassed myself for one day. Good night."

Parker breathed in relief a moment too soon, because as Mia was leaving the table she turned around one more time and said, "I do hope you're happy. Just because I can't figure out what you two could possibly have in common doesn't mean you won't be able to find a way to make it work out."

With that little backhanded bit of well-wishing, she left. Parker turned to Campbell and saw exactly what she feared she would. Her eyes, so bright minutes earlier, were now cold, and her expression was hard and distant. The walls that Parker had worked hard to get past were back up.

"I didn't mean for this to happen. I wanted to tell you in my own time. I should have explained about her sooner."

"Yes, you should have," Campbell replied, her voice emotionless.

"I knew she might be here this weekend, but I have no clue why she thought there was anything left between us."

"Two years of sharing your life with someone is a lot to walk away from," Campbell said softly as she stared down at her hands.

"It's not like that. We were never partners, not in the true sense of the word. I misread her involvement in politics as interest, and I got carried away. By the time I realized we were part of the same circles for different reasons, I was in too deep. We were living together. Our lives were all mixed up." Parker's voice was low and her heart heavy. Reliving these mistakes wasn't easy for her, but Campbell deserved to hear the truth.

"You knew you didn't want to spend the rest of your life with her, but you stayed in the relationship anyway?" Campbell refused to look at her, but Parker could sense the pain her words only hinted at.

"I don't know how to explain it," Parker said slowly. She struggled to put into words things she was only beginning to come to terms with herself. "Maybe I couldn't believe how wrong I had been about her. Maybe I hoped that the longer we were together, the closer our beliefs would become. Maybe I didn't want to admit what a horrible judge of character I was."

Campbell stood and looked her in the eyes for the first time since Mia had arrived. She held her gaze steady for a long moment, and Parker could clearly see the old hurt she'd hoped had begun to heal. "Or maybe you were killing time until something better came along."

Parker shook her head. She understood Campbell's pain, and she knew she'd made some mistakes in how she'd handled the situation, but she was tired of paying for Lynn's sins, too. She was in pain and angry that Campbell couldn't see past her own history long enough to realize she wasn't the only one who'd been hurt. Between the problems of their past, her conflict with Greg, and her uncertain career future, Parker wondered if her relationship with Campbell was becoming more work than it warranted. Now Campbell was adding her own accusations to events Parker already felt guilty about, and it was too much for her to take at once.

"Damn it, Campbell. Not everything's about you," she said, and walked away.

CHAPTER TWENTY

Campbell didn't get much sleep that night, and not for the pleasant reason she had become used to. She'd been restless all night in her cold, empty bed with only Badger to comfort her. She needed to talk to Parker about the conversation they'd had the night before, but she couldn't do it yet. The hurt was too fresh, and she didn't trust herself not to say something she'd regret. She'd projected her own history onto Parker and Mia's failed relationship, but it was hard not to.

She had finally begun to trust Parker, but she'd discovered Parker had kept a huge part of her past from her. Would Campbell have ever found out about Mia if she hadn't come to Bear Run? Parker had stayed in a loveless relationship rather than go through the trouble of breaking it off. Did she let Mia think everything was okay? Did she try to tell her they wanted different things from life? Sure, Mia had her own problems, but Parker had spent two years with her. What did that say about Parker?

Mia, though not the most objective source about Parker, had hit all of Campbell's fears, and it was impossible to ignore her insinuations about their differing personalities and background. Parker's past didn't suggest she'd be happy with a small-town ski instructor. If Parker needed the "high life" or "outgoing and driven" women, Mia was right. Campbell wasn't her type. People said opposites attract, but was attraction enough to build a relationship on?

As Campbell plodded to the slopes, Mia's words merged with Lynn's recriminations about having to choose between Bear Run and a lesbian relationship.

She didn't want to deal with Alexis's lesson, but she'd offered to help her, and she wouldn't break her word because she was upset with Parker.

"Good morning, Camy," Alexis said as she approached. "Does anyone ever call you Camy?"

"Not since I was three years old," Campbell answered truthfully.

"And why is that?"

"Do I look like a Camy to you?" The answer was implied in the question.

"No, I don't suppose you do." Alexis chuckled, then headed for the lift they'd taken the day before. "Let's get this workout started, shall we?"

Campbell sat beside Alexis and outlined their lesson on the way up the mountain. "You got off the hook yesterday because of Mia's little stunt, but don't think I didn't notice you were being modest about your ski level."

"Don't be silly. 'Modest' isn't a term I'm familiar with," Alexis said. "I simply had no interest in dragging Parker onto a black diamond slope. I chose to work on her level."

Alexis could pretend to be a hard-ass if she wanted, but it was clear she had a good heart behind her sharp wit. "Parker isn't here today. Why don't we take it up a notch and see if you can keep up with me."

"Trash talk is gauche, darling. If you want to challenge me, do it with your skis, and find something more useful to do with that pretty mouth."

Campbell laughed. Alexis was confident, but this was her mountain. No one could test her skills here. If nothing else, a good workout would help clear her head.

As they neared the end of the lift Alexis simply stated, "I'll be right behind you."

Campbell glanced back only once to see Alexis on her heels before she grinned and tilted her skis over the edge of the drop-off. It was the mountain's most challenging trail, narrow and steep, with its slightly uneven terrain left ungroomed where it wound through several patches of firs and evergreens. The old ski bums called it a cartilage killer because of the way it could rattle skiers' knees.

When Alexis sliced in behind her, she took several quick, sharp cuts, and her skis threw up a rooster tail of fresh powder. She thought that might be enough to impress Alexis, but she heard her call, "On your right," and fly past her. Alexis was in a full tuck to lower her wind resistance, which allowed her to go faster, but Campbell knew she'd have to ease up to take the turn they were bearing down on. She adjusted her line accordingly. When Alexis stood up, easing off slightly, Campbell was able to slingshot around her, laughing as she went.

There was another big dip before the trail flooded wide open into the main basin, and Campbell was certain Alexis would take it in a full crunch in the hopes of catching her, but Campbell didn't sacrifice style for speed. She took a slant only a native of the mountain would know. Instead of lining up on the inside track, she went wide toward the inclined bank of the final turn and used the height she got, along with her own momentum, to send her airborne. Her skis remained completely parallel and she crouched tightly as she exploded over the edge of the drop, a spray of snow in her wake.

She landed and immediately threw her skis sideways, a wave of powder arching up in front of her as Alexis slid to an equally abrupt stop behind her. "Well?" Campbell asked.

"Don't gloat, darling. It doesn't become that 'aw gee shucks' country-kid persona you do so convincingly." Alexis feigned uninterest, but she had a grudging appreciation in her eyes.

When they were once again headed up the mountain, Alexis said, "This time down I want you to show me how you took flight off that turn."

"Sure," Campbell agreed. Her heart rate began to return to normal after the exhilaration of the last run. "Anything else you want to know?"

"Well, I'd like to know why my best friend left the lodge visibly shaken last night."

Campbell was jolted by the sudden shift in subjects, and the harsh reminder of last night's conversation with Parker hit her like a punch in the stomach. She exhaled sharply before saying, "If you saw our departure, then you also saw Mia's. Doesn't that give you an idea of what happened?"

"Mia, I know all too well, but I also know she no longer has the power to upset Parker." Alexis regarded her pointedly. "But you're now the unknown entity."

"You'll have to forgive me, but I prefer to stay that way. I don't like to talk to near strangers about my personal life."

"Good, because I'm not interested in what you have to say about it. You and I are going to reach an understanding about your relationship with my best friend." Campbell started to reiterate her unwillingness to share the details of her love life, but Alexis raised a hand. "Let me clarify. By *we*, I mean I'm going to talk, and you're going to listen.

"Mia is a flake," Alexis said, and Campbell didn't feel the need to disagree. "I suspect you're twice as good for Parker as Mia ever was, but if you want to be around long enough to prove me right, you'd better pull your head out of that sweet ass of yours and pay some attention to who she really is."

"I suppose you're telling me she's a saint in all of this, or maybe she's bigger than me and this mountain," Campbell said. "Don't bother. I've heard it all before."

"I seriously doubt you've heard it all or you wouldn't be acting so daft," Alexis stated bluntly. "Parker wants to change the world, and she might actually do it if she had the right support in her life. Do you want to be that, or do you want to be just another in a long line of people who want to use her for your own selfish reasons?"

"Your suggestion that I'd ever intentionally hurt Parker shows how little you know me."

"And your implication that you haven't already hurt her shows how little you know about her." They were at the top of the lift, but instead of heading back toward the drop-off when they got off, Campbell skied to a stop in front of Alexis.

"What are you talking about?" Campbell asked. The thought of Parker suffering was enough to damper her own pain for a moment.

"Why don't you go ask her yourself?"

Campbell thought for a moment. She tried to picture Parker's face just before they parted the night before. She'd been so blinded by her own hurt that she'd barely registered the sadness in Parker's eyes. It didn't add up. She'd broken up with Mia, not the other way around. What did she have to be upset about? Campbell was immediately worried. What had she missed?

"Alexis, I hate to do this," she said, "but I have to have to cut this lesson short once again."

"How cute. You thought you were the one giving *me* the lesson." Alexis chuckled. "Go ahead."

This time when Campbell tore down the mountain, she didn't stop until she stood at Parker's office door.

❖

Campbell barged through the door to Parker's office and closed it behind her. "We need to talk."

Parker put down the papers she'd been staring at without comprehension. The dark circles under Campbell's eyes told her Campbell's night had likely been as long and restless as hers. She didn't want to talk. She wanted to hold her and be held by her. The look in Campbell's eyes had haunted her ever since she had stormed out of the lodge last night. She wanted to stay angry and felt she was entitled to, but a long night apart had weakened her resolve. "I know I should have told you about Mia sooner…" She didn't know how to continue.

Campbell gave a little quirk of a smile. "When I said we need to talk, I meant I was going to talk and you were going to listen."

"Oh, geez." Parker managed a weak smile also. She knew that line. "You've been talking to Alexis, haven't you?"

"Yes, I have, and you're right. You should have told me about Mia sooner, but I should have listened better to what you weren't saying instead of filling in the blanks with the worst possible scenario."

"Yeah, that would have helped." Campbell's sincerity was dispelling her remaining resentment.

Campbell pulled a chair next to Parker's desk and rested her elbows on her knees in her most attentive posture. "I'm listening."

"Do we have to go into this now?" Parker didn't want to relive her failures, especially to Campbell. "Can't we just kiss and be over it?"

Campbell shook her head. "We've been putting off the tough conversations for too long. If we want any chance at a real relationship, we need to put in some real effort, and I'm willing to do that if you are."

"You're right, but I'm afraid you'll think less of me when I tell you what happened between Mia and me."

"Try me," Campbell urged.

Parker took a deep breath and stared down at her hands. She couldn't bear to look Campbell in the eye. "You saw Mia at her worst yesterday, but you have to understand that in her element she can be quite convincing in the role of concerned young heiress to the Chicago Democratic network, and that's how I first met her."

"Because her father is a bigwig Chicago politician?"

"Yes, but that's not why we initially got together. I wouldn't use my lover to forward my career." She hoped Campbell knew that about her, but after their argument the night before, it was worth clarifying. "I fell for Mia because she shone in many of the social situations I did, though for different reasons. Mia was bred to be the wife of a politician. She is a brilliant hostess with an eye for details that I always forget—flower arrangements, catering, evening wear. She can parrot enough of what she's heard her father say about politics to hold brief conversations that make her appear credible without ever forming an opinion of her own, and that was enough to reel me in.

"We had a 'whirlwind romance' that was heralded as a 'match made in heaven.' Imagine, the young upstart who worked miracles behind the scenes politically falling for the daughter of the Chicago Democratic Party's elder statesman. We were the Democratic party's ideal couple. By the time I realized Mia's interest in politics was only superficial, I was already committed to her."

"You stayed with someone you didn't love because you didn't want to disappoint the Democratic party?" Campbell sounded bewildered. "I *am* trying to understand, but it sounds like you cared more about how your relationship came across to other people than how healthy it was for you and Mia."

"Campbell," Parker sighed, "you know me better than that. Listen to what I said. I made a public commitment to Mia and, by extension, her family and our friends who rewarded that commitment with their support. To walk away from Mia would mean admitting that I failed not only myself, but also Mia and all the people who supported us. I couldn't break that commitment without giving our relationship every chance to succeed."

"I see your point, but ultimately you did break that commitment. Why did it suddenly stop mattering?" Campbell didn't sound angry, only flustered by Parker's logic.

"I told you I was a political strategist for Tim Brady's political campaign, and I left over the sexual-harassment scandal, but I didn't tell you about the young woman who was caught in the middle of it all."

"No, I remember the news reports saying the girl was young and poor. They hinted that she was a gold digger."

Parker shuddered at that characterization as a mix of sadness and anger rushed over her once again. Her voice wavered. "She was an intern, a recent grad from Northwestern with a full academic scholarship, tons of potential, a real idealist—young, attractive, and smart, but naïve. Sound like anyone else you know?"

Campbell's face turned distinctly paler, and Parker took that as sign that she understood the connection. "She reminded me of myself, and I wanted to help her succeed. I personally recruited her for the campaign, and I threw her in the senator's company every chance I got. I was determined to make sure she had every opportunity she deserved. I thought that's what I was providing her with."

Campbell groaned. "And the whole time that dirtbag was trying to force himself on the girl."

Parker lowered her gaze again and her voice faded to a whisper. She could barely bring herself to give voice to the rest of the story. "She was ruined, Tim Brady was elected to the Illinois State Senate, and I'll never forgive myself."

"That's ridiculous," Campbell said vehemently. "You can't hold yourself responsible." Campbell seemed to remember who she was talking to because she immediately added, "It must have been hellish for you to think you'd been partially responsible for her downfall. It must have shaken your foundations."

Parker was once again amazed at how intuitive Campbell was. "I didn't know where to turn. Everyone I'd trusted was invested in seeing Tim Brady elected. My friends, my colleagues, my in-laws…even my girlfriend."

"Mia sided with that scum?" Campbell let loose a flash of outrage on Parker's behalf.

"Mia did exactly what she had been raised to do. She put on a pretty dress, plastered that fake smile on her face, and followed her daddy to the podium to address the press. She was on the front line of damage control for the party, which proved beyond question that all the hope and faith I'd invested to make our relationship a success had been one-sided."

When Parker looked up, she saw the tears in Campbell's eyes. "You poured your heart and soul into everything, only to have your personal and professional relationships destroyed all at once, and I had the nerve to suggest that you'd merely been 'waiting for something better to come along.'" Campbell groaned and jumped to her feet. "Can you ever forgive me for being so self-absorbed?"

"It wasn't totally your fault. You can't be expected to know something I never told you. I should have been more forthcoming. You didn't deserve to be blindsided by Mia."

"I do wish you'd told me sooner, not because you owed me any explanation, but to let me know what an ass I was. I was so wrapped up in myself I didn't stop to think that Mia might have hurt you. If I had, I wouldn't have listened to her ramble. I would have strangled her on sight."

Parker smiled, because it was funny, and probably true. Her mood was lightening with each of Campbell's comments.

"Here's where you're wrong, though," Campbell said, as she paced in front of Parker's desk. "You didn't hurt me. That was old hurt coming back up. You've never given me any reason to doubt your integrity. I should've taken the time to listen to you. I should've trusted you."

"I realize how it must have sounded to you. I know how Lynn hurt you. I don't blame you for reacting how you did. You were protecting yourself." Parker moved toward Campbell. She couldn't stand being away from her any longer. She needed to touch her.

"You're not Lynn. I have to remember that, but I was so busy protecting myself that I hurt you in the process." Campbell took Parker's face in her hands. "I didn't even realize how hard it would be for you to face Mia. I should've shielded you from that pain. Instead, I multiplied it."

Parker kissed Campbell. She couldn't resist any longer. She slipped her hands under Campbell's coat and slid it off her shoulders, then let it fall to the floor. "You didn't hurt me," she said between kisses. Then to reiterate her point, she pulled back enough to meet Campbell's beautiful blue eyes. "You have never hurt me."

"I should've been there for you." Campbell's voice quivered.

"You're here now. That's enough. That's everything." Parker

pressed her lips to Campbell's once again. She let her hands travel down Campbell's shoulders, grazing her breasts through the fabric of her shirt, then trailed her fingers along the length of Campbell's torso to settle on the curve of her hips. As the kiss grew more frenzied, their passion escalated beyond their control.

Parker breathed harder as their mouths continued to claim one another. Before she knew what she was doing, she ran her hand beneath the waistband on Campbell's ski pants. She hadn't intended to have sex right here in her office. She hadn't thought this through at all, but when she found the wetness already waiting, she lost all ability to think logically. With her libido now fully in control, she tugged Campbell's pants down, pushed her into the desk chair, and knelt before her. A mix of lust and astonishment played across Campbell's face just before Parker lowered her head. She wasn't sure which one of them moaned when she took Campbell into her mouth, but the sound only drove them both closer to the edge.

Campbell's hips rocked in time with the strokes of Parker's tongue across her clit and she laced her fingers though Parker's hair, holding her gently against her. The room was silent except for Campbell's increasingly ragged breath, but Parker could hear office conversations outside her door. As much as she didn't want this moment to end, the thought of someone interrupting them made her increase her pace. She pushed first one finger and then two into Campbell, who moaned her approval. Parker established a fast-paced rhythm with both her fingers and her tongue that had Campbell's muscles trembling in minutes.

"I'm going to come," Campbell gasped in a hoarse whisper as her body tightened and her hips bucked under Parker's mouth.

Parker stayed between her legs until all the tremors subsided. Then she rose and regarded her lover with a grin. "How'd you like our first attempt at make-up sex?"

"Is that what that was?" Campbell stood and pulled up her pants.

Parker nodded, pleased at the sated glow on Campbell's face.

"Then I think I have some making up to do, too." Campbell placed her hands on Parker's waist and drew her close.

"No, you don't." Parker pushed her away. "You have to get back to work and so do I."

"That's not fair." Campbell tried to pull her close again. "Come on. I can tell you want me as bad as I want you."

Parker laughed but moved farther out of her reach. "Yes, I do, which is why you have to get out of here right now or you'll miss your next lesson."

Campbell picked up her coat. "Okay, but only if you promise to spend the night with me tonight."

"I promise." Parker allowed her to get close enough for a good-bye kiss, but when Campbell tried to undo the top button on her blouse she swatted her hand away.

"You can't blame me for trying," Campbell joked, that full unguarded smile back on her face.

"Go," Parker commanded through her laughter, and playfully pushed Campbell out the door.

Once Parker was alone, she collapsed into her chair. Campbell was exhausting and exhilarating both physically and emotionally. She doubted they would ever overcome the endless challenges to their relationship, but at times like this she certainly wanted to try.

CHAPTER TWENTY-ONE

Campbell's stomach was in knots when she and Parker arrived at Nadia's cabin that evening. Nadia was an important woman who had likely sensed Parker's potential and was eager to include her in the pet project she mentioned. While Campbell didn't have a clue what the project entailed, she was certain it involved Parker returning to Chicago, and that scared her. Still, she couldn't keep Parker cut off from the rest of the world, and even if she could, that would be unfair.

Nadia took their coats and ushered them into a living room that blended into a dining area and was separated from the kitchen by a bar. It was one of the better-furnished cabins on the mountain, and Campbell knew it well. Either the familiar surroundings or the informal atmosphere Nadia had established with her warm greeting eased some of Campbell's tension.

"Let me introduce you both to the rest of our little group," Nadia said as the other women rose to meet them. "This is Hannah McBride, the director of social services for the greater Chicago area, and Marta Rodriguez, director of Mayor Daley's City Youth Program. Ladies, this is Parker Riley and her partner, Campbell Carson."

Campbell glanced at Parker as they all shook hands. This was the first time someone had put a label on their relationship. They were certainly lovers, but there was more to it than that. "Girlfriends" was probably accurate, but she liked the sound of "partner." That was how they were approaching this evening's meeting. Whatever was laid on the table, they'd promised to face it together.

"And I'm Alexis Reynolds, queen of all things," Alexis said. "What can I get you to drink?"

"Water for me," Campbell said.

"Sorry, darling. This is a business meeting. We never do business while sober," Alexis teased.

"Then I'll have what you're having," Campbell said, though she wasn't sure what that was.

"Same for me," Parker added as they took their seat at the dining-room table.

"Campbell," Nadia sat down across from them, "I've done my homework on Parker, but you're an unknown. Where are you from?"

"Here." Campbell took a hesitant sip of the scotch Alexis handed her. She'd never been a drinker.

"Here, as in Wisconsin?"

"I grew up on the mountain. My grandfather built this cabin. My parents live two houses down the road. My place is farther down the hill."

"That's impressive," Nadia said, and the sentiment sounded genuine. "It must be amazing to have your roots run deep in a place like this."

"It is. I've been blessed."

"It's good that you realize that. Most of the kids in the neighborhood I grew up in couldn't dream of visiting a place like Bear Run, much less living here."

Campbell realized that comment hadn't been made off-handedly. "You still represent that neighborhood, don't you, Alderwoman?"

Alexis chuckled. "I told you, she doesn't beat around the bush."

Nadia gave her an appreciative smile. "Very astute of you, Campbell."

"Southside Chicago?" Parker, who'd been quiet up until that point, leaned forward with interest.

"The area around Comiskey Park," Nadia confirmed, then clarified for Campbell. "It's economically depressed, plagued by high rates of unemployment and crime. We lose too many of our young people to violence, drugs, abuse, teen pregnancies, and incarceration."

"It's hard to rise above your current condition if you aren't exposed to any other way of life," Marta added, her Latina heritage evident in her soft accent.

Hannah joined the conversation as well. "We're ultimately products of our upbringing until we're shown something different."

"I couldn't agree more." Campbell thought of her own charmed childhood. Without that foundation she wouldn't be half the person she was today. She also knew Parker felt the same way about the opportunities her affluent upbringing had provided her.

"Then you'll understand the importance of the program we're here to discuss." Nadia pulled some papers off the bar and slid them across the table to Parker and Campbell. "The Broad Horizons Youth Initiative takes inner-city youth and provides them an alternative to the life they're living."

Campbell glanced at the brochure. It was filled with statistics and demographics that confirmed what she already knew. Young people trapped in bad situations tended to make bad decisions.

"What does it entail?" Parker asked as she ran through the statistics. Campbell recognized her business tone, the one she used frequently in early staff meetings as she tried to rapidly gather and evaluate new information.

"There are a lot of details about the psychology that you can read up on, but basically we take youth who've shown potential but are in high-risk living conditions and offer them a chance to spend a summer at one of our Broad Horizons sites, which are spread nationwide, mostly in suburban or rural areas," Nadia explained.

"While at the site, they receive counseling in a wide range of areas, from study skills to critical-thinking techniques and decision-making models," Hannah said excitedly.

"They also interact with positive role models, who teach basic employment and living skills that they don't have modeled for them at home," Nadia added.

"It's an opportunity to see themselves living a better life, an alternative way of conceptualizing their future," Alexis said. "No one can make the choice for them, but we can at least show them that they do in fact have one."

Campbell had to admit it sounded like a good program. Her time at the YMCA in Madison had taught her that the hardest thing to battle with disadvantaged kids was their overwhelming sense of hopelessness, and that was the key component of this program. It offered hope for a better life.

"And they travel in groups?" Parker asked.

"Absolutely. Ten to twenty kids per site," Nadia confirmed. "After they go home, they can hold each other accountable and have a support group when things get hard again."

"Is it a one-time event?" Parker was in full work mode now. Campbell could practically see her internalizing the information, and her enthusiasm escalated with each answer.

"No, we encourage the students to stay in touch with the hosts they build relationships with and return to their sites as many summers as they wish to," Hannah answered.

"That would give them something to look forward to each year, which in turn would help them stay on track," Parker concluded.

"It also gives the site coordinators a chance to use the positive experiences of the returning participants to acclimate the newer ones. It's a learning experience for everyone." Marta was feeding Parker's excitement.

"What about interest in the community?" Campbell asked. "Are kids from the south side of Chicago eager to get shipped off to the country for an entire summer?"

"These kids are hungry for a chance to succeed. They go through a rigorous application program and have to get recommendations from community leaders, and there's still a long waiting list. We have more kids than we have sites to place them in."

"Sounds like everything is up and running," Parker said, and Campbell could read the big question in her eyes even before she asked it. "What do you still need, Nadia?"

"What every charitable organization needs."

"Money," they said in unison.

"We need a lobbyist who'll get the program written into state and federal budget programs," Alexis explained, "someone who knows the system and people involved, but isn't tied to any one politician or special-interest group."

"It's a full-time position, Parker, and you'd have the full backing of Mayor Daley, as well as several high-ranking city officials. You'd be given access to all our resources and contacts. You'd split your time between Chicago, Springfield, and Washington D.C. and have the ear of legislators and dignitaries in all three cities."

Campbell's stomach turned over and her palms began to sweat. Chicago, Springfield, and D.C.? That didn't leave much time for Bear Run.

"I'm sorry, but I left politics for a reason," Parker stated emphatically. "I have no interest in working for dignitaries and legislators."

"Darling, you won't be working for the politicians. You'd be working for these kids," Alexis said, the barest hint of pleading in her voice.

"I know you've been let down by people in power before," Nadia added softly. "I wouldn't ask you to put your faith in another politician, not even me. I'm asking you to put your faith in these young people, and in a program that offers them a shot at the same bright future you and I were given."

Campbell knew that appeal would reach Parker because of how she felt about her own opportunities. She also knew that Parker probably wouldn't hesitate now if it weren't for her, and she didn't know if she should feel honored or guilty.

"I can't decide about this right now," Parker finally said.

"Of course not." Nadia sat back as if to signify her sales pitch had ended. "Take some time. The two of you talk it over. If you decide you want to hear more, give me a call and we'll set up a time for you to come visit our office, meet some of our supporters, and get to know some of our kids."

Campbell sat silently as the conversation turned to small talk about Nadia and Parker's mutual acquaintances. She knew Parker had just been offered something that would be hard to refuse, and she struggled to come to terms with what that meant for their relationship. The next time Alexis filled her glass, Campbell didn't hesitate to gulp the amber liquid. She wished the drink could drown the feeling that she was about to lose another woman she loved to a life she couldn't even begin to compete with.

❖

Parker was glad to see the conference end. She felt like she'd been running for three days without a break. She missed the peace and quiet she'd grown accustomed to at Bear Run and didn't know how she had lived at such a rapid pace for months during a campaign. A few days of such activity was enough to exhaust her. Still, she was proud that the event was successful and that people had begun to discuss booking the lodge for next year. The women of the Chicago Women's Democratic Caucus had enjoyed being able to ski, dine, and mingle without interruptions from the press or constituents, and the Carson family met all their needs. In return, the women paid well for their services and tipped generously for any extra attention. Everyone was happy with the arrangement. Parker had even seen Greg smile a time or two, and while she didn't plan to rub that reaction in, she was pleased to prove him wrong.

"You look awfully self-satisfied," Alexis said from the open doorway to Parker's office.

"And why shouldn't I be? The event we planned was a hit."

"Yes, it was." Alexis closed the door behind her. "I'm heading home this afternoon. Any chance you'll come?"

"Nope. As soon as all of you Chicagoans leave, I'm going to bed for two days."

"I would, too, if I had your hard-bodied ski goddess in my bed," Alexis said mischievously.

"She is divine, isn't she?" Parker felt dreamy at the thought of Campbell.

"That she is." Alexis nodded, but her smile faltered slightly. "I assume her divinity is what kept you from jumping at Nadia Baker's job offer."

Parker frowned. She'd done her best to ignore that prospect. She and Campbell had put off talking about it. Both of them sensed the gravity of the conversation, and neither was ready to face what Nadia's offer meant for them yet. Instead they'd spent the previous night making love and reveling in the joy of each other's company. "Alexis, I said I'll think about it next week."

"Bullshit, darling. You can't fool me. I know it's been on your mind constantly since the offer was made, maybe even before that."

"I like it here, Alexis," Parker said emphatically.

"I know you do, but I also know you're called to bigger things than marketing and sales. You know it, too." Alexis's voice was nothing but sympathetic. "This is the opportunity you've always wanted. If you pass up a chance to make a real difference in these kids' lives in favor of this comfortable cocoon, you won't be able to forgive yourself."

Parker stood up suddenly and finally said what had haunted her all night. "I can't do it to her, Alexis. If you knew what Campbell had been through, you'd understand why."

"You're going to short-change yourself again for some woman you don't even know if it will work out with?" Alexis chuckled.

"Don't do that." Parker raised her voice more in desperation than anger. "She's not Mia. She's nothing like Mia."

"I know she's not," Alexis acknowledged. "I like Campbell. I wish I didn't. This would be easier, but ultimately it's not about her. It's about you doing what's right for you, what you've always wanted to do, and this program is it."

"What if Campbell is what's right for me?" Parker asked quickly, her head and her heart warring within her, almost tearing her apart.

"This is your chance of a lifetime. Take her along for the ride."

Parker dismissed the idea immediately. "She wouldn't be Campbell without Bear Run. I can't ask her to leave her home, her family, for a dream that isn't her own. Can you imagine her being happy in some city apartment while I keep the ungodly hours this job would require?"

Alexis silently agreed.

"Honestly, Alexis, if I could be involved in the program without sacrificing all this, I'd jump—"

"So you plan to sacrifice yourself? If she loves you, she wouldn't ask that of you."

"She hasn't asked it of me. She hasn't said anything about it, but she's scared. I know she is, and she deserves better, Alexis." Parker's voice cracked with emotion.

Alexis rose. "As long as I've known you, you've searched for a way to make a tangible difference in the world, and now you have your shot. If you walk away, you'll regret it, and you'll resent her in the end. You *both deserve better.*"

There it was, the fear that had been in the back of Parker's mind. She could lose it all. She couldn't guarantee that staying would save Campbell from the pain she wanted to protect her from. This week had shown several reasons why their relationship could fail—their past mistakes, the differences in their personalities, the objections of Campbell's father. Any number of things could still arise to threaten their status as a couple. She could pass up this opportunity and still not give Campbell a relationship she was worthy of.

Alexis hugged Parker and headed for the door. Before she walked out of the office she said, "I'll see you in Chicago."

❖

Campbell knew something was wrong as soon as she saw Parker that evening. She was clearly exhausted, though that could be explained by the recent conference, or their lack of sleep because they couldn't keep their hands off each other. If she'd merely been tired, Campbell wouldn't have worried, but she was clearly sad, too.

"Hi." Campbell tried to force a smile as she placed a kiss on Parker's lips, but she stopped there. They couldn't put off the inevitable. Campbell took Parker's hand and led her across the room to the couch. She steeled herself for the conversation she'd been dreading and gently asked, "What have you decided?"

"Campbell," Parker said, then exhaled slowly, "I haven't decided anything for sure. We need to determine this together. If you tell me not to go, I won't."

Campbell shook her head, unable to find the right words. She'd been here before. She'd learned how it felt to hold on to someone whose heart was somewhere else. "I won't do that. I can't, and you know why."

"It's not like that," Parker said softly. "I don't want to leave. I love it here. This mountain feels almost like home now, and your family has been wonderful to me." She smiled weakly. "And you…"

Campbell looked into those deep brown eyes and saw her own pain mirrored there as Parker said, "You're amazing. You're the woman of my dreams."

"But," Campbell said what Parker couldn't, "you have other dreams, too."

Parker nodded as her tears started to fall. Campbell pulled her close and rocked her tenderly. She could barely breathe. She wanted to beg Parker not to go. She wanted to keep her in her arms forever, but if she did, things would never be the same. She wouldn't be Parker if she didn't chase her dream. Campbell might have fallen for Parker the first time she saw her—confident, proud, and beautiful at the softball game—but she'd also known that Parker was meant for a bigger life than Bear Run offered.

"It's not set in stone," Parker said. "I just need to give it a chance. Maybe when I learn more about the program it won't sound as good. I ran away from that life once because I couldn't do what I needed to do there. Maybe that's still true."

"I understand," Campbell whispered as she stroked Parker's hair. She did understand, but that didn't make it hurt any less. "When will you leave?"

"The day after tomorrow. Only for two days, to learn more."

"Will you stay with me tonight?"

"I'd like that," Parker said between sniffles.

"Me, too." Campbell kissed her again, this time more thoroughly. She didn't care what Parker said now. Once she left she would be gone for good. Even if she did come back to the mountain after the interview, her heart would already be gone This would be their last time together with nothing else between them. She wanted to savor every minute.

CHAPTER TWENTY-TWO

Parker had been at a standstill on Lake Shore Drive for over twenty minutes. The bumper-to-bumper traffic was maddening, and the freezing rain that had been falling on the city for the past hour didn't help. She'd been in the car for too long, since it was less than ten miles from Alexis's apartment on Grand and Michigan to Nadia's office across from Comiskey Park, or U.S. Cellular Field, as it was now named. She felt claustrophobic as she wound between skyscrapers and sports stadiums built among and on top of century-old warehouses. She'd always loved old Chicago, but today it was disorienting not to be able to see the horizon.

Someone laid on the horn behind her, as though honking would make the traffic disappear. She'd already seen two fender-benders, and several other drivers screamed or gestured with their middle fingers extended in the direction of their fellow commuters. The Carsons rarely raised their voice in anger.

She missed Campbell so much her chest ached. She missed sleeping with her, she missed waking up next to her, she missed watching her on the slopes. She still couldn't forget how Campbell's blue eyes shimmered with tears when they parted the day before. Alexis had done her best to take her mind off her loneliness by taking her out to dinner and then to the theater, but Parker hadn't had much appetite and wondered during the entire play what Campbell was doing. She'd picked up the phone to call her several times, but hearing her voice would only make things harder.

She circled the block that Nadia's office was on several times before she found a parking lot with space available and noted that it would cost her thirteen dollars an hour to leave her car there. When she entered the building, a polite but obviously busy receptionist greeted her and told her to have a seat, that Nadia would be with her soon. Parker reached into the leather briefcase she'd pulled out of her closet for this occasion and retrieved an antacid and two aspirin. She'd had a stomachache and a headache since she arrived in the city. Maybe it was stress, maybe it was the smog or the lack of sleep, but she felt terrible, emotionally and physically. She dry-swallowed the pills, a habit she had picked up on the campaign trail, and studied her surroundings. She was awfully miserable for someone about to have a lifelong dream come true.

The reception area was relatively bare, but some pictures on the opposite wall caught her eye. She crossed the room to examine them more closely. One showed several teenagers, all of them either black or Latino, standing around a tractor in an open field. They wore huge smiles, and Parker assumed the group was part of the Broad Horizons program. The next was of Nadia with a young girl in a graduation cap and gown. Parker searched the previous picture and realized the girl was one of the teenagers standing beside the tractor. The second picture testified to the success of the first, and Parker was glad to be reminded why she was here. She wanted to make a difference in the lives of young people like these.

The next picture, though, reminded her of what she was leaving behind. It was Nadia's wedding picture. Parker guessed her to be about ten years younger as she stood with her new groom on a hillside surrounded by their extended families. Tears once again formed at the corner of her eyes as she wondered which picture Nadia held more dear. If she'd been forced to choose, would she be in this office right now, or would she be on that hillside? She was still pondering that question when the secretary informed her that Nadia was ready to see her.

❖

Campbell lay awake for hours listening to the sounds of the ice storm outside while Badger paced nervously at the foot of the bed. It was probably the weather that bothered him, but maybe he missed

Parker, too. He could certainly sense Campbell's sour mood because he didn't try to follow her when she finally got out of bed.

She conferred with Sammy, and they decided to take a few early runs down the slopes to see if conditions were safe for the general public. They rarely shut down the mountain, but since ice could be deadly on certain trails, they occasionally had to restrict access to those areas. Campbell hated ice and dreaded having to ski the most challenging portions of the mountain on it while freezing rain pelted her in the face.

"Like this day wasn't shitty enough as it was," she mumbled as they hunkered down on the lift.

"You didn't have to come." Sammy pulled his hat down to his goggles and tugged the zipper on this coat over his mouth so that only the tip of his nose caught the cold, stinging ice pellets that swirled on the wind.

"I was only lying around feeling sorry for myself at home," Campbell admitted. She'd tried to get her mind off Parker's absence, but she couldn't let go yet. She should've known better than to put herself in this position in the first place. She should've seen it coming, and in many ways she had. She'd always suspected that when Parker's confidence returned she would move on, and still Campbell fell for her. Even knowing what she knew now, however much she hurt, she didn't feel any regret. She'd tortured herself all night wondering whether she'd take it all back if she could and finally decided she wouldn't trade the time she'd had with Parker for anything. But was she destined to make the same mistake time and time again?

After a few minutes of silence, Sammy said, "I know it's not the same, but I'll miss her, too."

"Thanks, Sam." Campbell would have never believed after that first staff meeting that Parker would have adapted to life on the mountain as well as she had. She even got along with the majority of her family. She would have made a great addition to the Carson clan if Campbell's father hadn't objected. It would have been nice if they could have made peace. She was sure her dad would have grown to like Parker if they had taken the time to see in each other what Campbell saw in each of them. Campbell cursed herself for dwelling on what could have been. It wasn't going to happen.

"It's not too late to ask her to stay," Sammy said so quietly that she could barely hear him over the wind.

"I won't do it, Sam," Campbell snapped. "If she wanted to stay, she would have chosen to."

"Sorry." Sammy shook his head. "I'm trying to help. There should be a better compromise, you know?"

It wasn't as though that thought hadn't crossed Campbell's mind, but it was just wishful thinking. You couldn't be both a power lesbian and a happy homemaker.

They reached the top of the lift and immediately headed for the drop-off. Because of the steep slope, narrow sections, and sharp turns, the trail would most likely be a problem on a day like this. They stopped at the edge of the trail as if asking which one of them would go first.

"Why not?" Campbell shrugged. "Can't be any rougher than what I'm already going through." She tipped her skis over the edge and angled across the slope. The sound of her metal edges scratching their way down a solid sheet of ice made her shiver. This slope would have to be closed for at least part of the day. She wished once again that she was back home safe and warm, snuggled in bed with Parker. Her chest seized up at the thought that she'd probably never do that again, and she immediately segued into anger that she'd been on the losing end of a choice between work and family again.

She wasn't completely certain what happened next, but as she made the turn around the last bend in the trail, her skis caught an edge and she was on the ground before she realized she was falling. The ice was unforgiving as her shoulder hit first, then her head. The fall knocked the wind from her, and she slid farther down the slope. She gasped for air, and when she finally stopped, something in her seemed to have snapped, and not in the physical sense.

Sammy was next to her in an instant. "Cam, are you hurt?"

"Yes, I'm hurt," Campbell said through gritted teeth.

"Where?" He pulled off his scarf and goggles and stared at her.

"Everywhere."

"Okay, I'll go get help. Stay where you are."

"I'm tired of staying where I am, Sam." Campbell sat up. "That's what got me in this mess in the first place, and it'll keep getting me in messes like this."

Sammy looked at her like the blow to her head had made her talk nonsense.

"I'm sick of coming in second, Sammy. Why am I lying here cold and hurt and alone? All I want is to live the life I want with the woman I love." Campbell stood shakily and clicked back into her skis. "I think I deserve that much."

"Did you say you love her?"

Campbell didn't even hesitate. "Yes, I love her. I'm in love with her," she repeated, letting the full impact of her words sink in. "Holy shit, Sam. I'm in love with Parker, and I didn't even fight for her. I told her to leave."

"You're going after her, huh?" Sammy's smile was broad and genuine.

"Yeah." Campbell's head spun. "I'm going after her, but I have to take care of something first."

Sammy stared at her for a second, then shouted, "Well, what are you waiting for? Go!"

❖

Campbell barged through her parents' back door without knocking. "Dad? Mom?" she called as she stormed toward the kitchen. Both her parents were sitting at the breakfast table, her father in flannel pajamas and her mother in a faded nightgown. They jumped up, startled by her boisterous entry.

"For God sakes, Campbell, what's wrong?" Greg asked.

"What happened? Where's Sammy? Are you hurt?" Her mother examined her carefully.

"I'm hurt," Campbell said in a rush, her emotions overrunning her composure. "I'm hurt because Parker is gone."

"Kiddo, I hate to say I told you so, but—"

"Then don't, Dad, because she's not the only one that hurt me. You hurt me, too."

"Because I called it like I saw it?" he asked, incredulous.

"No, because you had so little faith me, because you're still treating me like a child, because you act like you're the only one who cares about this mountain."

"What's gotten into you?" Her father was clearly astonished to hear her speak so bluntly.

"Love, Dad. I'm in love with Parker and I'm going after her." Campbell was surprised at her own force, but she didn't waver.

"I think you're making a big mistake, and I don't approve."

Then it's my mistake to make, and I'm not asking for your approval, but I'd like your support."

Irene cut in for the first time. "You've got my support. You're a strong, beautiful, capable woman, and Parker is lucky to have you."

"Thank you, Mom." Campbell kissed her forehead, then turned back to her father. "If Parker will have me, I'll be the lucky one, and I plan to make her part of my life, part of our lives for as long as she'll let me."

"What do you want me to say about that?" Greg asked. "You want to lie and say I'm happy for you?"

"I want you to say you trust me. You've raised me to care about family, and home, and the future of this mountain, but every time I try to act on those beliefs, all you do is criticize me." Campbell wasn't sure where the words had come from until she spoke, but it was becoming increasingly clear this conversation was more about her and her father than it was about Parker. "You find fault with every new plan for the business. You don't let me take my own role in how the resort is used, and when I finally find the nerve to try to make a family of my own, you interfere every chance you get."

"I'm sorry you feel that way, Cam." Greg rubbed his face with his hands and shook his head. "I guess you want me to just stay out of your life?"

"No, I need you in my life. I need you to be there for me, but I need you to respect me and stop trying to protect me. I'm ready to take my place in this family and on the mountain, and you need to recognize that I have as much invested in the future of our home as you do."

"Someday you'll have kids of your own. Then you'll understand how hard it is see your children as adults."

She smiled slightly at the softening of his voice. "I hope I do, and I hope I'll be half the parent to them that you've been to me. If I have, I'll trust them to make the right decisions."

"I do trust you, Cam. I'll just have to work harder at showing you."

"That's all I'm asking for, Dad."

He extended his hand and Campbell shook it. "It's not going to be easy, though. You may have to point it out to me if I'm not giving you your due."

Campbell smiled. She felt like she and her father had entered a new stage in their relationship. She only hoped he realized that, too. "I'll hold you to that."

He chuckled slightly and pulled her into a hug. "I do believe you will."

❖

After lunch Parker sat in Nadia's office for the second time that day. They had toured the neighborhood where most of the Broad Horizons youth lived, then met with program staff from around the city. They ate lunch with two of the program participants in a *taqueria* where they were the only ones speaking English. The experience reminded Parker again how much this world differed from the one where she grew up, only a few miles away. Parker's spirits rose when she talked with the young women who spoke passionately about their experiences in the program, the connections they'd made with their site coordinators, and the relationships they still shared with their fellow participants. Those conversations cemented in her mind that this organization was exactly what she'd trained her whole life to be a part of. But back in Nadia's office, Parker couldn't bring herself to formally accept the job offer.

As Nadia talked about the specifics of their budget, grants and government subsidies they'd already received, Parker's mind wandered back to Bear Run. She had been there only a few months, yet she couldn't imagine going home anywhere else at night. She thought of skiing the first tracks of the season with Campbell and wondered how it would feel to miss that next year. What would it be like when the first snow fell and she was in some city high-rise? Would she long for the slopes? Would she go back to visit Bear Run? How would it affect her to see Campbell and not hold her? Or worse yet, see someone else hold her? She had to swallow a lump in her throat at that thought.

Not wanting to lose her composure in front of Nadia, she focused on a poster on the opposite wall. It was a picture of Mahatma Ghandi, and under it ran his famous quote, "You have to be the change you wish to see in the world." Parker had heard the words many times, but this time when she read them something new struck her. You have to *be* the change, not fight for the change, not fund the change, not lobby for the change, but *be*.

Be.

If she fell back into a world that had made her miserable, she'd be doing exactly what Broad Horizons tried to save kids from. Sure, she wouldn't turn to crime or live in poverty, but Campbell had shown her a better way to live, an alternative. She'd given her hope for a brighter future, and Parker was turning away from it. No amount of good intentions could sugarcoat the hypocrisy in such a decision. She'd made up her mind. She would go back to Bear Run, to a better life, to Campbell.

Still, she wanted to be involved with the Broad Horizons program. But those young people deserved someone who could give their whole heart to their cause. And while she wasn't that person, she cared for those kids. It simply wasn't right that she was able to leave this city that suffocated her while the teens she'd met today were stuck here. She wished she could take them all with her.

"Take them all with me," she said aloud, and started to laugh.

"What?" Nadia asked, her confusion evident in her expression.

Parker could barely talk. The joy overwhelmed her as she said, "I'm not the right person for this job, Nadia. I'd be a hypocrite if I came back to the city after working at Bear Run. I'd be a terrible role model for the kids I'd be trying to help."

Nadia nodded, but her disappointment was clear. "I understand, but forgive me if I don't share your enthusiasm. The kids would have benefited from your expertise."

Parker could feel her grin stretch across her face. "I didn't say I couldn't work with the program. I said I wasn't the right person for *this* job."

Nadia leaned forward attentively. "I'm listening."

CHAPTER TWENTY-THREE

Campbell still wore her ski boots, which helped keep her foot heavy on the gas pedal for hours. She would have been at Nadia's office by now if she knew where it was, but after she talked to her parents she didn't even stop at her cabin for a change of clothes or directions. She'd followed the signs toward the ball park and found it relatively easily, but now she was driving around one of the worst neighborhoods she'd ever been in, searching for anything that resembled a city office. She waited for someone to stop and ask directions from, but the dismal weather didn't leave room for much pedestrian traffic. She was about to pull over and go inside somewhere when she saw two women under an awning up the road. She stopped alongside the curb and called to them, "Excuse me, can you tell me where Alderwoman Baker's office is?"

She was shocked when the women turned around. Even through the rain, she could clearly see Parker and Nadia's surprise. "Campbell?"

Campbell jumped out of the truck as Parker ran to meet her. They flew into each other's arms, the heat of their kiss making them oblivious to the frigid rain. Campbell clutched Parker's face in her hands so close, little more than a breath was between them. "I love you."

Parker immediately started to cry again, and Campbell worried that she'd misunderstood. "I didn't say that to make you stay. I want you to do whatever makes you happy, but I love you, and I won't let you leave my life simply because you've got to leave Bear Run."

"I love you, too," Parker sobbed, "and I don't want to leave you or your home, our home."

"What?" Campbell wasn't certain she'd heard correctly. Surely she was dreaming.

"You two have some talking to do, so I'll leave you to it."

"I didn't take the lobbyist job. I turned it down." Parker sounded giddy now that her tears had slowed.

"Why?" Campbell tried to process this new piece of information. "I don't want you to give up your dreams because of mine. We can find a way to have both. We can have a long-distance relationship. I'll come to Chicago in the off-season, and you can come to Bear Run when Congress isn't in session. I don't know all the details, but I know I love you." Campbell's emotions poured out along with her words.

"I love you, too, and I don't want to spend another night away from you. I want a relationship with you, full time, not one based on the ski season or the congressional calendar." Parker kissed her again.

"But what about changing the world?" Campbell asked.

"You have to *be* the change you wish to see in the world," Parker said seriously, then laughed at the confusion on Campbell's face. "Do you remember the meeting we had with Nadia when she said the only thing they needed as much as money was—"

"Site coordinators," Campbell said. She started to put the pieces together and wondered why she hadn't thought of the solution.

"Apparently places with room and work for a group of teenagers and a staff that can provide a family atmosphere are scarce. Can you think of any place better suited to that than Bear Run?" Parker asked, sounding slightly hesitant. "I mean, if you want to be part of this, too. I shouldn't assume that—"

Campbell silenced her with a kiss. "Yes, you should. You can always assume that if something is important to you, it's important to me, too. We can work out the details later."

"If we can get your father to agree," Parker said. "I don't want my plan to cause a rift between you and your family."

"It'll take some convincing, but I'm sure he'll come around. This is the right decision for us. Bringing Broad Horizons to Bear Run will be the perfect way to combine our passions."

Parker smiled mischievously. "I can think of another way for us to combine our passions."

Campbell was immediately aroused. "Care to demonstrate?"

"Care to take me home?"

The thought of being home with Parker made Campbell feel complete. "There's nothing I'd rather do."

About the Author

Rachel Spangler avoided getting a real job by staying in school for way too long, and she loved (almost) every minute of it. She holds degrees in politics and government, women's studies, and English, as well as a master's in college student personnel administration from Illinois State University. Throughout her college experience, she was actively involved with PFLAG, PRIDE, FMLA, and Safe Schools, all of which influenced various aspects of her first novel, Learning Curve. She also has a short story titled "Baby Steps" in the Bold Strokes Books anthology Romantic Interludes 1: Discovery.

Rachel and her partner, Susan are raising their son in western New York. During the winter they make the most of the lake effect snow on local ski slopes, a hobby that inspired the setting for her second novel, Trails Merge. In the summer, they love to travel and watch their beloved St. Louis Cardinals. Regardless of the season, Rachel always makes time for a good romance, whether she's reading it, writing it, or living it.

Rachel can be reached at Rachel_Spangler@yahoo.com or www.myspace.com/rlspang.

Books Available From Bold Strokes Books

Green Eyed Monster by Gill McKnight. Mickey Rapowski believes her former boss has cheated her out of a small fortune, so she kidnaps the girlfriend and demands compensation—just a straightforward abduction that goes so wrong when Mickey falls for her captive. (978-1-60282-042-5)

Blind Faith by Diane and Jacob Anderson-Minshall. When private investigator Yoshi Yakamota and the Blind Eye Detective Agency are hired to find a woman's missing sister, the assignment seems fairly mundane—but in the detective business, the ordinary can quickly become deadly. (978-1-60282-041-8)

A Pirate's Heart by Catherine Friend. When rare book librarian Emma Boyd searches for a long-lost treasure map, she learns the hard way that pirates still exist in today's world—some modern pirates steal maps, others steal hearts. (978-1-60282-040-1)

Trails Merge by Rachel Spangler. Parker Riley escapes the high-powered world of politics to Campbell Carson's ski resort—and their mutual attraction produces anything but smooth running. (978-1-60282-039-5)

Dreams of Bali by C.J. Harte. Madison Barnes worships work, power, and success, and she's never allowed anyone to interfere—that is, until she runs into Karlie Henderson Stockard. Eclipse EBook (978-1-60282-070-8)

The Limits of Justice by John Morgan Wilson. Benjamin Justice and reporter Alexandra Templeton search for a killer in a mysterious compound in the remote California desert. (978-1-60282-060-9)

Designed for Love by Erin Dutton. Jillian Sealy and Wil Johnson don't much like each other, but they do have to work together—and what they desire most is not what either of them had planned. (978-1-60282-038-8)

Calling the Dead by Ali Vali. Six months after Hurricane Katrina, NOLA Detective Sept Savoie is a cop who thinks making a relationship work is harder than catching a serial killer—but her current case may prove her wrong. (978-1-60282-037-1)

Dark Garden by Jennifer Fulton. Vienna Blake and Mason Cavender are sworn enemies—who can't resist each other. Something has to give. (978-1-60282-036-4)

Shots Fired by MJ Williamz. Kyla and Echo seem to have the perfect relationship and the perfect life until someone shoots at Kyla—and Echo is the most likely suspect. (978-1-60282-035-7)

truelesbianlove.com by Carsen Taite. Mackenzie Lewis and Dr. Jordan Wagner have very different ideas about love, but they discover that truelesbianlove is closer than a click away. Eclipse EBook (978-1-60282-069-2)

Justice at Risk by John Morgan Wilson. Benjamin Justice's blind date leads to a rare opportunity for legitimate work, but a reckless risk changes his life forever. (978-1-60282-059-3)

Run to Me by Lisa Girolami. Burned by the four-letter word called love, the only thing Beth Standish wants to do is run for—or maybe from—her life. (978-1-60282-034-0)

Split the Aces by Jove Belle. In the neon glare of Sin City, two women ride a wave of passion that threatens to consume them in a world of fast money and fast times. (978-1-60282-033-3)

Uncharted Passage by Julie Cannon. Two women on a vacation that turns deadly face down one of nature's most ruthless killers—and find themselves falling in love. (978-1-60282-032-6)

Night Call by Radclyffe. All medevac helicopter pilot Jett McNally wants to do is fly and forget about the horror and heartbreak she left behind in the Middle East, but anesthesiologist Tristan Holmes has other plans. (978-1-60282-031-9)

I Dare You by Larkin Rose. Stripper by night, corporate raider by day, Kelsey's only looking for sex and power, until she meets a woman who stirs her heart and her body. (978-1-60282-030-2)

Lake Effect Snow by C.P. Rowlands. News correspondent Annie T. Booker and FBI Agent Sarah Moore struggle to stay one step ahead of disaster as Annie's life becomes the war zone she once reported on. Eclipse EBook (978-1-60282-068-5)

Revision of Justice by John Morgan Wilson. Murder shifts into high gear, propelling Benjamin Justice into a raging fire that consumes the Hollywood Hills, burning steadily toward the famous Hollywood Sign—and the identity of a cold-blooded killer. (978-1-60282-058-6)

Truth Behind the Mask by Lesley Davis. Erith Baylor is drawn to Sentinel Pagan Osborne's quiet strength, but the secrets between them strain duty and family ties. (978-1-60282-029-6)

Cooper's Deale by KI Thompson. Two would-be lovers and a decidedly inopportune murder spell trouble for Addy Cooper, no matter which way the cards fall. (978-1-60282-028-9)

Romantic Interludes 1: Discovery ed. by Radclyffe and Stacia Seaman. An anthology of sensual, erotic contemporary love stories from the best-selling Bold Strokes authors. (978-1-60282-027-2)

A Guarded Heart by Jennifer Fulton. The last place FBI Special Agent Pat Roussel expects to find herself is assigned to an illicit private security gig baby-sitting a celebrity. (Ebook) (978-1-60282-067-8)

Saving Grace by Jennifer Fulton. Champion swimmer Dawn Beaumont, injured in a car crash she caused, flees to Moon Island, where scientist Grace Ramsay welcomes her. (Ebook) (978-1-60282-066-1)

The Sacred Shore by Jennifer Fulton. Successful tech industry survivor Merris Randall does not believe in love at first sight until she meets Olivia Pearce. (Ebook) (978-1-60282-065-4)

Passion Bay by Jennifer Fulton. Two women from different ends of the earth meet in paradise. Author's expanded edition. (Ebook) (978-1-60282-064-7)

Never Wake by Gabrielle Goldsby. After a brutal attack, Emma Webster becomes a self-sentenced prisoner inside her condo—until the world outside her window goes silent. (Ebook) (978-1-60282-063-0)

The Caretaker's Daughter by Gabrielle Goldsby. Against the backdrop of a nineteenth-century English country estate, two women struggle to find love. (Ebook) (978-1-60282-062-3)

Simple Justice by John Morgan Wilson. When a pretty-boy cokehead is murdered, former LA reporter Benjamin Justice and his reluctant new partner, Alexandra Templeton, must unveil the real killer. (978-1-60282-057-9)

Remember Tomorrow by Gabrielle Goldsby. Cees Bannigan and Arieanna Simon find that a successful relationship rests in remembering the mistakes of the past. (978-1-60282-026-5)

Put Away Wet by Susan Smith. Jocelyn "Joey" Fellows has just been savagely dumped—when she posts an online personal ad, she discovers more than just the great sex she expected. (978-1-60282-025-8)

Homecoming by Nell Stark. Sarah Storm loses everything that matters—family, future dreams, and love—will her new "straight" roommate cause Sarah to take a chance at happiness? (978-1-60282-024-1)

The Three by Meghan O'Brien. A daring, provocative exploration of love and sexuality. Two lovers, Elin and Kael, struggle to survive in a postapocalyptic world. (Ebook) (978-1-60282-056-2)

Falling Star by Gill McKnight. Solley Rayner hopes a few weeks with her family will help heal her shattered dreams, but she hasn't counted on meeting a woman who stirs her heart. (978-1-60282-023-4)

Lethal Affairs by Kim Baldwin and Xenia Alexiou. Elite operative Domino is no stranger to peril, but her investigation of journalist Hayley Ward will test more than her skills. (978-1-60282-022-7)

A Place to Rest by Erin Dutton. Sawyer Drake doesn't know what she wants from life until she meets Jori Diamantina—only trouble is, Jori doesn't seem to share her desire. (978-1-60282-021-0)

Warrior's Valor by Gun Brooke. Dwyn Izsontro and Emeron D'Artansis must put aside personal animosity and unwelcome attraction to defeat an enemy of the Protector of the Realm. (978-1-60282-020-3)